Now look at her, he thought with a wry shake of his head, *traipsing through the brush without a care for her dress and wearing that hat like a real rider.*

He could hardly believe they'd only met less than a week ago. It seemed more like a month with all they'd been through.

At the base of the rock spire, Delsie stopped. Myles came up beside her. Instead of the lofty height of the formation, her attention seemed riveted on the names and initials carved into the soft rock. There were dozens and dozens of them, some fresh, others growing faint from the effects of the sun, rain and wind.

"Just think how many people have passed by this very rock." Delsie reached out and traced a name with her finger. "All looking for a new life out West." Her voice held the same wistfulness it did whenever she spoke of her sister. Did Delsie hold out hope of possibly carving a new life out here, too?

Myles reached into his boot and withdrew his knife. "I say we add our names to theirs."

Delsie looked from the knife to him, then smiled fully. "All right."

Stacy Henrie has always had a love for history, fiction and chocolate. She earned her BA in public relations before turning her attentions to raising a family and writing inspirational historical romances. Wife of an entrepreneur husband and a mother to three, Stacy loves to live out history through her fictional characters. In addition to author, she is also a reader, a road trip enthusiast and a novice interior decorator.

Books by Stacy Henrie

Love Inspired Historical

Lady Outlaw
The Express Rider's Lady

Visit the Author Profile page at Harlequin.com.

STACY HENRIE

The Express Rider's Lady

HARLEQUIN® LOVE INSPIRED® HISTORICAL

LOVE INSPIRED BOOKS

Recycling programs for this product may not exist in your area.

ISBN-13: 978-0-373-28348-4

The Express Rider's Lady

Copyright © 2016 by Stacy Henrie

www.Harlequin.com

Printed in U.S.A.

Be strong and of a good courage; be not afraid, neither be thou dismayed: for the Lord thy God is with thee whithersoever thou goest.
—*Joshua* 1:9

For my three families—
the one I call my own, the one I grew up in
and the one I married into. Love you all.

Thank you to my agent, Jessica Alvarez,
the best advocate an author could ask for,
and to my editor Elizabeth Mazer, who was as
excited as me to see Myles and Delsie's story come
together. Thanks also to Giselle Regus for her
excellent editorial help and suggestions.
A final thanks to my readers, especially those of you
who've traveled with me from the Old West
to the battlefronts of WWI and back again.

Chapter One

~❦~

Saint Joseph, Missouri, June 1860

"Can I help you, miss?" The horseman cocked an eyebrow at Delsie, his surprise evident in each line of his weathered face. Clearly he wasn't used to finding ladies standing around the Pony Express Stables. Especially at this early hour.

Delsie forced her lips into a smile, despite the nervousness making her stomach roil. Good thing she hadn't eaten any breakfast at the hotel. "I'd like to speak to your fastest Express rider."

The man rubbed his stubbled chin. "I suppose that'd be Myles Patton, miss. But if you need a letter delivered right quick, you ought to take it to the office at the Patee House hotel."

"This concerns more than a letter." She drew herself up to full height, although the top of her rounded hat still didn't reach the man's shoulder. "May I speak with him please?"

The man shrugged. "I think he's inside the stables. His run begins in less than an hour. If you'll wait here, I'll get him."

"Thank you." She exhaled with relief. One obstacle down. Now if she could only convince this Mr. Patton to go along with her plan.

Delsie turned her back on the open stable doors and brought her handkerchief to her nose. The smell of manure, permeating the morning air, made her nausea worse.

Hold on, Lillie. Delsie clutched her leather valise tighter in her hand as she thought of her sister. *I'm coming.*

Her luggage held a change of clothes, a nightgown, a few toiletries, money she'd received in exchange for selling nearly all of her inherited jewelry and the most recent letter from her older sister. One of many unopened letters Delsie had just discovered inside her father's desk back home in Pennsylvania.

A man strode toward her, his face shadowed beneath his hat. He wore an elaborate riding uniform, complete with silver decorations and a scabbard hanging at his side. Delsie blinked in surprise; she'd been expecting a ruffian in a rawhide jacket and trousers.

"Mr. Patton?" She tucked her handkerchief into the sleeve of her blue riding habit.

He tipped up his hat, revealing black eyes and a dark beard that accentuated his strong jaw and bronzed skin. Delsie gulped. He was rather handsome, in a rough sort of way, minus the scowl on his face and the way he sized her up as if she were a pampered child.

"Who are you?" he asked in a tone bordering on rudeness. "And what do you want?"

He certainly wasn't taken in by the beauty of her dark hair or her midnight-blue eyes like her would-be beau Flynn Coppell always claimed to be. But perhaps that was a good thing. If this Mr. Patton agreed to help her they'd be spending a great deal of time in each other's company.

"My name is Delsie Radford," she said with feigned cheerfulness. "I'm here to request a ride."

"Livery stable's down the street." He turned away.

"Wait. You don't understand." She hazarded a step toward his retreating figure. "I need a ride to California."

He spun back, his eyes traveling the length of her again. Delsie tried not to squirm under his scrutiny. "I'm guessing that fancy getup you're wearing means you can read."

She frowned. "Of course I can read."

"Good. Then you'll notice the sign above the building here says Pony Express Stables and not the Overland Stagecoach. Good day, Miss Radford." He twisted on his spurred heel once more.

Throwing propriety to the wind, Delsie rushed after him. "I can't take the stage, Mr. Patton. That's a three-week journey and I must be in California in eighteen days. Not a day later."

"Can't be done," he barked over his shoulder.

Delsie finally caught up with him, close enough to reach out and grip his sleeve. He froze immediately at her touch. An almost panicked expression flickered across his shadowed face, but at least he'd stopped.

"I read about the incredible feat the Express riders performed with that first run in April. Bringing the mail to California in ten days." She hadn't exactly read the newspaper article herself—Papa didn't think perusing the paper a worthy pastime for women—but he'd read the news out loud to her and Flynn over dinner one evening.

Myles shook his head. "That wasn't done by one Express rider. We ride a hundred miles or more along our assigned routes. Then we return with the eastbound mail a few days later to our starting point and do it all over again."

He shrugged off her hold. "We carry mail, Miss Radford, not passengers. Besides, I've heard talk that Indian trouble has likely closed parts of the Pony Express between Utah and California—some of the mail might not even be getting through. What would you do once you reached Salt Lake City?"

"I am aware of the situation and the dangers, Mr. Patton." She'd heard plenty of talk—first on the stagecoach and later on the train after she'd left her aunt's home in Saint Louis. "But I'm willing to pay you."

He harrumphed. "I doubt you've got enough to make it worth—"

"How's five hundred dollars?" She patted the front of her valise.

His eyebrows rose and a flicker of emotion skimmed across his features. Was it interest?

"I recognize the absurdity of my request," Delsie admitted. He needed to know she hadn't worked out this solution with no thought to the consequences. "But I'm willing to pay you five hundred dollars, if you'll help me get to California by the twenty-first of this month."

With her request out in the open, she pressed her lips together and waited for his response. *Please, Lord*, she prayed through the ensuing silence. *I know this may be a foolhardy venture, but surely Lillian is that important to You, and to me, to make this work.*

Myles blew out his breath. Was he relenting? "What's so important you gotta get to California for?"

A flush heated Delsie's cheeks. "I'd rather keep the reason to myself."

"Look, miss." He readjusted his hat, pushing it up and pulling it back down again. "If I'm going to attempt this, even for five hundred dollars, I need to know what I'm getting myself into."

"So you'll do it, then?"

"Didn't say that. What's your reason for going all that way, Miss Radford?"

Delsie heaved her own sigh. "It's for my sister."

Myles frowned. "Is she dying or something?"

"No." But there were things that would die if she failed to reach California in time—like Delsie's promise to her mother on her deathbed and the chance to restore the close relationship she'd once shared with her sister.

A whisper of sadness swept through her at the reminder of their sweet and gentle mother. Lillian and their father, Owen Radford, were far more impetuous and stubborn, more prone to harbor a grudge. For this reason Delsie's mother had made her promise to look after the other two in Lydia Radford's absence.

Delsie had diligently done so, smoothing things as best she could between her father and sister for the past six years. At least until Lillian had refused to marry the man their father had chosen for her and instead followed her farmer beau to California ten months ago. Delsie hadn't known where her sister had been living or if Lillie was even all right until she'd found the letters her father had hidden from her. Now the only way to keep her pledge to her mother was to go after Lillie herself.

"I know it may sound silly." Delsie tilted her chin to meet Myles's stern look. "But it's imperative I be at my sister's wedding on June twenty-second. If I'm not there, I will never see her again. She and her husband are bound for Oregon the following day and I don't know where they'll be living once they reach their destination." Gripping her valise tighter, she added in a clear voice, "I'm willing to risk whatever this journey may bring to be there and fulfill a promise I made a long time ago. Surely helping family is something you can understand."

The lines around his dark eyes tightened. "I don't have any family."

Compassion filled her, but she schooled her tongue, certain he didn't want her pity. This loneliness must be what Lillie felt, without family there in California, thinking Delsie had no desire to contact her.

"Why me?" Myles asked, jerking Delsie from thoughts of her sister.

"That other gentleman said you were the fastest—"

"No. Why have *me* take you the whole way? Why not ask a different Express rider at each home station? Pay each one?"

"Because convincing one man to help me is proving to be most difficult," Delsie quipped. The barest hint of a smile twitched at his masculine lips before he suppressed it. "I also don't want to end up in the middle of Nebraska with no one willing to help me move forward or back."

He folded his arms, stretching his shirt tighter and hinting at the sinewy muscles beneath. Delsie glanced away. She watched the toe of his boot kick at a dirt clod and resisted the urge to do the same. Would he refuse to help her? If he did, there'd be no hope for reaching Lillie by the twenty-second—she'd be gone forever, assuming Delsie wanted nothing to do with her.

At last, Myles emitted a low growl and lowered his arms to his sides.

"Here's what I'll do, Miss Radford. I'll take you with me on my route today." A rush of gratitude prompted Delsie to step forward, with the intent of reaching for his arm again, but she stopped when Myles held up a hand. "I expect to be paid twenty-five dollars when we reach Guittard's tonight. I'll decide then if I think we can go the rest of the way to California."

She nodded. "Thank you, Mr.—"

"I wouldn't thank me just yet." He pulled off his hat and ran a hand through his thick, black hair. "We have a hundred and twenty-five miles to ride, changing horses every ten to twelve. I can't deliver the mail fast enough if we ride together, so you'll have to ride your own horse."

"I know how to ride."

A glimmer of amusement flashed in his eyes as he replaced his hat on his head. "We'll see. Since the station owners know me, I think we can get you a fresh mount each time I get one. But it'll cost you a few dollars for the extra horse and we don't waste time at any of the stations. We're in and out in two minutes or less. The moment you start to slow me down, I'll drop you off at the next station and collect you when I return to Saint Joseph. Is that clear?"

The reality of what she was about to do pressed down on her, momentarily bringing doubt and a panicked throbbing to her pulse. Could she really do this? A hundred and twenty-five miles in one day sounded suddenly daunting—and she had eighteen hundred to go to reach California.

The memory of Lillie's tear-stained face as she'd ridden away from the house rose into Delsie's mind. This same image still haunted her dreams. Surely she could endure anything to help her sister and keep her promise to their mother.

"I'll keep up," she said, infusing the words with haughty confidence, even if she didn't feel it.

The merriment returned to Myles's gaze, though she wasn't sure if it meant he, too, doubted her abilities or if he found her show of bravery humorous. No matter, he'd agreed, at least for today's ride.

"In that case, Miss Radford," he said, doffing his hat

and giving her a mocking smile, "let me be the first to welcome you to the Pony Express."

Myles had plenty of reasons to suspect Delsie Radford, determined as she was, would falter in her resolve to travel to California—and soon. She was the epitome of a wealthy young lady, with her fine clothes, spotless gloves and a bag containing more money than he could make in six months working for the Pony Express.

Just like Cynthia. Myles ground his teeth against the thought.

Sure enough, the first crack in Delsie's confident facade came the moment he led the horses out of the stable.

"You…um…don't have a sidesaddle, do you?" She eyed the trimmed-down saddles on the two horses.

"Nope." Myles walked toward her, his spurs clinking, his scabbard and revolvers bumping the legs of his decorative trousers. The morning sun glittered off the silver decorations adorning his uniform and his horse. He plucked at his collar with one hand, counting down the minutes until he could change out of the fancy getup. "We use these lighter 'California tree' saddles with the shorter, broader saddle horn. Not a sidesaddle in sight." He stopped the horses beside her. "Change your mind?"

He saw her visibly swallow, then a grim smile graced her mouth. "If you'd be so kind as to help me up, Mr. Patton."

Myles cocked an eyebrow. Did the girl possess more gumption than she first appeared to? He quickly dismissed the idea—all these rich girls were alike. She'd be lucky if she made it the fifteen miles to the Troy station, let alone the hundred and twenty-five to Guittard's home station by tonight.

Once he'd helped her sit astride her horse, Myles swung up onto his own. Delsie did her best to pull down the hem of her dress, but she couldn't quite hide her button-up shoes or the section of her lower calves clad in stockings that peeked above them. Myles jerked his gaze away.

"We'll ride to the office at the Patee House to collect the mail, then we'll—"

The blast of a cannon from the direction of the hotel silenced the rest of his words. It was time to go. He nudged his horse in the direction of the Patee House.

Glancing back over his shoulder, he made sure Delsie guided her mount behind his. The only telltale sign of her embarrassment at straddling the mare could be seen in the pink blush that stained her cheeks. But she kept her ridiculously flowered hat tilted high, even as they rode down the street past the few people out and about at this hour.

"Wait here," he told her when they reached the office. He swung down and went inside to collect the mail. "Morning," he called to the man at the counter.

"Morning, Patton. Here's the mail from back East." The man handed over the leather *mochila* or knapsack, which fit over the horse's saddle and contained the mail inside four padlocked boxes.

Myles grunted in response. If he hurried out, maybe the other fellow wouldn't notice Delsie outside. He figured the less he had to explain about his tagalong passenger, the better. He exited the office, the *mochila* in hand, but the other man followed him outside.

"Looks like a nice day for a—" The man's friendly remark died the moment his eyes caught sight of Delsie. "Morning, ma'am." He removed his hat. "Are you in need of directions?"

The color in her face increased as she shook her head. "No. I'm waiting for Mr. Patton."

Myles felt the man's gaze boring into his back as he placed the knapsack over his horse's saddle.

"Didn't know you had yourself a new girl, Patton…"

Myles scowled and mounted his horse again. "I don't," he bit off the words. "Let's go, Miss Radford." He swung the animal around. "We ride full out down the hill to the river. The ferry will be waiting."

Not stopping to see if she followed or not, he charged his horse forward. They tore through the street at a full gallop. The *boom* of the cannon sounded behind him, signaling to the ferry that he was coming. He and his mount raced down the hill. The wind tore at his face and hat, and he had to keep a hand on the brim to keep from losing it. A few passersby cheered as he rode past and he lifted his chin in greeting.

At the river, he jerked his horse to a stop. The beast danced with energy from the spirited ride. Myles twisted in the saddle to see Delsie gallop toward him. Just when he thought her mare would ram into him, she yanked back on the reins and stopped the animal. Her hat had slipped off her hair to hang down her back by its ribbons, but her blue eyes, the color of deep twilight, glittered.

"Do you always ride this fast?" she asked, her voice breathless.

"No. Only when we're being pursued by Indians." Myles climbed out of the saddle. "It's mostly for show—like my outfit here."

He went to help her dismount. As he placed his hands on her trim waist and assisted her to the ground, Delsie frowned, her eyebrows dipping toward her pert nose. Did she look down on him and his lowly station in life as Cynthia had? Myles pulled his hands away and practically dropped her onto her feet.

"I know you're trying to scare me, Mr. Patton," she said, bracing herself against the saddle.

He tipped his hat up. "Come again?"

"With your remark about Indians." She righted her own hat and tucked a few strands of hair back into the elaborate coil at the back of her neck. "I told you I am aware of the dangers, but I'm still intent on reaching my sister for her wedding on the twenty-second."

She knew of the dangers? Myles resisted the impulse to laugh at her naïveté. "Can't say I didn't warn you." He took the reins of his horse and started toward the waiting boat. "Come on. It's time to board the ferry."

Once the mounts were situated on the boat and it had pulled away from the bank, Myles excused himself.

"Where are you going?" Delsie asked, a note of alarm in her voice.

"I'm not up and leaving. Like I said, this uniform is only for show. We always change on the boat."

Her face relaxed, though he noticed lines of worry still pinched her eyes.

"You ever been on a boat before?"

She shook her head. If a short ferry crossing made her this nervous, how in the world did she expect to survive the next eighteen days? Myles battled the urge to ask the captain to take Delsie back to the Saint Joseph shore. He'd given his word to accompany her all the way to Guittard's, though, and he'd do it. Not only because his stepfather had ingrained in him the importance of integrity, but Myles had also sworn an oath as a rider to conduct himself honestly.

He ducked into the room the Express riders used for changing and traded the fancy uniform and scabbard for a trail-worn shirt and a buckskin jacket and trousers, though he kept his Colt revolvers. Despite loving Cynthia, he'd always loathed the idea of having to dress up if they married. He much preferred the ease and comfort of his riding clothes, and the absence of stiff collars and scratchy fabrics.

When he emerged from the changing room, he was surprised to find Delsie standing at the railing. Her gloved hands held the metal rail in a vise-like grip, but she stood there nonetheless, her face turned toward the western horizon.

"Is trying new things a first for you?" he couldn't help asking.

She glanced at him, without loosening her hold on the railing. "Is it that obvious?" Her lips curved into a crooked smile. "Lillian, my sister, was the adventurous one. I was more content to stay near the house or our governess. But eventually she would coax me to join her in some harebrained scheme, in which one or both of us ended up dirty or in tears."

A feeling of loneliness cut through Myles at the familial picture she presented. His parents had both died of illness before he turned five. He'd been taken in by his stepfather after that. Charles Patton had lost his wife and new baby a few months earlier. The man soon became the only father Myles could remember—so much so that he'd taken on Charles's last name as his own. His stepfather had taught him everything he knew about horses and had encouraged Myles's dream of owning a horse ranch one day. Even five years after his death, Myles still mourned the man and the loss of the only family he'd ever known.

He cleared his throat to ward off the emotion collecting there. "Does your sister know you're coming to her wedding?"

Delsie shook herself as though she'd been caught up in memories, as well. "No…she doesn't. I considered writing, but when I heard the mail wasn't necessarily getting through out West, I decided to go in person instead. I didn't want to risk a letter not reaching her in time."

"Suppose that makes sense."

The ferry bumped against the shoreline. Myles led his horse down the gangplank, Delsie and her mare following behind. "Welcome to Kansas," he said drily.

"What do we do now?" Delsie asked as he assisted her into the saddle again.

"We ride."

Myles climbed onto his horse and urged it forward,

whistling for his sparrow hawk, Elijah. He'd let the bird fly off earlier, as was his custom, to collect some breakfast of its own. A few seconds later, the brown-and-blue hawk swooped over the wharf and landed on Myles's shoulder. The bird would remain there most of the trip, except when Myles changed horses at the different swing stations or when it felt more inclined to fly ahead.

"Is that your bird?" Delsie nudged the mare closer and eyed the hawk with obvious fascination.

"I found him, out on the prairie, if that's what you mean." He rubbed the speckled breast of the hawk. "He was hurt, so I brought him home and fixed him up."

"Does the bird have a name?"

"Elijah," Myles muttered.

"Elijah? That's an unusual name for a pet."

He frowned at her remark, not wishing to get into the particulars. "Pick up the pace, Miss Radford. We've got mail to deliver."

Without waiting to see if she complied or not, Myles urged his horse to move faster. A few people called out in greeting to him as he made his way swiftly through town. Myles tipped his hat in response. If anyone thought it strange that a woman, and a well-dressed one at that, dogged his heels, no one said so. He'd have enough explaining to do at the stations along the route today.

Once the people and buildings gave way to open prairie, Myles pushed his horse into the usual slow gallop. The sunshine had burned away the coolness of the early-morning air and now it glistened off the dewdrops dotting the grass. The clean, fresh smell of wind and prairie filled Myles's nostrils and he sucked in a deep breath, filling his lungs completely. Only out here, charging across the plains, did he feel at home, with the sky, the earth and Elijah for companions.

Of course he couldn't entirely forget the woman riding several feet behind him. He shot a look over his shoulder to ensure Delsie was keeping up. Her hands seemed to grip the reins as tightly as she had the boat railing, but her wide-eyed stare appeared to hold more interest than fear.

"It's so big…and wide," she called to his back. A few moments later her horse drew alongside his. "I'm from Pennsylvania, you see. It's very different than this. Are you from Missouri originally, Mr. Patton?"

"Yes."

"Have you ever been back East?"

"No."

"What's the farthest west you've been?"

"Nebraska."

He eyed her with mounting irritation. Did she plan to talk the entire one hundred and twenty-five miles to Guittard's? He wasn't accustomed to hearing much but the thud of the horse's hooves beneath him and the occasional trill of birds in the distance. Elijah watched her, too, his head cocked to the side as though trying to figure out the strange creature tagging along with them today.

"How far is it to the first station?"

Was she already uncomfortable? He stifled a groan. She rode well enough, despite the absence of a side-saddle. "The Troy station is about fifteen miles from

Saint Joseph," he answered. "It's at the Smith Hotel. We'll change horses there and head on to the hotel in Syracuse."

A smile quirked her lips, though she tried to hide it. Myles got the instinct impression she was laughing at him. "Something funny?"

She shook her head, but her deep blue eyes danced in a way that belied the gesture.

He raised his eyebrows in silent question.

"I was only thinking that was the longest speech I've heard from you since we started riding." She drew herself up in the saddle and glanced away at the distant trees. "I was beginning to think you couldn't sit a horse and talk at the same time."

Myles watched her shoulders rise with stifled laughter, bringing a low growl from his throat. This only added to her fit of merriment. He scowled at her hat. What had he gotten himself into by agreeing to bring her along?

"I'm sorry," she said, turning to face him again. "That was…unkind."

"Not at all." He feigned a forgiving smile. "If we could all talk a streak like you, Miss Radford, news would travel even faster than the Pony Express."

Her mouth fell slightly open and her eyes narrowed. Myles tried to maintain a deadpan expression, but he couldn't hold back his chuckle for long. If she could dish out the sarcasm, she could certainly learn to swallow some herself.

With another chuckle, he pulled his horse ahead, relishing the pounding of the hooves against the prairie sod and the blessed sound of quiet from behind.

Chapter Two

The Smith Hotel, in Troy, Kansas, appeared ahead. Myles rode straight to its large barn and jumped to the ground. One man held the reins of his next horse, while another yanked the *mochila* from the saddle to throw it over the new one.

"I need a second horse," Myles explained as Delsie stopped her mare beside them. The two men gaped openly at her.

The man holding the new horse's reins recovered first. "What's wrong with this one, Patton?"

Myles hurried over to help Delsie dismount. "Nothing. But I need another horse—for the lady here." When the man shot Myles a bewildered look, he added, "I'll explain later, Rogers. Just get us another horse. She'll pay to ride it."

Thankfully, the man brooked no more complaint and raced into the barn to collect the second horse. Myles climbed into the saddle again, turning an expectant gaze on the hotel. Right on cue, a young lady exited the building and ran toward him. In each hand she held one of the fried pastries the Troy station was known for.

"Thank you," Myles said, accepting the treats. He immediately handed one down to Delsie, then bit off a bite of the chewy, sweet dough. "Delicious," he murmured.

Delsie sniffed at the pastry, then took a delicate bite. Myles rolled his eyes at her prim manners. Did she honestly think she could make it across half the country when she couldn't even— The unfinished question died within his mind as he watched the fried treat disappear between her lips in less than a minute.

A startled laugh escaped his mouth. If Delsie heard it, she didn't react. She simply stood there waiting for Rogers, looking as imperial and composed as a duchess, as if she hadn't just devoured her pastry in two bites.

Well, I'll be, Myles thought with a rueful shake of his head. She'd clearly been starving, though she hadn't let on one bit. He glanced at his own half-eaten pastry and extended it toward her.

"No, thank you," she responded politely, though she wouldn't quite meet his gaze as she sipped water from the canteen one of the riders had found for her.

At that moment, Rogers led her new horse out of the barn. Delsie handed him a few dollars before he helped her into the saddle. Myles kneed his horse forward and they were off again.

The next four relay stations brought more of the same routine, minus the pastries. He'd ride in first, tell the men he needed a second horse, then he'd wait while they gawked a few seconds at Delsie before scrambling to collect and saddle another mount. Delsie seemed to take it all in stride, paying for the horses and climbing back into the saddle each time without hesitation and even offering courteous smiles to the other Express workers.

When they reached their fifth station, though, Myles could see she was beginning to wilt like a flower in the height of summer. Once astride her new horse, she paused and squeezed her eyes shut. He knew from his first few Express runs the discomfort of being in a saddle for so long. But it couldn't be helped—not if he was to deliver the mail on time and not if she planned to ride this way from here to California.

Elijah left his shoulder to go hunt for a mouse or a smaller bird, reminding Myles of the hardtack he kept in his jacket. The Troy pastries and the promise of a full meal at Guittard's was sufficient food for himself, but he imagined Delsie wasn't used to such a long day with so little to eat.

With the ease of practice, he managed to remove the hardtack without slowing his horse. "Hungry?"

Delsie took a long moment to answer, her hand rubbing at the back of her neck. She'd been doing that more and more the past two hours. "Yes…thank you." She took the piece of hardtack he handed her, and without hesitation or inquiry as to what it was, she bit into it.

After she'd finished off that piece, he extended the other to her. "Aren't you hungry?" she asked, her gaze moving from his hand to his face. He couldn't recall ever seeing another woman with such dark blue eyes. They were nearly black, like her hair, but still blue enough to add contrast.

"I don't usually eat much till I get to Guittard's. This is just for emergencies."

"If you're sure…"

When he nodded, she took the rest of the biscuit from him. Again, she lifted her hand to rub at her neck as she ate. She had to be sweating bullets in the thick fabric of her high-collared dress, and her silly hat barely shaded her eyes.

Myles reached for his canteen, an idea forming. "You got a handkerchief with you?"

Delsie reached into one sleeve and removed a white piece of cloth. "Yes, why?"

"Can I see it?"

She studied him quizzically, then handed him the handkerchief. Leaning slightly to the side, Myles poured a little water from the canteen onto the cloth and squeezed out some of the excess.

"Try putting this around your neck. It oughta help keep you cool." He pressed the damp cloth into her gloved hand.

Delsie obeyed, draping the wet handkerchief against the exposed skin at the base of her neck. An audible sigh of contentment reached his ears and her eyes fell shut. "That feels…wonderful."

Myles allowed himself a smile at her obvious relief, especially since she couldn't see him. "You're welcome."

She opened her eyes to look at him. "Thank you." The words were quiet and genuine, reminding him of the woman herself. At least when she wasn't talking a mile a minute. To her credit, though, she'd spoken very little the past few hours, only breaking the silence between them with an occasional question about the landscape or the next relay station.

"How far have we come?" she asked, looking around them at the rolling prairie. The sunshine had held and the blue sky arched bright and cloudless overhead.

"When we reach Seneca in a few more hours, we'll have come eighty miles from Saint Joseph."

"So we'll have forty-five more to go after that?"

He tipped his head in agreement, impressed with her quick figuring.

"Does that mean you aren't going to leave me behind, then?" Her words were coated with as much teasing as they were challenge.

Myles cut her a look before facing forward again with a grin. "We'll see, Miss Radford. We'll see."

"That's Guittard's Station there."

Myles's words took a moment to penetrate past the fog inside Delsie's mind caused by the endless riding and movement and pain. She lifted her chin from where it drooped nearly to her chest. Ahead of them in the evening sun, past the woods and creek, she spied a two-story wooden structure with a front porch and plenty of windows flanking its sides. A large barn was also visible. While the place might appear rustic standing beside the ornate hotels back East or her own brick house back in Pennsylvania, Delsie couldn't recall a more welcomed sight. Her first day on the trail was finally at an end.

They rode to the stable, where Myles dismounted

first before coming to assist her. She was too exhausted in mind and body to pay much heed to the open stares from the other Express workers who'd come to collect the horses. She'd grown accustomed to the surprised looks or words exchanged at each station along the route when the men discovered her riding beside Myles and on a Pony Express horse, no less.

Myles lifted her to the ground, but when he released her waist, Delsie found her legs would no longer support her. Her knees crumbled beneath her riding habit, and she would have fallen onto the hard-packed dirt if Myles hadn't gripped her arm.

"Careful," he murmured, his voice surprisingly gentle. "You're likely a little stiff by now."

Stiff? She gave an unladylike snort. The single word didn't even begin to explain what she felt at the moment. Somewhere back on the trail, the throbbing ache in her back and legs had finally numbed, bringing temporary relief. But as she hazarded a step, with Myles still holding on to her elbow, sharp prickles of pain lanced through her lower body. She almost preferred the numbness.

Delsie bit her lip to keep from crying out as she hobbled next to Myles—she didn't want the triumph of the day marred by complaint. But, oh, how she longed for her bed at home, with its laundered sheets and feather-soft mattress.

"Myles!" An older man approached them from the direction of the house. A gray beard and a friendly smile graced his weather-beaten face. His blue-gray eyes widened when he noticed Delsie limping alongside the Express rider. "Who's this young lady?"

Myles stopped walking, forcing Delsie to follow suit. She didn't think she could manage a single step on her own just yet. "Good to see you, Amos. This is Delsie Radford." He motioned to the other man with his free hand. "Miss Radford, meet Hank Amos. Express worker, avid explorer and accomplished harmonica player."

Hank Amos chuckled and extended his hand. "Guilty as charged. Pleased to meet you, Miss Radford."

Delsie shook his hand. "Nice to meet you, too, Mr. Amos."

His laughter deepened. "Not to contradict a lady, Miss Radford, but call me Amos. Everybody does." He glanced at the sky. "Elijah off hunting?" he asked.

Myles nodded. "He flew off before we rode in."

Amos considered Delsie, his gaze lingering on the spot where Myles still held her arm. "What brings you West…with Mr. Patton?"

Myles released Delsie's elbow at once and took a deliberate step to the side. She swayed a moment, but her feet held firm. "I promised to escort her to Guittard's today."

Delsie threw him a questioning glance, but he wasn't looking at her. He'd told her he would consider tonight whether to take her the rest of the way to California. She hoped he hadn't already made up his mind. While she felt nigh unto death, she'd certainly kept up her end of the bargain by not slowing him down.

"Are you catching the stage from here, Miss Radford?"

"No. We're actually going—"

"To be late for dinner," Myles interjected. "Let's get you some real food, Miss Radford." With that, he clutched her elbow again and led her at a trot toward the house.

Delsie frowned up at him. Did he really care that much about her well-being? He had offered her his hardtack hours ago and helped her cool down with his wet-handkerchief trick. But something about his thoughtfulness right now struck her as false. Why hadn't he let her tell his friend about her plans? She opened her mouth to ask him, but the words were forgotten the instant she inhaled the tantalizing smell of cooked ham and rolls floating from the house.

Her stomach grumbled in response, resurrecting the gnawing sensation she'd felt for hours. She placed a hand over her middle to squelch it. "That smells absolutely scrumptious," she muttered, though not softly enough.

Amos gave another throaty chuckle. "Tastes even better."

"I think if shoe leather smelled that wonderful, I'd eat my fill and die perfectly happy."

There was a low rumbling that sounded in her right ear, not unlike distant thunder but more jovial. It took Delsie several seconds to realize the noise came from Myles—he was laughing at her remark.

Though she knew it shouldn't, the sound of his laughter and the knowledge she'd solicited it filled her with momentary pleasure. Her father would be displeased at her errant thought. She was supposed to be deciding if she loved Flynn Coppell, the man who managed her father's bank, not entertaining ideas of how to make some other man laugh once more. Of course what she was or wasn't thinking would likely be the least cause for worry, if Owen Radford could see her now. Alone in Kansas, having ridden one hundred and twenty-five miles with a man she'd never met before this morning.

Myles steered her toward the back entrance. Inside the kitchen, Delsie found herself seated at a large wooden table beside Myles and across from Amos. Her backside instantly protested the return to a seated position, especially on the uncushioned seat, but Delsie chose to be grateful that neither the chair nor the table would be moving any time soon.

They were served ham, eggs, rolls and coffee by the station owner's wife, who, upon discovering another woman in her kitchen, made a motherly fuss over Delsie. Uncertain why Myles wanted to keep quiet about her plans, she answered the woman's questions, and those from the other Express workers as they trailed in, with the simple explanation that she was going to visit her sister in California.

Delsie ate everything on her plate and even accepted seconds of the ham and eggs. Her father would have been horrified by her ferocious appetite, but he'd never ridden so far in a single day.

Though she longed to sequester herself in a room upstairs and wash away the dust from the day's ride, she lingered at the table, listening to the Express riders' stories. The tales they told of dodging Indian arrows, riding through thunderstorms or racing buffalo across the prairie sent tremors of fear and excitement up her spine. Would she encounter all these experiences herself? The conversation soon turned to the Indian troubles farther west and the speculation on how the other Express stations and riders were faring.

"Come, now, boys," the station owner's wife gently scolded in her slight French accent as she refilled the coffee mugs. "No more of that kind of talk." She tipped her head at Delsie. "Especially in the presence of a lady."

Delsie scooted her chair back and stood. "That's all right, Mrs. Guittard. I believe I shall retire for the night. Thank you for the delicious dinner. I can honestly say it was better than anything I've eaten back home in Pennsylvania."

The woman blushed at the compliment. "I'll show you to your room, Miss Radford."

Delsie glanced at Myles, as did everyone else in the room, but he was gazing into his coffee cup. "I just need to locate my valise first…"

Myles scraped back his chair. "I'll get it."

After bidding the rest of the workers good-night, she followed Mrs. Guittard up the stairs to a large and tidy bedroom. "I'll get you some water to wash up." She exited the room, pulling the door shut behind her.

Delsie unpinned her hat and set it on the bureau. The mirror revealed a stretch of pink across her nose and upper cheeks. She touched the sunburned flesh with a sigh. *Oh well.* She'd likely only get browner as the days went by.

All for you, Lillie, she thought ruefully as she went to peer out the window. She pushed back the curtains and spied Myles talking with Amos near the barn. He shook his head at something the older man said, then removed his hat and ran a hand through his dark hair. His entire manner breathed agitation. Were they talking about her?

As if they sensed her watching, they both glanced at the house. She jumped back and let the curtain fall into place. A knock at the door alerted her that Mrs. Guittard had returned with the promised water. Delsie let her in and the woman emptied the pitcher she carried into the basin on the bureau.

"There you go, my dear. Let me know if you need anything else." She crossed to the door, where she paused. "Will you be leaving early?"

"I believe so…" Delsie wished Myles had been more forthcoming about what to expect for the second day of their journey, but either way, she imagined they would be departing as early as they had today.

Once Mrs. Guittard left her, Delsie unwound her hair and released the top button of her collar. The simple act brought instant relief to her tender head and flushed neck. With the aid of a small towel, she bathed her face and hairline.

She was so caught up in the luxurious feel of the cool water against her heated skin that she yelped in surprise when someone pounded on her door. After dropping the towel into the basin, she threw open the door and found Myles standing there, her valise in one hand and his hat in the other.

"I brought you your…" His gaze shifted from the floorboards to her face and his eyes rounded in shock.

Belatedly she remembered her unbound hair and loose collar.

Fresh heat burned her face as Delsie brought her hand up to cover her exposed throat. "Yes, my bag. Thank you." She plucked it from his grip, prepared to retreat in mortification, but he didn't make a move to leave. "Is there something else you needed, Mr. Patton?"

He shifted his weight from boot to boot. "Well, you see—"

"Oh, your money," she finished for him. She lowered her hand to open her valise. "I believe we agreed upon twenty-five dollars…"

His hand closed over hers before she could locate the cash. The gentle, almost caring, touch felt different than the times he'd helped her on and off the Express horses today and succeeded in derailing her thoughts. A strange flurry of sensation churned inside her, similar to what she'd felt on the ferry ride that morning.

"I don't want your money, Miss Radford."

"You don't?" The color of his eyes reminded her of warm, liquid chocolate, the kind she liked to sneak from the kitchen and drink in her room after her father was asleep. Myles released her hand, bringing clarity back to her muddled mind. "B-but I promised to pay you for today."

"Look." He ran a hand through his disheveled hair, mussing it more. "You did…pretty well today, Miss Radford."

Pretty well? She cocked an eyebrow at him in defense. How many women did he know who could keep up with an Express rider for a hundred and twenty-five miles?

His lips twitched when he caught her look. "All right. I can give credit where it's due." He blew out his breath. "You rode as well as…as well as a new Express rider might."

It was Delsie's turn to hide a smile. "Seeing as you are a man of few words, Mr. Patton, I'll take that remark as a compliment."

"As you should." The merriment in his dark eyes faded and his expression returned to one of complete somberness. "That being said, I think this is a fool's errand." She started to protest, but he held up his hand to stop her. "Let me finish. Whether it's plain crazy or admirable that you want to be at your sister's wedding on the twenty-second, it can't be done."

Spikes of alarm shot through her. "But what about today?"

"Today was different." He jammed his hat on his head and began to pace the hall in front of her door, his boots clomping against the floorboards. "I know these station owners. But that ends tomorrow. No one past Guittard's knows me. You'll have to pay—possibly double what you did today—to take a horse at every station. Two horses." He held up two fingers as if she didn't remember. "And another thing. Like I told you before, I've never been farther west than Nebraska. I don't know the terrain, the stations or the dangers beyond that."

Myles stopped pacing to face her directly. "The time

it would take to learn all of that, to convince these station owners to lend you their Express horses…"

The dread that had tightened her stomach when he'd first begun his little speech grew worse, even before he half whispered his next words. "You won't make it to California when you need to."

"I…I have to." She clutched the valise to her chest, hoping to stop the panic rising into her throat and spilling over into tears. "There must be a way."

He shook his head, his look bordering on compassion. "Even if you rummaged up a guide and a couple of horses, the poor beasts wouldn't make it that far that fast. It's impossible. That's why we change out animals every ten to twelve miles. Besides, the supplies you'd need to strike out on your own would weigh the horses down too much."

The need to cry was growing stronger, the sting of tears forcing Delsie to blink. Had she left behind everything familiar, in order to reach Lillie, only to be turned back now?

"I'm sorry, Miss Radford." For once his voice held nothing but kindness. "If you'd like, we'll take it slow heading back to Saint Joe tomorrow."

"What I'd like is to go to California," she whispered, but she knew he heard her by the way he glanced at the floor again.

"Good night." He lifted his gaze to hers and held it for a moment. Though he didn't say it, Delsie sensed he, too, had experienced the bitter disappointment of having a dream ripped from one's grasp. "I'll see you at breakfast."

She gave a wordless nod and stepped back to shut the door. Alone once more, she sank onto the neatly made bed, her valise still crushed in her arms. She'd never felt such fatigue, such despair. Every muscle in her wearied body seemed to echo Myles's sentiment, *It can't be done.* The first of her tears skidded down her cheeks. In seventeen more days, her sister would be lost to her forever and her promise to their mother would be broken. There was nothing she could do to change either one.

Unable to hold back the sobs any longer, Delsie dropped onto the bed and buried her head in the pillow to muffle the sound. She'd managed this first part of her journey without crying once, despite the new and somewhat terrifying things she'd experienced since leaving her aunt's house.

Aunt Cissy had assumed Delsie was returning straight to Pennsylvania, after her two-week stay in Saint Louis, and Delsie hadn't bothered to correct her. She'd been so full of optimism once she'd concocted her plan to go to Lillie, just as she had today when she'd convinced Myles to take her with him. But now… The failure tasted worse than the hardtack she'd stomached earlier.

Twisting onto her side, she stared at the room's nice furnishings, not so different from the opulence she was accustomed to at home. What sort of room did Lillie live in? Did she enjoy being on her own as she'd claimed to in the letters Delsie had discovered?

Her eyes narrowed in on the book lying on top of the low table beside the bed. Delsie released her bag to the floor and sat up. She pulled the book onto her lap.

Her own Bible would've weighed her luggage down too much, so she hadn't brought it, but she was grateful to find one here.

She flipped aimlessly through the pages, wondering where to read, where to find solace. At her aunt's house, she'd been working her way through Hebrews. Delsie turned there now and located the last place she recalled reading. She began in chapter 10, but her mind was as much on her predicament as it was on the words before her. Until she reached verses thirty-five and thirty-six.

> Cast not away therefore your confidence, which
> hath great recompence of reward. For ye have
> need of patience, that, after ye have done the will
> of God, ye might receive the promise.

A feeling of warmth began near her heart and spread all the way to her tired fingers and toes as she reread the two verses. She'd felt that confidence from the moment she'd decided to go to Lillie and at every step up to now. Why should she doubt, then? If God wanted her to be in California before the twenty-second—and everything inside her said He did—then she had to trust and be patient that He would make that possible. That she would receive the promise, the reward, of fulfilling their dying mother's wishes and reuniting with Lillie before it was too late.

Delsie set the Bible on the bed and stood to pace the room, her arms tucked tight against her. Myles thought it impossible to either procure horses at every station or to travel with their own for so long. But was there a third solution they'd overlooked? One obvious to the Lord?

"Please help me see it, too," she prayed in a soft voice.

Calculations appeared in her mind's eye like figures on a chalkboard, the way they always did—the number of miles they had to go, the number of miles a horse could reasonably trot before needing to rest. She dug through her valise to find a pencil and Lillie's last letter. Using the back of one of the pages, Delsie wrote down the numbers in her head. She began playing with them, organizing them, rearranging them.

And then she saw it—the answer—as plain as day and as clear as the sky had been earlier. So simple and yet so hidden until this moment. A ripple of excitement and gratitude ran through her. *Thank You, Lord.* One problem solved. Now she only needed a guide and three horses.

She left the paper on her bed and crossed to the window again. The yard sat empty, though light from the open doors of the stable attested to someone's presence. Weariness had certainly affected her mind when she and Myles had ridden up earlier, but Delsie thought she recalled seeing a number of filled stalls inside the barn. Would the Guittards allow her to purchase three of their horses?

A figure exited the stable. It was Amos. As Delsie watched, the man lifted his arm and whistled, his eyes toward the western sky. Elijah soon appeared and swooped down to settle onto Amos's arm. She hadn't seen the bird come to anyone else all day, except Myles.

Clearly the creature saw something in both men that others might not.

What was it Myles had said about his friend? *Express worker, avid explorer and accomplished harmonica player.* Was it possible Amos knew the terrain beyond Nebraska?

Delsie studied the man's face as he gently ran his finger over the feathers on Elijah's head. Though she knew next to nothing about him, she instinctively sensed kindness within him, as the hawk obviously did. Just as she'd sensed integrity and honor within Myles, despite all his gruffness and sarcasm. Would the old man agree to join them? Would Myles be willing to split his money from her if Amos came along, too? There was only one way to find out.

Determination welled inside Delsie and she spun away from the window. She quickly did up her collar and arranged her hair in a hasty twist at the nape of her neck. There'd be enough time later on to finish washing and dressing for bed. Right now, she needed to corner Amos and present him with her new plan before Myles came to collect his bird.

She slipped into the hallway, down the stairs and out the front door without encountering anyone. As she stole around the side of the house, her eyes went to the streaks of pink and orange smearing the darkening sky overhead. The same sun was setting over Lillie. Delsie smiled at the thought. The assurance she'd felt earlier while reading once again filled her heart. Tomorrow she'd be back on her way to California and to her sister—she just knew it.

Let the West do its worst, she mused. She had Someone far greater on her side than all the Express riders and horses and hazards from here to the coast.

Chapter Three

Myles pushed his eggs around his plate, his appetite not its usual hearty self. Sleep had eluded him for several hours last night, as it had after Cynthia's betrayal two months earlier. He kept thinking of Delsie's soulful eyes filled with disappointment and grief when he'd conveyed the impossibility of her plans. She was clearly disheartened, but she hadn't raged at him or laid blame at his feet as he might've been tempted to do.

Her quiet acceptance of defeat wasn't the only thing that had kept him awake. He'd had a difficult time erasing the image of her unbound hair and cream-colored skin from his memory, too.

So she's pretty, Myles thought, scowling at his half-eaten breakfast. *Any man would say the same.*

Not for the first time since meeting Delsie the day before, he felt some relief at the knowledge that they would be parting company very, very soon. She kept surprising him, acting in ways that contradicted his opinions about rich folk, and he didn't like it one bit. He liked routine, consistency and taking risks only when he knew for certain what the outcome would be.

Funny that she'd all but admitted to being the same way on the boat yesterday. Except this harebrained scheme of hers clearly meant she'd thrown her normal caution out the window.

"Thank you for the breakfast, Mrs. Guittard." He stood, hoping she didn't take offense to him not finishing everything.

The woman smiled. "You're welcome, Mr. Patton."

Myles glanced at the kitchen doorway. "Should I let Miss Radford know it's time to eat?"

"She's already had her breakfast."

"Oh." He'd suspected she would sleep in, especially knowing how sore she'd be today.

"I believe she's in the stables," Mrs. Guittard added over her shoulder from where she was working over a pot of something at the stove.

Myles put on his hat and let himself out the back door. Apparently Delsie was as anxious to get back to Saint Joseph as he was. The thought erased some of his guilt over frustrating her plans, however unintentionally.

Good thing he hadn't let Amos in on her notion to reach California before the twenty-second—the man would have tried to make it work, no matter the foolhardiness of the venture. Amos hated to see a woman in distress. Myles suspected it was the fatherly nature in him, one he hadn't been able to practice on with his own children. Amos and his wife, who had passed away seven years earlier, had remained childless, despite a strong desire for a family.

The lightening sky overhead promised to be as clear and blue as the day before. The sight brought a whistle to Myles's lips, a tune he'd heard Amos play plenty of times on the harmonica. Elijah swooped down over the stable roof and landed on his shoulder.

"You get breakfast, boy?" He ran his hand over the bird's head, his gaze on the western horizon.

For one brief moment, he considered what it would've been like to travel farther than he'd ever been, all the way to California. His stepfather used to tell him a place like that, so far west, would have enough room for a horse ranch.

Someday.

Myles turned toward the stables. It was time to return to Saint Joseph and his current life. The longer he stayed with the Pony Express, the more money he'd make—money he could use to purchase that sprawling horse ranch in the future. Now that Cynthia no longer wanted to marry him, the ranch was his only dream and focus. It was the reason he'd considered Delsie's proposal to take her to California in the first place. But he'd just have to be content with earning the money slow and steady instead.

The whistle returned to his lips as he entered the nearest stable. Inside Delsie stood talking quietly to Amos, but she closed her mouth the moment Myles walked up. She had on a different dress than yesterday, her hair pinned up again beneath her ridiculous flowered hat. He looked past them and spied one, two…

three?…saddled horses. His merry tune ended on a sour note. Something was afoot.

"You planning a trip to Saint Joe?" he asked Amos with an attitude of nonchalance, despite the wariness churning inside him. Delsie avoided his gaze.

"Nope," Amos answered. The glitter in the man's blue-gray eyes only heightened Myles's suspicion.

"What's with the third horse, then?"

"Can't very well walk to California, can we?"

We? Myles scowled at Delsie's bent head. Sure enough she'd convinced Amos to go along with her wild scheme, just as he'd feared last night. Well, he'd put a stop to all this nonsense right now. "Miss Radford, we talked about this last night. It can't be done."

"But you said if we had our own horses—"

Myles tightened his jaw in exasperation. Had the woman heard the rest of his explanation? "I said even *if* we had our own horses, it still wouldn't work. They can't go fast enough."

"Not necessarily. I've figured out—"

"The supplies you'd need to travel that far will weigh them down. At that slow pace you wouldn't reach California until—"

"Myles?" Amos said, quietly but firmly.

"What?" he growled. Elijah ruffled his wings as if startled.

"Let the lady finish. She's come up with a plan that might work."

Myles took a moment to swallow back his irritation, then through ground teeth he managed to ask, "What do you propose, Miss Radford?"

Delsie glanced between him and Amos and back to him before her chin rose a notch. "I calculated everything out last night." She lifted her hand and showed him a piece of paper with numbers scrawled all over the back of it. "We can average a hundred miles a day, if we rest the horses for an hour about every fifteen miles. If we start at six in the morning, we could reach one of the Express stations, at that pace, by eight o'clock that evening."

"And supplies?" he countered, mostly in an attempt to hide how impressed he was with her calculations. Clearly Delsie Radford was more than a pretty face with a sudden penchant for adventure. She'd managed to come up with a fairly logical plan...so far.

"Instead of paying to use the stations' horses, I'll pay them for room and board and feed for the animals for the single night we stay there."

Myles scrubbed a hand over the stubble on his face. He hadn't bothered to trim his beard this morning in his anticipation of getting Delsie back to Missouri. "What about water or feed for the horses during breaks?"

Delsie slid a glance at Amos. "That's where Mr....I mean, Amos comes in. He's familiar with the route. He knows most of the rivers and creeks along the way, as well as the Express stations."

A sardonic laugh nearly escaped Myles's lips. She'd clearly thought of everything, the little conspirator. While he'd lain in his bed awake last night, feeling guilty as he'd imagined her heartbroken and weeping in her room upstairs, Delsie had actually been scheming behind his back. And doing a decent job of it as evidenced by her clever equations and her solicitation of Amos's help as a guide.

"What do you need me for, then?" He crossed his arms over his chest as a feeling he couldn't quite name settled there, tight and uncomfortable. It reminded him of the taunts he'd experienced as a child at school, about being an orphan, about how Charles wasn't his real pa. He'd quit going at age ten.

"Because I promised to pay you first..." Myles frowned, ready to argue with her. While the money would be nice, even if he got less than she'd originally offered after she paid the station owners and Amos, he wouldn't be pitied. "And because you know the most about horses," she added before he could protest. "Amos told me you worked for years at a livery stable. You know better than either of us when to rest the animals, when to push them. So you see, I need you..."

An attractive blush stained her cheeks at her words. The image of her long hair and exposed collarbone from last night entered Myles's mind again. "What I mean is *we* need you. Me, Amos and my sister."

Myles blew out his breath and absently rubbed Elijah's feathers. Did he still want to help her? A good portion of him preferred climbing into the saddle and heading east, never to see Miss Delsie Radford again. But the other part of him, growing more insistent the longer the silence stretched between them, wanted to see if she—if they—could really do this.

Could they reach California in seventeen more days? The challenge, and the chance to earn more money for his future ranch, was as alluring as the woman watching him with those dark blue eyes. Eyes framed with long lashes, above a slightly pink nose. If anything the sunburn only added to her beauty.

Careful, Myles, he warned himself.

He'd fallen for a pretty face once before, only to be spurned. Clever and attractive as Delsie might be, Myles knew all too well the impossibility of their two worlds ever coexisting. It had been that way with Cynthia and it would be no different with any other spoiled rich girl who came along.

"All right, Miss Radford. I'll send word to Saint Joe that I'll be gone for a few weeks. But mind you, if I lose my job over this, I'll hunt you down and demand more money." He regarded her with a level look. "Got it?"

A slight smile toyed with her mouth. "Yes, Mr. Patton."

He tugged his hat lower onto his head. "What do you want to do now?"

"Now," she said, smiling fully, "we ride."

If she'd thought she was sore after her first day of riding more than a hundred miles, Delsie knew better now. Nothing could compare to the pain and stiffness of a second day in the saddle. Her limbs felt as heavy as logs and as hard and unyielding as granite. Every rise and fall of the prairie ground seemed to radiate from her mare's hooves up through her back and all the way to her stiff neck. Sheer determination, coupled with the constant memory of her sister's tearstained face on the day Lillie had left, kept her from begging Myles and Amos to turn around.

Their pace nearly matched that of yesterday's, except for the rests that, according to Amos's fancy pocket watch and Myles's knowledge of horses, they were taking every hour and a half. Even Amos, riding behind her, didn't look the least bit uncomfortable, though he had to be in his early fifties. Perhaps by the time they reached her sister, Delsie would be just as seasoned on a horse.

She shifted in the saddle, hoping to find a position that didn't chafe her legs or add to her pain. Up ahead, Myles remained silent and alert as he had the day before, his bird perched on his shoulder. Delsie had fully expected him to refuse to accompany her any farther, despite her new and improved plan. But then he'd surprised her by agreeing.

Why is he really here? she wondered, not for the first time since they'd set out. Why hadn't Myles left her and Amos to fend for themselves?

Amos had told her his reasons for coming—the promise of adventure and a soft spot for helping women. She'd found herself telling him more about her sister, and why she had to reach her, than she'd confessed to Myles. Not that she trusted Amos more. But the older man seemed to grasp—and appreciate—her willingness to face whatever obstacles to help Lillie and her family by keeping her promise. It was something she sensed Myles didn't quite understand. Delsie could still visualize his hardened expression when he'd declared he had no family. The memory filled her with the same measure of sadness his words had on the boat.

Was it this pain and loneliness that made him hide behind a mask of curtness and annoyance? For it surely was a mask. She'd seen a glimpse here and there in the past twenty-four hours of a different man. One who possessed integrity and determination but also kindness and compassion. At other times, though, she could almost believe she'd imagined this different side to Myles. He hadn't spoken more than a handful of words to her since they'd begun riding. If he disliked her company so, why wasn't he headed straight back to Missouri?

With an amused sniff, she realized her questions had come full circle again.

"The horses need to stop soon," Myles called over his shoulder.

"Let's rest by those trees there," Amos answered.

In the distance Delsie spied a patch of trees alongside the river they'd been riding beside—according to Amos it was called the Little Blue. She sighed with relief at the thought of a rest. Perhaps some walking would ease the continued agony of riding.

Amos drew alongside her and examined his pocket watch. Shaking his head, he grinned. "Look at that. An hour and a half almost to the minute. The man's got a way with horses."

Just not with people. She instantly regretted the unkind thought. "How long have you known Mr. Patton, Amos?"

The older man squinted up at the blue sky. "Let's see, it's been about seven years now. Right after my wife died, God rest her soul."

"I'm sorry…about your wife. Did you have any children?"

"No." A wistful look passed over his weathered face.

"Not for wanting, that's for sure. We hoped and prayed for a family, but we came to realize that God had other plans." His gaze traveled from her to Myles. "Myles is the closest thing I have to family now. He's the one who encouraged me to hire on with the Pony Express, despite my being up there in years—as he likes to remind me." His mouth curved up in a broad smile.

Delsie rubbed at the back of her neck. As soon as they stopped, she'd wet her handkerchief, as Myles had done yesterday, to help prevent a sunburn. The longer she rode, the more she realized the impracticality of her stylish riding hat. Maybe she could trade it somewhere for a wide-brimmed one like the two men wore.

"Has he always been…um…" She searched for the right word.

"Hard-edged?" Amos supplied with a chuckle.

She bit back a smile and nodded.

"No, he hasn't." Amos wiped at his brow with his sleeve, then tugged his hat lower. "His folks died when he was real young, but he was raised by a good and godly man—his stepfather, Charles Patton. Myles took his stepfather's death pretty hard." He glanced at Delsie. She'd told him last night about her mother dying when she was thirteen. "But things really turned bad for him two months ago when his girl, this rich young lady from Saint Joe, refused to marry him after stringing him along for six years."

Delsie turned her attention to the man in front of them, riding tall and straight in his saddle. What had the man at the hotel in Saint Joseph said yesterday? *Didn't know you had yourself a new girl, Patton.* No wonder Myles had looked ready to pummel him.

Would Flynn feel the same, angry and bitter, if she returned home and told him she couldn't marry him? She couldn't picture him acting that way, but then again, did Flynn truly love her as it seemed Myles had this wealthy woman?

Flynn had told her she was the most beautiful woman in the world and would make him the happiest man alive she if agreed to marry him. But was it her that he truly looked forward to having or was it her inheritance? She'd been asking herself that question ever since she'd left Pennsylvania to visit Aunt Cissy in Saint Louis.

Now that Lillie had been struck from their father's will, Delsie stood to gain a great deal of money. Some she would inherit when she married, the rest she would receive upon her father's death, and Flynn knew the particulars. Despite her father's encouragement of the match, the thought that Flynn might be more interested in her wealth than in Delsie herself brought a mixture of unease and confusion to her stomach.

When they reached the trees Amos had indicated, the older man helped Delsie off her mare. She stumbled forward and braced herself against a nearby tree trunk as she waited for her legs to work properly again. Myles led the three horses to the riverbank and let them drink.

"Shall we eat the food Mrs. Guittard gave us?" Delsie asked. She didn't know if it was time for lunch, but the hunger in her middle could no longer be ignored.

"Fine by me," Amos said, taking a seat in the shade.

Myles gave a grunt of approval as he looped the

horses' reins around several low-hanging branches. He removed the simple meal of bread, cheese and apples from one of the saddlebags.

Delsie eyed the ground, trying to decide if she preferred sitting or standing at the moment.

"You're going to get dirty, Miss Radford," Myles said with a shake of his head, "so you might as well start now."

"But I wasn't…" She pressed her lips over her defense and glared at his bent head as he set out the lunch things. The man could truly be insufferable, even if he had good reason to be.

Chin up, she stepped away from the tree and plopped right onto the dirt as unladylike as possible. A cry barreled up her throat as pain shot through her spine, but she swallowed it back when she saw Myles quirk an eyebrow at her. Was that amusement or admiration glittering in his dark eyes?

She accepted the food he handed her, then waited until he and Amos had their portions before she spoke up. "May I say grace?"

Myles leaned back against the tree trunk and scowled in response.

Maybe he needed an explanation. "I'd like to give thanks for the food…and for a safe journey so far."

"Let her pray, if she wants, Myles." Amos removed his hat and nodded at Delsie.

She looked at the younger man, waiting for him to take off his hat, as well. They locked glares for a moment before he removed his hat and dipped his head. Fighting a small smile of victory, she bowed her head, as well. "Thank You, Lord, for this good food. And thank You for keeping us in Thy watchful care. Please bless Lillie and help us reach her in time. Amen."

Amos echoed her amen. Myles remained silent as he jammed his hat back on and started in on their meal. At least he hadn't put up too much protest about her praying. She bit into the homemade bread with relish. Quiet descended over their group, but it wasn't uncomfortable. A nice breeze gently swayed the trees and cooled her sunburned face.

Elijah, who'd flown off earlier, landed beside Myles. Something small and limp dropped onto the ground in front of him. As she watched, the bird began tearing into the rodent with its beak. Delsie's stomach twisted at the sight, robbing her of the rest of her appetite.

"I think I'll walk a bit." She stood and managed to get beyond the trees without limping.

Out of sight, though, Delsie slowed her steps to a faltering walk as she massaged the backs of her legs. She followed the river, enjoying the chance, however painful, to move on her own.

The blue sky and rolling prairie were so vast, so endless. Myles might scoff at her for thinking so, at least out loud, but she saw the hand of the Lord in the beauty of it. Something inside her stirred and responded to this new open world—something she didn't feel at home within the confines of her family's elaborate parlor or in the midst of a grand party.

Was it this restlessness that had come over Lillie, prompting her to leave her family and home behind and strike out after her beau, Clay Weeks? Delsie hadn't understood at the time why Lillie would defy their father's wishes or ignore his threats to disown her if she ran off to find *that farmer*. Her older sister had confessed she loved Clay, and if the rigidness of their society life and their father's disapproval wouldn't allow her to be with the man she loved, then she'd go West with him. And so she had.

Now looking over this wide country, Delsie felt for the first time a piece of what Lillie must have felt. Her life at home suddenly felt a bit stale and narrow when compared to what she'd seen and experienced in the past two days.

A low whistle sounded from behind. She turned to see Myles motioning for her. It was time to ride again. A loud sigh fell from her lips. Too bad she couldn't walk just as quickly to California. Even the thought of climbing back into that saddle sent tremors of fresh pain shooting through her legs and back.

"Only for you, Lillie," she murmured. "And for Mother."

When she reached the grove of trees where they'd stopped, she allowed Amos to assist her back onto her mare. Being the first to mount, she decided to move away from the trees to the open prairie, where she'd wait for the two men.

Delsie nudged the horse forward, dodging tree branches to keep from getting smacked in the face. One particularly long branch she pushed aside as far as she could while she passed by. But instead of swinging harmlessly through the air when she let go, the branch swung back and struck the rump of her horse with a loud *thwack*. The poor creature reared in fear. Delsie yelped and clung to the reins, her heart crashing hard against her ribs. The mare landed back onto all fours, then charged from the trees at a full run. From behind someone shouted, but she couldn't make out the words.

Squeezing her knees as tightly as she could, she managed to stay in the saddle, despite the horse's wild dash across the grass. The skin on her inner thighs stung with the effort. She tried to slow the mare by pulling back on the reins, but the frightened beast would have none of it. If anything, their careening pace increased.

Delsie held on, her fingers and hands aching, her pulse pounding as hard and as fast as the hooves below her. Would the horse eventually slow down or would she be forced to jump off in order to save herself? She peeked at the ground rushing dizzyingly beneath her and gulped. If she broke a bone, or worse, how would she manage to keep riding for the next seventeen days?

Oh please, Lord.

It was the shortest prayer she'd ever prayed, but she figured God understood why and what she was asking.

Off to her right, huge brown masses began turning tail and running at the approach of the runaway mare. Buffalo! Delsie managed only a quick look at their giant wooly frames, dozens of them, before they fled over a rise in the prairie. At least she could say she'd seen them, before it was too late.

The buffalo interrupted the mare's path of retreat, causing it to angle back toward the river instead of the open plains. Ahead Delsie spied another thick grove of trees. If the horse made a dash through them, she'd surely be knocked off or struck in the head.

Time to jump, then. She eyed the ground again. The thought of striking the earth at this intense speed made her want to vomit with fear. But it couldn't be helped.

She pressed her eyes shut, hoping the temporary blindness might squelch her nausea and ignite some confidence. She took a deep breath and leaned to the side. If she lived through this, she planned to share a few choice words with Lillie, though she instinctively knew her predicament was no one's fault but her own.

Just as she was about to release the reins and leap to safety, or to her death, something jerked the mare hard to the right. Delsie scrambled to keep hold of the reins and opened her eyes. Myles rode next to her, his hand gripping her horse's bridle in a firm fist. He didn't let go, even as the mare tried to shake off his grasp. Eventually the scared creature was forced to slow its pace in order to follow Myles and his mount.

When her horse, at last, came to a shuttering halt, Delsie realized she was shaking.

"Are you all right?" Myles asked, still keeping a hand on the animal's bridle.

Her teeth were chattering too much to speak, so she settled for a quick nod. When had it gotten so cold? She shivered and forced her fingers to release the reins. They would hardly uncurl from their clawlike grasp.

"Let's get you down." Myles finally released the mare's bridle and dismounted. He talked soothingly to the horse, all the while rubbing its nose and patting the side of its head, before he circled around to help Delsie off.

For some unknown reason the sight of him calming the mare, instead of her, sparked anger inside her. His next words didn't help. "You're shaking, Miss Radford," he said as he set her on her feet.

The tiny flame of anger roared to life. She'd come so close to being maimed or nearly killed. Her legs and skin hurt horribly from hours and hours in the saddle, and her face and neck were tender from the hot sun. And now this man had the audacity to turn his nose up at a little shivering after all she'd been through?

"Yes, I am, Mr. Patton," she snapped. "Unlike you, I'm not accustomed to riding a hundred miles a day or dealing with frightened horses or having my skin clawed by that uncomfortable saddle." Her voice hitched with unshed tears and she swallowed hard.

"I didn't mean—"

"Please. I just need to…" She caught sight of Amos riding up. She didn't want to dissolve into tears before them both. "I think I need to walk…"

Without waiting for Myles's reply, she marched past them and the horses, heading west. At least if she was slowing them down, she was moving in the right direction. She walked as fast as she possibly could, in spite of the tremors that still shook her body. Folding her arms, she tried to ward off the cold inside her. A sob raced up her throat and she covered her mouth with her hand, willing the tears back. She was alive—no use wasting tears on what might have been.

Delsie spied a flat rock in the grass and sat down on

it, her eyes on the western horizon. She'd only been on this portion of her journey for a day and a half, but already, it felt like months ago since she'd left Aunt Cissy's house or her own home in Pennsylvania.

Measured footsteps approached. Delsie cut a glance in their direction, surprised to see it was Myles walking toward her and not Amos. What did he wish to say now? Probably more comments about how unsuited she was for this trip.

She turned away from him and set her jaw. If she didn't speak, maybe he'd take the hint and leave her in peace to finish working through her earlier fear and adrenaline.

Something warm and leatherlike in smell settled over her shoulders. She recognized the buckskin jacket Myles wore. "Thank you…" she admitted begrudgingly. Her shivers began to subside as she pulled the jacket tighter around her.

He circled the rock and stood watching her from beneath his hat. "It gets easier."

She tilted her head to give him a quizzical look.

"The riding, the soreness. You might want to get a pair of leather trousers, though." He kicked at a clump of grass. "That'll help with the chafing."

Her cheeks flushed at his words, but she didn't break eye contact. "I will not be wearing trousers, thank you."

One side of his mouth lifted. "I meant under your dress."

The heat on her face intensified. She ducked her chin and stared at the ground, hoping he would leave.

"Look, I didn't mean anything unkind back there."

Myles removed his hat and ran a hand through his hair. She'd seen it mussed more times on their short journey than lying flat or slicked back like Flynn wore it.

Myles squatted down in front of her, his hat dangling between his knees. "I only mentioned the shakes because...well, because I wanted to be sure you really were all right. That horse was going mighty fast when I caught up."

"Yes, it was." Delsie toyed with the hem of his jacket, her anger deflating in the wake of his explanation. "Thank you...for coming to my aid. I was about to jump." She gave a nervous laugh, grateful again she hadn't been forced to fling herself from the mare.

His chocolate-colored eyes glinted with respect before he looked away. "You kept a level head, that's for sure."

"Is that another compliment, Mr. Patton?"

A deep chuckle erupted from him as he shook his head. "You are not what you seem, Miss Radford."

"And neither are you." She spoke the words so softly she wasn't sure he heard, especially when he made no reply. The question she'd been asking herself all day resurfaced in her mind. "I know what you think of me and my privileged upbringing, so why are you helping me?"

He fiddled with the brim of his hat. "I need the money. For the land I want to own someday. A lot of land, out West maybe, where there's fewer people." His face had softened with his answer, its usual hardness transforming into earnest vulnerability for a brief moment.

Did she have a dream? Delsie wondered. Something

to work toward? Right now it was reaching Lillie, of course, and continuing to fulfill her promise to her mother, but what about beyond that? Did she want to return to the sameness of her life at home? The thought brought another shiver of cold sweeping through her.

"You ready?" Myles asked as he stood and offered her his hand.

With a nod, she placed her hand in his. He pulled her gently to her feet, which brought her nearly toe-to-toe with him. Delsie peered up at his shadowed face. His gaze had lost its guard, if only for a moment. She'd thought him quite handsome before, even with his scowl, but his nearness and the glimpse at this gentler side of his had her middle erupting into flutters.

He broke contact first, releasing her hand and stepping back. "Shall we get you to that sister of yours, Miss Radford?"

She took a deep breath to steady her emotions. Clearly the horse escapade had played with her head. She wouldn't follow in Lillie's footsteps by choosing a man her father would never approve of. Not only would it break his heart, but it would be going against her promise to look after her papa.

"Yes, Mr. Patton." She smiled and fell into step beside him. Only when they reached Amos and the waiting horses did she realize he hadn't asked for his jacket back.

Chapter Four

When they arrived in Nebraska that evening, at the home station known as Liberty Farm, Myles discovered Delsie had fallen asleep in the saddle. And no wonder. For someone unaccustomed to riding more than a hundred miles in a single day, she had to be exhausted. She didn't even stir when her mare—Amos had traded her horses after her other one had gotten spooked—came to a stop outside the stable.

Amos glanced over at her and chuckled. "You want me to wake her?"

An unfamiliar twinge of protectiveness rippled through Myles, then faded. "No, I will." He released Elijah into the sky to hunt.

"I'll go explain our situation to the owners," Amos said, dismounting. "See how much they'll charge for room and board for the night."

Myles nodded and climbed off his horse. Taking the reins of both his and Amos's animals in hand, he approached Delsie. "Miss Radford," he called quietly so as not to startle her. "We're here, at Liberty Farm. You can get down now."

When she remained still, he crossed to her side and gave her arm a gentle shake. "Miss Radford?"

At his touch, her chin rose and her eyelids blinked open. She stared in confusion at the yard around them and the still-bright sky of the summer evening, then down at Myles. Her blue eyes lit with recognition and a smile angled one side of her lips. "Did I fall asleep?"

That smile, combined with the soft expression on her face and the way her hair had come loose in places beneath her hat, sent a jolt of feeling through him. *Watch it, Myles*, he warned himself. *Money and a pretty face only lead to trouble.*

"We need to get the horses in the stable," he replied in a slightly gruff tone. "I'll help you down."

She complied, swinging her skirt over the side of the mare and allowing Myles to help her to the ground. Once her feet struck the dirt, she peered up at him, her lips parted as if to speak, but instead she remained silent. The open, earnest look on her face matched the one she'd worn earlier on the prairie after he'd rescued her. Awareness of her, both then and now, along with their close proximity, quickened his pulse and dulled the warning still ringing in his mind.

A strange terror had seized him as he'd watched Delsie and her horse burst from the trees and go charging at reckless speed over the plains. He kept imagining her being thrown and injured. His heart had beaten with as much fear as adrenaline when he'd jumped on his own steed and gone after her. Thankfully, he'd reached her in time, especially after hearing how close she'd come to leaping off.

Why should he care that much for a complete stranger, though? He mentally shook his head. Maybe *stranger* wasn't the right word anymore—not after spending two full days together. He'd told himself he'd saved her today out of human decency and the money she'd promised to give him at their journey's end. And yet, his logical reasoning didn't explain the bizarre need growing inside him to look after her. Though truth be told, there were moments when he wondered if she needed his protection at all.

A smile curved his mouth at the thought. This tiny woman, regarding him solemnly, had the courage of a hundred trained soldiers. She hadn't let out a single scream as her mare had spirited her away or fallen into uncontrollable sobs afterward. Myles couldn't help but think if it had been Cynthia in that situation things would have gone much differently.

"What are you smiling about?"

Delsie's innocent question broke whatever trance he'd been under. Myles stepped away from her and added her horse's reins to the others in his grip.

"Nothin'," he said over his shoulder as he walked toward the stable. "Amos is inside the house. You can join him in there."

He didn't wait to see if she'd listen or not. Instead he entered the structure through the open doors. The smell of hay and horses greeted him with all the familiarity and comfort of a friend. Memories of working with his stepfather at the livery stable rushed over him, clearing his mind of a certain dark-haired beauty.

As a young child, he'd trailed Charles everywhere around the spacious barn, doing the small jobs he was given. Myles had loved looking at the horses, feeding them, riding them when he could, even mucking their stalls. His stepfather had taught him to respect the power inherent in such creatures but also their fear and stubbornness.

There were other lessons Charles had imparted to him, ones he'd largely ignored since his stepfather's death. Things like looking for God's hand in his life or keeping his heart open and receptive to God's will. His jaw hardened at the turn of his thoughts. God didn't care any more for him than Cynthia had.

"Howdy, stranger," a young man called out to him from the other end of the stable. He held a pitchfork in one hand.

"Evening." Myles stopped the horses and quickly explained they were passing through and would pay to have the horses cared for tonight.

The boy, for he couldn't be more than fourteen or fifteen, agreed to feed and groom the animals, if it was all right with the station owners. "For now, put them in those empty stalls."

Myles did so as Amos appeared. "Everything's taken care of," the older man said. "For us and the horses."

"Where's Delsie?" Myles kept his voice devoid of interest.

"Inside, starting on supper. You coming?"

He wasn't ready to be near her again, not until he had

a stronghold on this growing attraction for her. Eying the three horses, Myles shook his head. "No, go ahead. I'll help settle them in."

Amos studied him for a moment, while Myles fought to keep his expression impassive. Finally his friend shrugged. "We'll try to save you some." With that he left the barn.

The young stable hand offered to help, but Myles encouraged him to join the others inside. He wanted the comfortable solace of a quiet barn, with no one else around except the beasts in the stalls.

Once the boy showed him where the tack and feed were located, he started in on grooming Amos's horse. He ran the brush down its chestnut-colored sides, talking soothingly as he did so. When it gleamed as fresh and new as a colt, he brought the beast some hay, then started in on his horse next.

Soon his thoughts moved back to Delsie. That was the trouble with doing something so familiar—his hands stayed busy but his mind didn't.

He had to remind himself, hourly if needed, that this journey to California was nothing more than a business arrangement. Acting on any possible attraction he felt for Delsie would be entirely futile. Her father, like Cynthia's, wasn't likely to approve of any interest in someone as poor and unconnected as Myles. Besides, a life out here in the West, with him or any other horseman or farmer, would likely drain her of whatever vitality and beauty she currently possessed. His life was about survival and weathering hardship, not choosing whom to invite for tea or which social engagement to attend on the weekend.

"Business," he muttered to himself, causing the steed's ears to flick backward. Myles reached out and ran a hand down its nose. "That's all it'll ever be." A measure of relief filled him now that he'd gotten his head in the right place. But the tiniest sliver of disappointment cut through him all the same.

Delsie slipped inside the stable. Though she was growing more accustomed to the smell, the trapped heat and scent of manure still had the power to make her wrinkle her nose in protest. Down the line of occupied stalls, she caught sight of Myles standing next to his horse.

"You missed supper," she said as she walked toward him.

He flinched as though struck, but he didn't glance at her. "I thought I'd see to the animals first."

Guilt trickled through her at his explanation. She'd been half-asleep when they'd arrived and had momentarily forgotten about the horses.

Delsie came to a stop beside the stall where he stood. Tentatively she lifted her hand to the steed and let it smell her.

"Where'd you learn to do that?" Myles asked, his voice bordering on sharpness.

She pulled her hand back. "Is that wrong?"

He'd removed his hat, giving her a full view of his face and beard. "No, that's exactly what you're supposed

to do, but most people don't know that, especially..."
He let the words trail off.

"Rich people," she supplied.

He frowned before picking up a brush and exiting the
stall. Delsie stepped back to allow him room.

"I think it was Lillie's beau, Clay, who taught us that.
He was a farmer."

"Your sister had a beau?"

"Still does. That's who she followed to California
and who she's marrying on the twenty-second." And the
next day, Lillie and Clay would head to Oregon. Never
to see or contact the family again, according to Lillie's
last letter, if she didn't receive some word by then that
Delsie still cared.

Myles entered the stall where Delsie's mare stood.
"Let me guess—your father didn't approve of him." His
voice sounded flat, bitter. His manner was so different from when he'd woken her up in the saddle earlier.

Heat layered her face. "Papa had hoped she'd marry..."
It was her turn to swallow back the rest of her words. She
found she suddenly couldn't say someone rich or of the
same social circle as her family. Someone like Flynn.

"I get it," Myles said, his tone no longer harsh but
full of resignation. Silence descended between them as
he began brushing the mare. Delsie watched him, mes-
merized by the movement of his hands and the gentle
murmurs falling from his mouth. Here he was in his
element, like a duke in his castle.

"May I try?"

He jerked his head in her direction as if he'd forgotten her presence. "What? Brushing?"

She nodded. "I own them now, which means I ought to know how to care for them."

Myles looked from her to the brush in his hand as if making a weightier decision than whether to teach her horse grooming or not. "All right."

Smiling, Delsie entered the stall. "What do I do?"

"Stand beside the horse," he said, moving behind her and pressing the brush into her hand, though he kept both in his grip. "Start up here on the animal's neck..." He lifted his arm, bringing her hand and the brush along with it, then he placed both against the mare. "Now you brush from front to back."

Together they moved the brush along the horse's side. "Then you repeat the motion," Myles said near her ear.

Gooseflesh rose along her arms, which thankfully, her long sleeves hid from view, at the low murmur of his voice and the warmth radiating from his solid chest behind her. When he leaned forward to help her again, his breath grazed the skin at the back of her neck. Delsie shivered, despite the temperate air inside the stable.

Myles stopped their motion, though their joined hands still held the brush to the horse's coat. Even the mare itself stood perfectly still. Delsie held her breath, anticipating something, though she didn't know what.

A soft touch skated her hair above her ear. Her heart drummed faster against her rib cage as she realized Myles was breathing in the scent of her hair.

"It smells like..." His nose skimmed her hair again.

"Lavender?" she whispered. After another full day of riding, she was surprised to learn she still smelled like her favorite soap and not just sweat and horse.

"Yes, lavender." His voice held a smile. "Smells better than gardenias."

Gardenias? Was that what his girl had worn, the one who'd bludgeoned his heart? Intent on asking him just that, Delsie lowered her arm and twisted slowly. Myles still held her hand over the brush and stood so close she could see where the sun had lightened some of the hairs of his beard. What would those dark bristles feel like beneath her fingertips? She lifted her free hand to find out.

A throat cleared behind them, as loud as a gunshot in the quiet barn. Myles jerked his hand from hers so fast that she dropped the brush into the hay at their feet.

"Came to see if you needed help," Amos announced.

Delsie bent to retrieve the brush and hide her flushed face. Myles practically bolted from the stall. "I think you got the hang of it," he said when she straightened. He wouldn't look at her. "Amos can show you how to feed them. I'm gonna get me some supper."

Moving to the other side of her mare, she tried to ignore the sound of Myles's retreating steps and the searching glances Amos kept throwing her way. She ran the brush over and over across the horse's coat, fighting a sudden desire to cry.

Why should she waste a single tear on that ornery Express rider? They came from two completely different worlds, as Myles himself seemed to enjoy pointing out. Even if her heart should stray from what her father wanted for her, she'd witnessed firsthand what Lillie's choice had done to him. While Delsie didn't agree with his decision to disown her sister for going after Clay, deep down, she recognized he'd only wanted the best for Lillie. His wrath had masked his fear. She wouldn't follow the same path and tear apart what remained of their small family.

"You all right, Miss Radford?" Amos held a pitchfork in his hand.

"Of course." She kept her head tilted high, but she sensed the older man saw through the bluff.

Why did she have to feel this attraction toward Myles, one stronger than any she'd ever felt for Flynn, and after only two days? She needed to place all her energies and focus on reaching Lillie in time, and nothing more.

"Will you show me how to feed the horses?" she asked, infusing as much cheerfulness as she could into her tone.

Amos watched her, his blue-gray eyes keen. What did he see? Did he read the hurt on her face over Myles's rude behavior just now, how he'd acted as if nothing had happened between them? Could Amos see how hard she was trying not to care? Finally, the older man nodded and motioned for her to exit the stall.

The lesson proved to be the perfect distraction. Amos patiently taught her how to pitch the hay into the stall and how to feed some carrots to the mare. Perhaps she'd take more interest in the animals and in riding, when she returned home.

By the time they left the stable, Delsie had almost forgotten Myles and his shifting moods—until they met up with him on the front porch. He sat on the bottom step, feeding Elijah pieces of meat from his supper. Amos took a seat beside Myles and removed his harmonica from his pocket.

Delsie caught Myles glancing at her, but when she turned his way, he busied himself with his bird. A wave of exhaustion engulfed her, restoring her earlier sleepiness. "I think I'll head inside."

"Good night, Miss Radford," Amos said. "We'll see you at breakfast."

"Please, call me Delsie." She cut a look at Myles. "Both of you."

"'Night, then, Delsie." Amos tipped his hat at her, a kind smile on his face.

"Good night, Amos. Mr. Patton." When the latter made no response, she blew out a sigh and entered the house. *I'm doing this for Lillie,* she told herself. *Just remember that, Delsie.*

She entered the room the station owners had told her to use and started to close the door behind her. Amos and Myles would bunk in one of the outbuildings.

"Delsie?"

Myles's voice drew her back to the doorway. "Yes?" She couldn't quell the sudden speeding of her pulse, no matter how much she wanted to.

"I...um..." Those dark eyes observed her in a way that reminded her of their close moment in the barn earlier. But she wouldn't let it go to her head—or her heart—this time.

"Do you need something, Myles?" She kept her tone nonchalant and businesslike.

A corner of his mouth lifted, ruining her attempt at

being stoic. That lopsided smile made her insides flutter. "I'm not *Mr. Patton* anymore?"

Belatedly she realized she'd called him by his first name. "Would you rather I still call you that?"

He shook his head. "No, ma'am. Myles suits me fine. Just like Delsie…suits you."

"Very well," she said, trying to discount the pleasure his veiled compliment gave her, "what do you need, Myles?"

"Do you have a lock on your door?"

"A…lock?" She stared in confusion at him.

He motioned for her to move aside so he could examine the door. She saw that it did possess a latch. "Be sure to lock it tonight."

"Why?"

"Because there aren't any other women at this station."

"So?"

Myles ran a hand through his hair. "I don't…we don't…know the character of these men at this station or any other station from here to California. You need to be careful."

Understanding dawned, bringing warmth to her cheeks. "Oh. I see. Yes, I'll…lock it."

"Good." He turned to go, but she had a request of her own.

"Myles?"

He faced her again, his expression holding its usual guarded quality. Would anyone ever be able to help him shed his pain?

"I only wanted to thank you for rescuing me today…

and for agreeing to come along." She fiddled with the dirty cuff of her riding dress. "While I understand everything about this arrangement is wholly unconventional…I would very much like it if you and Amos and I…could be friends."

She steeled herself for his refusal, and she couldn't blame him if he gave it. After all it was another woman, a wealthy one like herself, who had betrayed his friendship.

"I know it's silly," she added into the gaping silence. "But I don't know anyone out here, except for the two of you, and I just thought…"

He shifted his stance as if to walk away. Disappointment cut through her. She'd been silly to think they could, at the very least, be friends.

"You trust us, right?" he asked over his shoulder.

"Yes."

"So isn't that what friends do?"

He didn't wait for her answer. Instead he moved down the hall toward the front door. Delsie heard it click shut behind him. A few moments later she heard the soft, languid sounds of Amos's harmonica coming from the direction of the porch.

She closed the door to her room and locked it, her mind in disorder. Myles hadn't exactly accepted her offer of friendship, but he hadn't refused it, either. Certainly that was a good sign.

His actions earlier in the stable and his obvious desire to protect her were also proof he might be warming up to her. The thought filled her with a measure of hope as she readied for bed.

Despite the fatigue and aches that continued to plague her body, she found sleep wouldn't come easily. Instead she lay awake for some time listening to Amos play his harmonica and picturing a pair of haunting, chocolate-colored eyes.

Myles returned to the porch and took his seat on the step again. Out of the corner of his eye, he caught sight of Elijah perched on a corner of the house's sloping roof. Amos continued to play his instrument, performing one melancholy ballad after another. Myles gritted his teeth in annoyance. The music didn't help erase the memory of Delsie standing close as they'd brushed the horse together or the teasing scent of her hair.

He ran a hand over his face and released a frustrated breath. What had come over him that he'd given in to smelling her hair or testing the silkiness of it against the tip of his nose? And then she'd gone and asked to be his friend. Myles didn't want to be friends with her—that path would only lead to further regret and pain. Better to keep his distance, although he hadn't actually denied her request, either. He'd wanted to, but the honesty and innocence shining in those big blue eyes of hers had killed whatever refusal he might have made.

"Can you play something else?" he snapped, rising to his feet. "A livelier song, maybe?"

Amos lowered the instrument from his mouth. "I can. But first, you wanna tell me what's got you wound up tighter than a noose?"

Myles stepped away from the porch into the empty yard. He didn't want to talk. Doing so would only mean admitting he'd let his feelings get the better of him where a woman was concerned—and here he'd sworn them off only eight weeks before.

"This likely doesn't need to be said…" Amos stood and joined Myles in the yard, slapping his harmonica against the palm of his hand. "But you need to remember Delsie isn't Cynthia."

"I know." Myles glanced at the stars above.

"Do you?" Amos countered.

Myles shifted to give his friend a level look. Amos never could leave well enough alone. "All right, old man. What have you got to say?"

Amos gave an innocent shrug. "Not much tonight." Myles crossed his arms and waited—he sensed a lecture. "I'll only say this. I know you got reasons for not liking the kind of people Delsie comes from, and that's fine."

"But…" Myles prompted.

"But go easy on her. She isn't some simpering female like Cynthia."

Myles uncrossed his arms as irritation sliced through him. If Amos had harbored reservations about Cynthia Grover, all these years, the man should've voiced them long before now. "You mean to tell me, you—"

"Yes, I didn't care for her." Amos pocketed his harmonica and turned his attention to the starry sky.

"Why didn't you say something sooner?"

The older man shrugged again. "I probably should have." Silence filled the space between them for a minute or two before Amos continued, "About Delsie, though."

That twinge of protectiveness, the one that had prompted Myles to have her lock her door, rose inside him again. Did Amos sense it? Myles had never felt a driving need to be sure Cynthia was all right. "What about her?"

Amos chuckled. "There you go, being surly again. I only wanted to say she's proven her strength these last two days."

Myles grunted in agreement. He never would have guessed she'd make it this far when he'd first seen her standing outside the Express stables in all her finery.

"She needs a friend."

The words so closely echoed Delsie's that Myles threw Amos a sharp look. Had the older man overheard their conversation and Myles's noncommittal response? He swept his hand through his hair—he'd left his hat in the stable in his hurry to leave earlier. Being friends with Delsie Radford sounded dangerous and difficult— not unlike this journey they were taking now. Could he do it, though? Could he put a portion of his heart on the line to be her friend?

Amos rested a hand on Myles's shoulder, much like Charles used to. A lump lodged in his throat at the recollection. The man standing next to him was the closest thing in the world he had to a father or a family anymore.

"Just think on it," Amos urged. "That's all I'm asking."

Myles hesitated only a second or two, then nodded.

His friend strolled back to his earlier seat on the porch. The harmonica came out again, but this time,

Amos played a rousing tune. As he listened, Myles's thoughts drifted through the events of the day, settling on Delsie's passing mention of her chafed skin. With only that fancy dress between her and the saddle, it was no wonder she was in pain.

A sudden idea filled his mind. "What's the next place we come to where we can buy a few supplies?"

Amos paused in his playing. "We'll pass Dobytown tomorrow. Why? What do you need?"

He gave a lazy shrug that belied the spark of enthusiasm growing inside him. "Nothing much." Amos let the noncommittal answer go unprotested and returned instead to playing another lively tune on his instrument.

Crossing back to the porch, Myles sat down once more. He might not be ready to fully embrace a friendship with Delsie, but he could try to look out for her and ease her discomfort a little. And now he knew how.

Chapter Five

"I don't understand. Why can't we stop?" Delsie twisted in the saddle to watch the adobe buildings of Dobytown receding behind them. They'd charged right past Fort Kearney two miles back, as well. "It's time to the rest the horses anyway."

She turned back around in time to catch Myles's scowl. "I told you earlier. Dobytown is no place for a lady."

"But it isn't like I'd be alone. I have the two of—"

"No."

Delsie glared at him, irritation making her skin as hot and itchy as the sun did. Who did he think he was, ordering her around like a servant? She opened her mouth to argue further when Amos joined the heated conversation.

"What Myles is trying to say…" The older man shot Myles a pointed look, which solicited a momentary expression of contrition. Delsie needed to master such a look if it put him in his place. "Is that it might not be safe. Like I mentioned last night, Dobytown is usually rampant with drunks and harlots. We'd rather keep you outside its borders, than risk anything by entering them."

She tipped her chin upward in her best imitation of a haughty matron. "I suppose when you put it that way." But annoyance still simmered under her choking collar. She'd only wanted to take a peek at the fort or the city, not move in.

The conversation ended in strained silence as they followed the line of the Platte River. After another mile or two Myles announced it was time to stop.

Amos helped her dismount, and though she welcomed the feel of solid ground beneath her shoes, walking around only intensified the chafing of her dress against her legs. Would her skin ever feel normal again? She'd tried scratching her thighs, discreetly, during their last stop, but that had only made matters worse. Now her legs felt raw and prickly as if a thousand pine needles had taken up residence inside her skirt.

After they'd eaten the small lunch she'd paid the last station owners to provide them, Amos spread out in the shade to take a nap. His snores filled the air almost immediately. Delsie was considering how to pass the time herself when she noticed Myles climbing back into his saddle.

"Where are you going?" she asked.

Without looking at her, he wheeled his steed around. "There's something I need to buy back in Dobytown. I shouldn't be long."

"Buy? Why didn't you just get it when we…" She bit her lip as a sudden thought penetrated her confusion.

An awful, shocking thought. Anger followed quickly on its heels. "Myles Patton, you took an oath as an Express rider. And I will not be party to—to riotous behavior on your part. I won't pay you a dime, so help me, if you're planning to go—"

"Good grief, woman." His exasperated tone cut off the rest of her indignant speech. "I'm buying a few supplies. That's all."

"Oh." Her face felt twice as sunburned. "What about the horse? Isn't he going to lag if you don't rest him?"

"I'll ride slowly." He nudged the mount forward.

"But I didn't think we needed anything else." Why was he being so mysterious? She was paying him, after all, to get her to California quickly, not take in the sights. Not unless he planned to take her along, too, which he clearly wasn't. "What do you need that's so important?"

"I'll be back soon," he called over his shoulder. "Stay near Amos while I'm gone. I don't want you walking around by yourself out here. Not this close to the city."

Delsie's jaw tightened as she glowered at his back. She wasn't a child. Had he so easily forgotten how well she'd held her own the past three days?

"Oooo, that man," she muttered as she whirled around, her hands balled into fists. One moment he had her feeling weak in the knees over his kindness and handsome face, and the very next he had her so mad she wanted to throw something at him.

She eyed her mare, debating whether to follow after him or not. He'd likely just drag her back the moment he noticed her coming up behind him.

Her gaze wandered to the river. The cool liquid looked so inviting she couldn't resist the idea of wading into it. What if she took a quick swim instead? Amos would still be napping for a while longer—the man could sleep heavily anywhere, anytime. She could hike up the river a short ways, take a dip in her chemise and return before anyone was the wiser.

Myles's warning repeated in her mind, but Delsie brushed it aside. She wouldn't be too far away.

The thought of ridding herself of the grime and sweat of three days was too appealing. Surely it would help her chafed skin, too. Her mind made up, Delsie gathered her skirt in one hand and stole softly into the brush.

Myles fought to breathe through his mouth, instead of his nose, to avoid smelling the foul odor emitting from the trapper standing behind him. He was used to strong scents, having worked for years in the livery stable, but this man's aroma surpassed anything he'd known before. The man was tall, too. His coonskin cap and long, greasy hair hovered a good six inches above the top of Myles's hat. And the profanity spewing from the man's chapped lips was as foul as his aroma.

Not for the first time since entering the confines of Dobytown, he felt relieved he'd convinced Delsie to stay behind. Though he'd nearly had to tell her his secret because of it. The woman could be downright determined when she wanted.

Raucous laughter filled the trading post. Myles's lips curved upward, but not at the drunken joviality. The horrified look on Delsie's face, when she'd suspected him of wanting to participate in one of the unseemly businesses offered in Dobytown, resurfaced in his mind. Wouldn't she be surprised, and a little humbled, when she learned his real reason for coming back had to do with her?

When his turn came, he made his request to the clerk. "I need a pair of leather trousers and a good hat. Both in the smallest size you've got."

The man moved away to collect the items. Myles let his gaze wander over the crammed shelves of the trading post. Was there anything else they needed or that Delsie might like? He thought of the lavender scent on her hair. Would she appreciate more soap?

"Anything else for you?" the man asked, after naming the price of the items he'd slapped onto the counter.

Myles leaned forward. "Do you have any soap? Maybe lavender scented?"

"Lavender soap?" the man repeated in a loud voice, his bushy brows nearly reaching his hairline. "What do you think I'm running here, a mercantile?"

The trapper behind Myles hooted. "Hear that, fellows. The Express rider here is gonna show us up with the ladies by buying one of 'em some soap."

Myles ignored the ribbing, letting the man's sarcastic tone roll off him. "Any nice soap will do."

"I might have something in the back." The clerk walked away, grumbling under his breath and shaking his head.

Would Delsie be pleased or angry with him for coming here to purchase things for her? Myles hoped the former. While he enjoyed seeing her dark blue eyes spark with determination, he liked her smile best of all. Or maybe hearing her laughter. Or taking in the sweet scent of her hair.

Myles frowned. He was acting like the friend she wanted, nothing more. Even the soap could be considered a friendly, kind gesture—if the clerk had any. He shifted his weight in impatience at the same moment a thought nudged him hard. *Delsie's in trouble.*

Myles shook his head, dismissing the notion. She'd been fine when he left. There was no sense conjuring up false concern.

But try as he might, he couldn't completely rid his mind of the thought. Then a sense of urgency seized him with a vicelike grip. He needed to leave—now. Something wasn't right.

Jerking his money from his pocket, he hollered for the clerk. The man lumbered back into the room, a scowl on his face. "Here's what I owe you for the trousers and hat." Myles plunked the money onto the counter and grabbed up his purchases.

"What about the soap?"

"Maybe next time."

After elbowing his way out of the crowded trading post, he untied his horse. He swung into the saddle and set off at a gallop down the street, his purchases clutched under one arm. He had no idea what awaited him—only that his need to reach Delsie, to ensure she was all right, intensified with every passing minute. He only hoped he wasn't too late.

Delsie lay on her back in the water, not caring that she'd soaked her chemise from neck to knee. Her toes kept her anchored in the sandy river bottom. With her face turned toward the warm rays of the sun, she shut her eyes and focused on the gentle rush of the water as it flowed past her head and ears. She spread her arms out and let the river slide over and through her fingers. A feeling of freedom, of complete contentment, spilled out of her in the form of a soft laugh. Perhaps she'd have to make this a habit when they stopped.

Sitting up, she wrung out her unbound hair. She might have washed it properly, if she'd remembered to grab her soap. But she'd been so focused on the thought of being clean and cool after so many dusty hours in the saddle that she had slipped away without bringing anything with her.

Oh well, next time. Delsie scooped up some water in her hand and let it dribble back to its source. She didn't want to leave yet, but she needed to wrestle back into her riding dress, wet as she was, and return to Amos before he woke up. Or worse, before Myles discovered she'd gone off on her own. Even if it was just a short distance. With a sigh, she started to climb to her feet.

"Well, howdy there, girlie," a gravelly voice intoned.

She whirled around, a startled gasp rising toward her mouth. The sound tangled in her throat when she saw three men watching her from the other side of the river. They appeared to be trappers, rifles hung loose over their shoulders, their beards unkempt, their eyes keen. Eyes that stared with undisguised interest at her.

"Out for a little dip?" the tallest continued. "A little far from town, aren't you?"

Myles's warning rang like a bell through Delsie's

mind and sent her heart crashing in panic against her rib cage. She shouldn't have wandered off, at least not without telling Amos where she'd gone.

"Not a real talker, are you?"

Delsie glanced over her shoulder at the nearby bank. It didn't seem so close now. Could she make it to the trees and back to Amos before the men overtook her? Perhaps the trappers were merely being friendly, though their attentive stares suggested otherwise.

Eyes trained on the men, Delsie tried to slow her pounding heart as she scooted a few inches across the river bottom toward the bank. Hopefully, her movements would go unnoticed until the last moment when she would have to jump up and sprint. To her horror, though, the tall trapper set down his rifle and stepped into the river.

"Why don't you come on over here, girlie? We're not so bad, once you get to know us." One of his companions snickered and jostled the other in the ribs.

Fear prickled across Delsie's skin, turning the pleasant water to ice. How could she have been so foolish? She scrambled backward, no longer caring if they saw. The trapper continued his deliberate advance toward her, his smile large and leering.

Delsie eyed the bank again. She might not be able to outrun the man, especially in her wet chemise, but she had to try. The sand beneath her hands registered in her fear-clouded mind. Scooping up a handful, to hurl at the man if needed, she bolted out of the water and pushed through the meandering current at a clumsy run.

"Hey," he cried from behind, "what's your hurry? Come on back here."

Her toes at last sunk into the mud at the bank's edge and she scrambled from the water, her breath coming so fast and hard she could hardly breathe. Her feet caught in the hem of her chemise and she tripped. *No, no, no.*

"You can't hide for long, girlie."

Delsie threw a quick glance at her pursuer as she struggled to free her feet. He was halfway across the river by now, his large boots eating up her lead.

"There's no one else out here—"

The sudden cocking of a gun preceded Myles's loud command, "Leave her alone."

Relief washed over Delsie with such intensity she nearly cried out. The sight of Myles standing above her on the bank, his gun aimed at the trapper, stilled her frantic movements. Shivering, she dropped the sand and wrapped her arms around her sodden gown and knees.

The trapper had stopped, his arms lifted halfway. "You know you ain't the only one with a gun here." Sure enough, his friends had drawn their weapons, which were now pointed at Myles.

The hard look on his face didn't waver for a second. "True. But you'll be a dead man before you ever find out if your friends succeeded in shooting me, too."

Delsie held her breath as the two men glared at one another, as frozen as stone. At last, the trapper backed up, his hands reaching higher. "She's all yours then. Not worth the trouble."

Myles didn't lower the gun or look her way until the trapper had joined his companions on the other side of the river and the three of them headed back the way they'd come. By then, Delsie's shivers had grown worse. Her teeth had begun to chatter behind her tightly pressed lips.

"Get your dress and shoes," Myles ordered, his tone sharp with barely concealed fury.

Was he angrier at the trappers or at her for not listening? Too exhausted and chilled to ask, she collected her riding dress, took the hand he offered her and climbed onto her trembling legs.

Once Delsie stood erect, Myles turned his back to her. "Go ahead and get them on."

After several false starts at getting the dress over her wet chemise, she finally had the gown on. Her fingers shook so hard she could hardly do up the buttons. The relief she'd felt at Myles's appearance was fast fading in the wake of the shock coursing through her at what might have happened if he hadn't come along. As she pulled on her shoes, tears blurred her vision and she hurried to brush them away before he noticed.

"Done?" he asked after several minutes.

"Yes." She wasn't sure he heard her whispered reply as she started past him.

Myles's hand seized her arm in a firm grip, turning her toward him. His eyes blazed dark beneath his hat. "What were you thinking?" The edge had returned to his voice. "I told you not to wander off. Do you know what they could have done?" He released her to run his hand over the stubble covering his jaw and chin. Only then did Delsie notice his own fingers weren't as sure and steady as normal.

"I—I didn't think anything would happen—"

"That's the problem. You didn't think."

"I wasn't trying to court trouble, Myles." She folded her arms against another bout of tears rising fast toward her throat and eyes. "I just wanted to…to wash up. I didn't mean—"

"Why did I even bother warning you?" He yanked off his hat and plunged his shaking hand through his hair. "You're clearly going to do whatever you please. Including walking right into a group of trappers, dressed in just your…" He waved a hand at her, his face momentarily flushing before his expression hardened again. "Might as well have ridden into the fort and announced you were taking callers."

An angry spark lit inside Delsie, stoked by Myles's stubborn refusal to listen. It wasn't as if she'd chosen to swim with an audience of onlookers. "I admit I was wrong to go off alone, and for that I apologize. But I refuse to stand here and let you reprimand me another minute."

"Reprimand? I'm trying to talk sense into you. Something I'm beginning to think you left back in Pennsylvania."

Hands on her hips, she glowered up at him. "I'm sorry if my lack of sense requires you to keep rescuing me, but you agreed to come along. Not the other way around. Need I remind you that I'm not used to this way of life?"

He reared back as if slapped. "You're right," he said slowly. "Which is why…I'm trying to protect you."

Her anger, and her strength, ebbed at his admission.

"You may also recall—" her voice wobbled a bit "—I was nearly kidnapped and accosted back there and I don't know that my knees can hold me much longer. I'm going to find Amos…"

Delsie moved away from him but not before a sob leaked from her lips. Covering her mouth, she stumbled forward. The luxury of being clean no longer held any appeal—she felt only wet and cold, her feelings brittle. The magnitude of her journey weighted her footsteps and dragged at her head and heart. Would she continue to skirt danger, in the nick of time, to reach Lillie alive and well? Or was this truly a fool's errand?

She tripped, unseeing, over something, but before she landed on the dirt, Myles caught her elbow. This time his touch exuded only gentleness.

"I left my horse right over there, Delsie. You can ride back."

She tried to find the animal, but she couldn't see much through her tears. Then Myles's strong arms were around her, holding her in a comforting embrace. Delsie pressed her cheek to his jacket, breathing in the familiar scent of leather, and let her sobs flow unchecked.

"It's all right," he soothed, as if she were one of his horses, "you're all right. No one's going to hurt you."

"I'm sorry. I'm so sorry. If you hadn't come right then…" She shuddered in horror.

He tightened his hold and ran his hand down her wet hair. "Shh. Don't think about it. You're safe with me and Amos."

After another minute, her tears were spent and she

stepped back. Myles offered her a bandanna to wipe her damp face.

"Thank you."

He nodded, seeming to understand she was expressing gratitude for more than just his gentlemanly gesture.

Delsie followed him to his horse. There on the ground sat a hastily dropped pile of clothes. Myles picked them up and thrust them at her. "These are for you. From the trading post. They oughta help."

She accepted the hat and trousers, too surprised to form an immediate response. Myles had gone back to buy her more appropriate riding gear? Surely that meant he believed in her and her attempt to reach her sister. She glanced up at him, but he wasn't looking at her. He was staring in the direction of the river.

"I would have got you soap, too, but…"

She shook her head, pressing the things to her wet bodice. "No, no. This is wonderful. Thank you, again."

"I knew you were in trouble." His voice was low and tinged with wonder. "Knew it as sure as if someone had said it out loud. Riding back across the prairie, I couldn't seem to go fast enough. I had no idea what was wrong, but I knew…" He finally returned his gaze to hers. "I knew I had to reach you."

He lifted his hand and ran his thumb over the drying tears on her cheek. "Just promise not to wander off like that again." Something warm spread through Delsie, burning away the last remnants of cold, both inside and out.

"I won't," she whispered back.

The earnest look on his chiseled face, the warmth of

his touch on her cheek, the gift of the new clothing told a different story from the one Myles wanted people to believe—he cared. In spite of his occasional brusqueness, he cared about her. The realization rocked her nearly as much as her harrowing experience earlier.

He cares as a friend, she told herself. For that was all they could ever be—especially after their journey was over. Myles would never be content to live in her world, and her father would never allow her to live in his. But it was enough to know he was her friend.

Even when he lowered his hand and the guarded look returned to his dark eyes, even when he hastily lifted her onto his horse, she told herself it was enough to know he cared. As long as she stuck with Myles, she would be fine.

Chapter Six

Myles cast a glance at Delsie over his shoulder—the
fourth or fifth time in the past hour of riding. After the
events at the river yesterday, he was simply making
sure she was still behind him and holding up. He told
himself it had nothing to do with how charming she
looked in her new hat or with her trousers sticking out
the bottom of her skirt.

She caught his eye and smiled, though the gesture
lacked her usual spark. At least her face had lost its
paleness and her shoulders had returned to their normal upright posture. If he hadn't heeded that thought
of warning…

Facing forward again, he stared grimly at the open
prairie before them. He and Delsie had agreed to keep
the details vague when they'd explained their absence
to Amos the day before—Delsie had gone swimming
and Myles happened by at the same moment some trappers wandered up on the opposite side of the river. If
the older man had known the truth, Myles didn't doubt

Amos would wrestle the men's descriptions from him and hunt them down. He was still of a mind to do the same. The lurid look in the one trapper's eyes still had the ability to turn his gut to ice and his hands to fists—ready for revenge, even in memory.

One thing he knew for certain. God might not remember him, but He was watching over Delsie. That was the only explanation that made sense to him when he thought back on his earlier intuition about Delsie being in trouble.

The responsibility to protect her settled like a heavy saddle blanket over Myles's shoulders. Would he and Amos be able to keep her safe over the next fifteen days? What if something happened to one or both of them, and she were left on her own? The possibility filled him with enough horror to constrict his breath for a moment.

No, he wouldn't let that happen. He rubbed at Elijah's feathers as the bird playfully pecked at his hat. No matter what lay ahead, Myles vowed to get Delsie to her destination, well and whole. To do that, though, he would need to teach her how to handle herself in this unfamiliar world. His world. Could she do it? he wondered. Cynthia never would have.

He set his mouth in a hard line. Delsie had to. Any other thought or plan was unacceptable. He would best keep her safe by helping her help herself. Starting today.

At their first resting spot, Myles slid from his horse and removed one of his Colt revolvers from the saddle holsters. He waited for Amos to help Delsie down before he announced, "You need to learn how to shoot a gun."

"Now?" Delsie's eyebrows rose in surprise as she removed the wide-brimmed hat he'd bought her and hung it on the saddle horn.

"If you ever need to shoot something or someone—" he gave her meaningful look "—you'll know how."

She visibly swallowed. "But I don't own a gun."

"You're never far from one. I've got two revolvers, and Amos has one, too."

The older man nodded and pulled back his jacket to reveal the gun stuck into the waistband of his trousers.

"It's more than shooting, too." Myles motioned to the horses. "You need to know how to saddle and unsaddle your mare, and how to climb on and off without assistance."

Her blue eyes appeared troubled. "All right, I'll learn. However, I don't see the reason. If you and Amos are right here…"

Myles let his gaze flit past her to the western horizon, a rare feeling of uncertainty eating at him. "We most likely will be," he said, not wishing to scare her. "But if something should happen to either of us, or both of us, you can still make it on time yourself."

From the corner of his eye, he saw her studying him, as if trying to put a name, or a reason, to his insistence. But he couldn't explain it himself. All he knew was that he felt a responsibility to help her reach her sister, no matter what lay ahead, that went deeper than the promised money or adventure.

"I agree with Myles," Amos interjected as he gathered the horses' reins to lead them to the river. "I'll tie up the animals, but be sure you're shooting that revolver a ways off."

Myles nodded and started in the opposite direction. When Delsie didn't immediately follow, he turned back. "Coming?"

Her brow pinched in a determined way. "Very well."

He led her north toward a distant stand of trees. A tin can or two would've been nice for target practice, but Myles figured he could improvise. When they reached the trees, he went to the thickest and pointed to a particularly large knot in the wood. "This is your target."

Moving closer, she scrutinized the marking, then nodded.

He paced off ten steps. "Stand back here." Delsie threw another glance at the knot before coming to stand next to him. "Here's the gun." He set it in her hand.

Her gaze went wide like a spooked animal. "But I don't know what to do."

He released a soft chuckle. "Right now, I just want you to hold it. Get used to the weight of it."

Something more than determination etched her pretty face. Myles realized with a start it was trust. She trusted him, through and through. How long had it been since he'd inspired that sort of confidence? Since someone had relied on him? Not since Charles's death.

A soft exhale of breath pulled his attention back to Delsie. "I think I'm ready to try shooting it."

"Then face the tree." When she did so, he stepped directly behind her. "First thing you want to do is cock the hammer. You'll do that each time you shoot." He indicated the hammer on the gun and waited while she clicked it back. "Next you want to bring the gun to shoulder level and line up the notch on top of the hammer with the bead on the end of the gun."

Delsie lifted the gun and aimed at the tree.

"Now, when you're ready, you squeeze the trigger. But remember the gun will kick—"

The sudden explosion of the revolver ended his warning. Delsie slammed back against him with a cry. Instinctively, Myles gripped her waist to steady her. A whisper of lavender still scented her hair, reminding him of the moment they'd shared while brushing her mare two nights before. Had it only been two days ago? The more time he spent in her company, the harder it was to believe he hadn't always known her.

"Are you all right?" So much for his warning about the gun kicking back.

She twisted to look at him, her eyes as large as wagon wheels. "I think so. Did I hit the tree?"

Releasing her from his grip, Myles walked over to the tree and examined the trunk. A couple feet above the knot, he found the dent from the bullet. "You hit it here," he called back to her, indicating the spot on the tree.

Delsie's expression lit up. "Really? I didn't think I hit it at all."

"Let's have you try again." She swung the gun up to shoulder level, causing Myles to leap out of the way. "Wait a minute, woman. Don't shoot until I'm behind you."

"Sorry." Her cheeks flushed, but she threw him an impish smile.

The action coaxed a smile from him, as well. Learning to shoot might be serious business, but that didn't mean he couldn't enjoy it.

"Don't forget to cock it, either," he reminded as he positioned himself behind her.

Delsie cocked the hammer, lifted the gun again and took aim. This time, when she fired, she rocked back only a few inches.

"I think you were closer." Myles moved to the tree, Delsie trailing him. Sure enough the mark of the bullet stood only four inches above the knot.

"Again," she declared. Myles bit back a chuckle at this sudden desire to best herself.

They resumed their places and she pulled the trigger for a third time. Myles started to step past her to see where she'd struck the tree this time, but she motioned him back with her free hand. "I think that one was a little closer, but still to the left. Let me try once more."

She fired the revolver again, then joined him at the tree. The bullet had hit the outer edge of the knot. "Look at that." Her entire face lit up with pleasure as she fingered the dent in the trunk. "How many bullets do I have left?"

"Two."

"Then I want to see if I can be consistent."

Myles nodded in appreciation—Delsie didn't do things by half. It was another trait to add to the growing list of her redeeming qualities. Too bad he wouldn't get more than two weeks to discover all of them. She made for an intriguing puzzle of contrasts. Rich but humble, pretty but strong, unskilled but determined to learn.

Delsie waited a moment after he'd moved to stand

behind her before she cocked and fired the revolver in rapid succession, twice. When she'd finished, she lowered the weapon and rushed to the tree as fast as her long skirt would allow.

"I did it," she declared over her shoulder.

Sure enough two bullet holes marred the knot, one almost dead center and the other slightly to the right. Myles ran a finger over both, disbelief and pride weaving through him. He'd expected to take the whole hour to teach her to shoot. Instead she'd mastered the skill in less than half that time and with a consistency that rivaled some of the Express riders he'd observed doing target practice.

"You sure you've never shot a gun before?" he asked, taking off his hat and brushing at his forehead with his sleeve.

She shook her head. "Does that I mean did all right?"

"All right?" Myles plopped his hat back on and chuckled. "You shoot nearly as good as Amos and me. And that's after one lesson. I don't think any nefarious characters stand a chance against you."

"Really?" A brilliant smile lifted her lips and turned her eyes as stunningly blue as the sky overhead.

Locks of her hair had escaped their pins, several curling against the creaminess of her cheeks. Myles fought the urge to feel one and lost. Lifting his hand, he fingered one long black curl.

"My hair must look a sight." Her voice sounded breathless. He swallowed a grin at the idea that he might be the cause. Perhaps there were a few things in this world that unsettled Miss Delsie Radford just a bit.

"I like it this way." The words were no more than a murmur, but he knew she'd heard him when the hand she'd self-consciously lifted to touch her hair fell to her side and a pretty blush stained her cheeks.

She gave a delicate cough. "Thank you for the lesson."

Whether she meant to or not, her gratitude had the power to jerk him back to the present and the task at hand. He needed to prepare her, not stand here ogling.

"That's just the first one." He let go of her soft curl and stepped back, ignoring the feeling of emptiness that settled in his gut. "Now you need to know how to saddle your mare."

With that he took his gun back and clomped toward the horses. There were a couple of lessons he needed to get through his own head, too. Like how to avoid falling for another pretty face with a full purse. That path only meant further pain. Because all he had to offer a rich young lady was a hard life and little money.

If he let his feelings for Delsie run deeper than his promise to see her safely to California, he would simply be reliving his experience with Cynthia. And that was something he wouldn't allow.

After saddling and unsaddling her mare and climbing on the mount unassisted at every stop along the trail, Delsie's arms ached. Now that it was evening, she could hardly hold the reins. But at least Myles seemed satisfied with her efforts. Or so she hoped.

His face had hardened into familiar lines and the camaraderie they'd shared during her shooting lesson that morning had given way to determined quiet. She tried to coax another smile or laugh from him, but he remained solely intent on her instruction. While she was grateful for his help, even touched that he'd thought to teach her, she wished for the affable Myles to return.

Thank goodness there was only one more rest period before they stopped for the night, at a place known as O'Fallon's Bluff. She didn't know if her sore arms could last any longer. Her legs, on the other hand, were rapidly adapting to so much time in the saddle. The trousers Myles had given her helped, too, relieving her from the horrible chafing. She rather liked her wide-brimmed hat, as well. It certainly kept her face shaded from the beating sun.

Amos soon announced their stop, and Delsie gratefully slid to the ground. She stretched her arms above her head and behind her back to work out the soreness.

"I have a lesson for you, too," Amos said.

"What? No more saddling or unsaddling my horse?" She shot a rueful look at Myles, who was feeding Elijah pieces of jerky.

Amos chuckled. "I think you've got the hang of it now. Doesn't she, Myles?"

Myles grunted in agreement.

"All right. What's the lesson?" Delsie walked over to Amos, but she froze when he lifted a dead rabbit into the air.

"How to cook your supper."

She tried not to look at the lifeless eyes. "Where did you get that?"

Amos shrugged. "Two stops back, while you were

working on saddling your mare." He motioned for her to follow him away from the copse of trees back onto the prairie. "First thing, you want to do is to clear a patch of grass, then you need to collect some dry wood for a fire."

Swallowing her revulsion for the dead animal, Delsie set her jaw. She could do this.

She tore up handfuls of grass until she had a circular plot of earth. Then she searched back near the trees for twigs and branches. Once she had an armful, she returned to Amos's side. He produced some flint and steel and patiently taught her how to use them to produce a spark. The tiny flame she finally manufactured filled her with immense pride. If only her father and sister could see her now.

Following Amos's instructions, Delsie fed the small fire with prairie grass and sticks until it doubled in size. "Now you've got to skin the animal," the older man explained.

"Skin it?" A clammy feeling crept over her, making her shiver despite the summer heat.

He simply nodded and handed her the knife he'd pulled from his boot. "You'll need to skin and gut it so you can get to the meat."

Delsie bit her lip. *No different than our cook at home would be doing*, she tried telling herself. But the sickish feeling grew worse as she accepted the knife and knelt beside the rabbit. She momentarily shut her eyes to gather her resolve, then opening them, she pushed the blade into the limp creature.

The sight of the crimson trail trickling from the

punctured fur made her turn and retch in the grass beside her. A kind hand settled onto her shoulder, bringing comfort even as she continued to spill her previous meal. At least it was Amos, and not Myles, who had witnessed her humiliating reaction.

When there was nothing left in her stomach, she shakily wiped at her mouth with the back of her hand. A part of her longed to flee and forget this whole wretched task, but another part wanted to prove she wasn't the spoiled, rich young lady Myles still saw her as. Resolute, she picked up the knife she'd dropped in her queasiness and squared her shoulders.

"You want to continue?" Amos asked gently.

Delsie bobbed her head once, her jaw clenched so hard it hurt. With his quiet voice filling her ears with instructions, she set about skinning the rabbit. Another wave of nausea washed over her as she proceeded to gut the creature, but Delsie clamped her teeth against it. She was too close to finishing to quit now.

At last the small hunk of rabbit meat lay ready for cooking. She stuck the blade into it and lifted it for Amos to see. "Done." She threw him a triumphant smile, which made him chuckle. Her dress and hands might be spotted with dirt and blood, but she'd skinned and gutted her first animal.

"Good work." His blue-gray eyes were warm with approval. When was the last time her father had looked at her that way?

The sense of true accomplishment coursing through her nearly made her dizzy. "What do I do next?"

"Now we cook it." Amos showed her how to make a

spit over the fire to roast the meat. While she sat beside it, he graciously removed the rabbit's remains. He returned with a water canteen and Delsie used it to rinse her mouth and wash her hands and skirt hem.

"You've done real well today." Amos took a seat on the ground next to her.

Myles's curtness during the paddling lessons came back. She plucked at a long piece of grass and twisted it around her finger. "I'm glad you think so."

Amos shot a look toward the trees, where Delsie could barely see Myles dozing, his hat over his face. "He thinks so, too, for all his gruffness. My guess is you surprised him, and he doesn't like surprises."

"I did?" She laughed. Annoyed him was probably more accurate. Although he did occasionally act as though he wanted to be her friend and protector.

"You don't fit his prejudice against rich folks, and it's unsettling to him."

Delsie eyed the fire and the meat. Did she really unsettle Myles? A small smile curved her mouth at the thought of keeping him on his toes, instead of the other way around.

"Don't give up on him." Amos's entreaty was low and heartfelt. "He needs your friendship. Maybe even more than you need his."

She shot a look at the older man's weathered face. "How can I possibly help *him*? I only learned how to cook my first meal today." She tossed her piece of grass into the fire with a smirk.

Amos rubbed at his bristled chin. "Maybe," he mused.

"But I got a feeling God has the two of you here together for more than just reaching your sister."

The surprising thought seeped into her heart, but before she could respond, Amos examined the meat and pronounced it was done. Removing the rabbit from its spit, he used a nearby flat rock to cut off a few sections. He popped one in his mouth, murmuring, "Tastes delicious."

Delsie accepted the piece he offered her on the end of his knife and took a bite. The meat, while not as seasoned as what she was used to at home, didn't taste as gamey as she'd thought it might. "Not bad."

"Why don't you see if Myles wants a piece, while I douse the fire? It's about time to ride again."

With a nod, she picked up the remaining meat and walked toward the trees. Myles was still dozing. Though his hat covered most of his face, she could see enough of it to notice the relaxed quality of his jaw and the way his handsome features were slack with sleep. He looked so peaceful. And she likely looked a fright. Her hair hung as limp as the rabbit had earlier, her dress still soiled in places from her cooking lesson. But she'd accomplished something she'd never done before today—three things, actually. The reminder renewed her confidence as she used her shoe to tap Myles's boot.

Immediately he scrambled up, wildly looking around. "What's wrong?"

She couldn't help a laugh. "Nothing. I have something for you to eat." She held out one of the pieces of meat.

Myles glanced at it, then up to her face. "Is it going to kill me?"

She shook her head. "If so, Amos and I will be joining you soon. Come on, try it."

"It's good," Amos said, approaching them.

Myles took the piece and tossed it into his mouth. Delsie watched him as he chewed. A flicker of surprise filled his dark eyes before he schooled his expression. "Not too shabby for rabbit," he conceded.

"Not too shabby for her first cooking lesson on an open fire, either," Amos added.

"Did you skin and gut the thing for her?"

Delsie placed one hand on her hip and glowered down at Myles. "He most certainly did not. I did it completely on my own."

"Is that so?" he studied her, his lips tweaking at the corners of his mouth. "In that case, my hat's off to the cook."

The caution had fled his gaze, replaced by blatant admiration that darkened the color of his eyes. Delsie's stomach quivered in response and her face felt suddenly warm. It was the same reaction she'd had earlier when he'd touched her hair and told her he liked it down.

"Thank you," she murmured quickly before turning her attention to Elijah and offering the bird the last morsel of meat. Had Amos been correct—did she unsettle Myles as much as he did her? Did he really need her friendship?

She glanced at him from the corner of her eye and caught him doing the same, his respect still evident on his face. Though he might not say it exactly, he was proud of what she'd accomplished. The realization set her heart thumping a little faster and couldn't erase her smile as they climbed onto the horses and struck out again.

Come what may, she wouldn't give up on Myles, just as Amos had admonished. Friendship, at least, was one thing that came easily to her. Even with a gruff Express rider.

Chapter Seven

Dark clouds bunched together in the western sky, bringing steady unease to Myles. They were in for a storm, and reading the charged tension in the air, it wouldn't be a mild summer one, either. From the corner of his eye, he saw Amos watching the clouds, too, his mouth a hard line.

Slowing his steed, whom Myles had jokingly named Moses for taking him into the wilderness, he motioned for Amos to join him in front. "What do you think?"

Amos glanced back at Delsie, who was moving at a steady clip several paces behind them. "It might be best to wait it out, but…"

"We won't be able to make up the difference tomorrow," Myles finished for him.

"Better ask Delsie." The older man twisted in the saddle and called back to her. "Come on up here, Delsie."

She guided her mare next to Myles, looking for all the world like a horsewoman through and through, except for her fancy dress. But even that was showing signs of wear after five days of long travel. Still, Delsie hadn't lost one ounce of beauty.

"What's wrong?" She gazed at him, then at Amos, a slight frown on her lips.

Myles pointed at the sky ahead. "There's a storm coming. A good one, by the looks of it. We can wait it out, but that'll mean covering fewer miles today. It's your call."

As the men had done, Delsie scanned the darkening sky before them. A flicker of hesitation entered her eyes before her expression tightened with resolve. "I think we ought to keep going."

"Let's pick up our pace, then. The sooner we're through it, the better." Myles dug his heels into Moses's flanks and spurred the steed faster. Amos and Delsie followed suit.

A short time later the first drops of rain began to fall. The sudden rumble of thunder overhead made both Myles and his horse flinch. Elijah swooped down and took refuge on Myles's shoulder, hunkering down like a feather ball beneath his hat.

Gripping the reins tighter, Myles kept Moses moving at a steady gallop. The rain soon dampened his jacket and trousers, but thankfully, his hat kept his face—and Elijah—mostly free from the moisture. He'd ridden through storms before during his short time as an Express rider, and yet, the black clouds crowding each other like boulders overhead stirred unfamiliar uneasiness in him.

The rain had become a blustery drizzle, causing cold drops to slide down Myles's collar, when Amos an-

nounced it was time to stop. The three of them sought
shelter in a small stand of trees, but even those didn't
block the water completely. One look at Delsie told him
she was beginning to feel as miserable as he was. She
folded her arms tight against her soaked dress. Strands
of wet hair lay down her back and shoulders.

"Here." Myles removed his jacket and draped it
around her shoulders.

She shot him a look of gratitude and gripped the
leather garment between both hands. "Th-thank you,"
she said, her teeth chattering. "Do you think it'll get
any worse?"

Myles hated to lie. "Most likely."

"We shouldn't linger," Amos interjected, his gaze
on the sky. "We can slow the horses to make up for not
resting the full hour."

Delsie passed around some jerky they'd acquired at
the home station that morning. No one spoke—Myles
guessed the other two were paying as much attention
to the driving rain and churning sky as him.

Once the dried meat was gone, he led the horses to
a nearby creek. Though small, the rain had swelled the
stream beyond its banks. He let them drink their fill,
then led them back to the group. A nod from Amos sig-
naled the brief rest period had come to an end. It was
time to brave the weather again.

He saw some of the determination fade from Delsie's
face as he helped her back into the saddle. She made a
move to return his jacket to him, but he shook his head.
"You keep it for now."

She rewarded him with a tiny smile before turning

her mare around. Back in the saddle, Myles let Amos take the lead this time. The rain soon had him and Moses lowering their heads in a vain attempt to avoid the sheets of water. The only parts of him not wet were the patch of hair beneath his hat and the spot on his shirt where Elijah roosted.

They plodded on, alternating the horses between a walk and a trot. A shiver cut through Myles. He couldn't remember the last time he'd been this drenched. He looked beside him at Delsie, but she wasn't there. Twisting in the saddle, he saw she'd fallen behind. In the driving rain, he hadn't noticed. A prick of alarm raced through Myles as he turned Moses around.

"Delsie," he called as another crack of thunder filled the air. She jerked in the saddle, making her mare dance to the side. Her hands were pale where they held the reins. "What happened? Are you all right?"

Her chin dipped, but Myles could see it was quivering from her chattering teeth. She had no color to her face, either. "J-just c-cold. But I'll b-be all right."

Myles couldn't argue about the cold. "Can you keep up?"

She gave another wordless nod. But he couldn't shake his concern that she wasn't all right. He coaxed Moses to quicken the pace and was relieved when Delsie did the same with her mare.

After that Myles lost count of how far they'd gone or how much time had passed. The rain was the only constant across the waterlogged prairie. Amos didn't signal for them to stop again, so Myles kept Moses moving, although he let the animal set its own pace now and then.

Sometime later a sudden sting against his hand had him lifting his gaze to the sky. The rain was fast becoming pea-sized hail. Moses whinnied in protest and Myles fought the urge to do the same. No wonder the sky had looked ominous before. He hunched his shoulders, bringing Elijah to rest against his neck, to avoid some of the hailstones. Ahead Amos was doing the same, though he kept right on setting a steady pace for all three of them.

Myles glanced to his left, expecting to see Delsie there as she'd been the past while. All he saw, though, was open prairie and leaping icy stones as they struck the ground. She'd fallen behind him again.

He craned his head to see her. Her horse plodded along at least a hundred yards back. But it was the unnatural bounce of its rider that resurrected Myles's earlier fear.

Jerking Moses around, he hollered at Amos, then galloped back to Delsie. She appeared to be dozing, despite the hail, her arms no longer holding the reins but folded inside his jacket. Her entire body appeared to shake with the cold. He reached for her reins and stopped her mare. Only then did Delsie startle awake.

"Ar-are we there?" she rasped out from lips Myles thought looked more blue than white now.

"No. But you're riding with me." He passed the reins to Amos, who'd ridden up beside them. "I think she's too cold," he told the older man in a low voice. "I don't want her freezing to death."

The raw concern in Amos's blue-gray eyes mirrored

the emotion tightening his own lungs. "I'll tie her horse to mine," Amos offered.

Myles passed him the reins, then he scooped Delsie off her saddle and onto his own. After removing his jacket from around her shoulders, he draped it around them both, cocooning her as best he could within its warmth. She settled back against his chest, her entire body trembling with cold, as Elijah readjusted his perch on Myles's shoulder. He wrapped his arm around her waist, gripping the reins with his free hand.

"Let's go, Moses," he urged, prodding the animal forward.

By now the hail had ceased, replaced by the steady rain once more. At least that was something to be grateful for, Myles thought wryly. He glanced down at Delsie, but all he could see was the top of her hat.

Please help her be all right, he found himself thinking, almost like a prayer. The idea of no longer having her in his life cut deeper than he'd ever thought possible five days earlier. *Because she's become as good a friend as Amos*, his mind argued. But his heart, thrumming fast within his chest, told a different story. It had been weeks since he'd last held a woman in his arms, and yet, the experience of embracing Cynthia had never inspired this sort of contentment, despite the precarious situation.

"Delsie?" he said, bending to speak near her ear.

Several long seconds passed before she answered, "Hmm?" Sleepiness laced her voice, provoking fresh anxiety within him.

"You've got to stay awake, sleeping beauty." The endearment rolled without effort off his tongue, though he wondered if she even noticed it in her dozing state. "At least until we can get you out of the rain and get you warm."

"But I'm just…so tired…Myles."

He pressed her tighter to him, hoping his own warmth would add to hers. "I know, but I need you to stay awake for me. All right?"

She murmured something inaudible, then seemed to shake herself. "You could tell me a story."

"A story, huh?" He searched his memories for one. There were plenty of sad tales, but could he think of a happy one? "I remember the first time I got bucked off a horse. Landed so hard on my backside, I couldn't sit at the table for two days." He thought he heard her chuckle. "I told Charles, my stepfather, I would never ride again. But he said, 'Son, life's all about getting bucked off. You can't let it make you wallow in the dust, though. You gotta get yourself back up there and show it you ain't afraid.'"

Myles paused, the recollection filling him with a trace of happiness he hadn't felt in a long time. While he missed Charles, perhaps he'd been mistaken in not remembering the man more often in an effort to avoid the continued grief of his passing. Yes, there was pain in recalling some parts of the past, but there were plenty of joyful moments, too, like the one he'd just shared.

"So did you?" Delsie prompted, her voice still faint but no longer sounding so sleepy. "Did you get back up on the horse?"

"I did, and he never bucked me off again."

He could sense the smile on her face when she said, "Good for you, Myles. Do you have another story?"

"Plenty."

"Then I want to hear them."

The conviction in her tone warmed him through and through.

Delsie tried to focus on Myles's tales, some funny, some thought provoking, but the lure of sleep tugged at her again and again. She'd never felt so cold in her life. Even with the heat of Myles's jacket and his solid, warm chest behind her, she could hardly keep her body from shivering and her teeth from rattling. At least she was mostly protected from the rain.

Biting her frozen lip, she shifted in the saddle, hoping to keep herself awake. She knew she ought to be mortified about riding with a man like this. But she couldn't muster up any real emotion except a strange glimmer of satisfaction. What was it Myles had called her minutes or hours ago? *Sleeping beauty.* Did he really think her beautiful? She exhaled a soft sigh. Within the shelter of his arms, she felt safe, protected, comforted. If she weren't so chilled, she might be content to ride in this fashion all the way to California.

"Delsie?"

Myles's voice pierced her thoughts. "Yes?"

"Just making sure you're awake."

His concern brought a limp smile to her mouth. "Trying, truly."

"Good," he murmured, tightening his grip around her

waist. She leaned back. A feeling of contentment drifted over her. She was powerless to keep her eyes open.

Sometime later she sensed a change in Myles's voice. He was no longer telling her a story but talking urgently to Amos. "Are those lights up there? We've got to get her out of this weather. I can't keep her awake."

But I can hear you, she wanted to say. And yet, to speak the words out loud would take more energy and effort than she could muster.

"That's Julesburg," Amos was saying, "but we can't stop there."

"Why not?" Myles demanded.

Amos continued in his calm, unflustered way, "There's been talk of trouble, outlaw trouble. We can't afford to have the horses stolen."

A breath of resignation washed over her, heavy with defeat and fear. "Fine. But we've got to pick up the pace, Amos, even in the rain. I don't know how much longer she'll last out here."

I'll be fine, she wanted to reply. No harm would come to her when she had someone as good and decent as Myles around. Before she could attempt to voice her thoughts, though, the blanket of sleepiness descended once more.

The next thing she knew she was being jostled awake by the sudden stopping of the horse and the absence of Myles behind her. Delsie pried her eyelids open wide enough to see a lantern cutting through the wet darkness.

"We need one of your dugouts," Myles called to someone before he gently pulled Delsie from the saddle and settled her in his arms. Still cold and sleepy, she shut her eyes once more and rested her head against the crook of his neck. The bristles of his chin tickled her forehead as he carried her.

"Meat and coffee are needed, too." The other person made a reply that was lost to Delsie, but she didn't miss Myles's thunderous answer. "I don't care. The lady is sick, and we'll pay you double for whatever you can rummage up."

A grumbled murmur she took for consent drifted to her ears as Myles continued walking. A few moments later the battering rain disappeared, and she sensed she was no longer outside. With great effort, she opened her eyes. They were inside what she presumed must be a dugout. One wall butted up against a hillside and was comprised of solid dirt. The other three had been papered over entirely with newspaper.

"I'm going to set you down on the bed." Myles eased her onto the lumpy tick mattress, then stepped back, his face full of concern in the lamplight. A stove in the middle of the room gave off some heat, but she still shivered. "You need to change out of those wet clothes."

She nodded. "W-will you get m-my bag?"

"I'll be right back with it. Stay put."

Delsie nearly smiled. How would she possibly go anywhere on her shaky limbs? Besides, the fire, though weak, had begun to melt the frigid cold from her bones. There wasn't anywhere else she wanted to be. Except maybe in Myles's strong arms again. Her face flushed at the thought. Thank goodness he couldn't read her mind.

Myles returned sooner than she'd expected and thrust

the bag at her. Delsie forced her frozen fingers to close over it. "There's no woman here to…to help you."

"I—I can do it."

He looked skeptical, but finally he gave her a curt nod and moved toward the door again. "I'll be right outside."

"Th-thank you, Myles."

The moment the door was closed, Delsie scooted to the edge of the bed. She removed her other traveling dress from her bag, grateful to find it was still dry, and began the laborious process of peeling off her wet clothes. Her fingers shook so badly she could hardly make them work, but after several starts and stops, she had the dry gown on and the wet one laid over one of the boxes serving as a chair to the nearby table.

"Delsie?" A knock followed Myles's call from the other side of the door.

"You can c-come back in." Her teeth were chattering less and less, though she still felt chilled to the core despite the dry clothes.

Myles and Amos both ducked inside, their hands full. Elijah flew from Myles's shoulder and alighted on the back of the only chair in the dugout. "We got the station owner to give us some coffee and some biscuits," Myles explained as he and Amos set the food on the table.

"Sounds good." When was the last time she'd eaten? Not since the jerky they'd shared when the rain had first started. She moved toward the table, but Myles shook his head, his mouth a fierce line.

"You need to be in bed. You can eat there."

Delsie wanted to argue, and yet, her knees had begun

to tremble again. With a sigh, she woodenly moved to the bed and sat down. Myles dropped a large buffalo robe onto her lap and legs. Immediately the warmth began to thaw her.

"Here's a biscuit and some coffee." Amos handed her the food and cup. Then he and Myles took their seats on the boxes around the table.

Delsie lowered her chin and silently blessed the food before thanking the Lord for their safe arrival. She was too exhausted to insist both men join her in prayer tonight. When she opened her eyes, she found Myles watching her, a slightly amused spark in his dark eyes.

"You gonna say one for all of us?"

A jolt of surprise ran through her. He was inviting her to pray? "Of course." She bent her head a second time and quietly repeated the words she'd just said. "Father, bless this food. Thank you for our safe arrival and for Your watchful hand over our journey. Bless us this night. In Thy Son's name. Amen."

The repeated amens, especially from Myles, filled her throat with a lump of gratitude that the coffee couldn't quite wash down. She likely owed her life tonight to these two men.

She managed to drain her cup and finish off her biscuit before her energy began to wane once more. Lying down on her side, Delsie pulled the buffalo robe nearly to her chin. The fur smelled stale, but she wouldn't begrudge its warmth.

At any minute, she expected Myles and Amos to head off to their own dugouts. A measure of loneliness filled her at the thought. The cold had eased considerably within her, but she still felt weak and vulnerable. Instead of leaving, though, once the food had been eaten and the lamp turned low, both men pulled more buffalo robes from the corner and spread them out on the dirt floor. Each one removed his boots and hat before lying down on his respective fur. Amos immediately shut his eyes.

"What are you doing?" Delsie asked Myles in a whisper. He'd taken the spot nearest the bed.

"Someone needs to keep the fire going all night." He placed his hands behind his head, his gaze toward the ceiling. "My turn is first."

Surprise, and tear-filled relief, washed over her. She tried to blink back the moisture, but a few droplets escaped her efforts and slid down her warm cheeks. Myles and Amos were going to keep the fire going all night for her.

Her father would be furious if he could see her now, sharing this small space with two men who'd been complete strangers to her less than a week ago. But Delsie couldn't muster up any amount of embarrassment, only weariness and more tears.

"I'm sorry I've been such a burden," she admitted in a soft voice that wobbled with emotion. She'd been so determined to reach Lillie that she hadn't stopped to think about what trouble a city girl such as herself might cause two seasoned riders.

"Delsie." Her name sounded as much a chastisement as a gentle touch. Though the shadows hid his face, she still sensed that intense gaze leveled on her. "There aren't many women who could've survived a single day of this kind of travel. Let alone five." She watched him twist onto his side to face her. "Some Express riders haven't even gone through half of what you have."

The honest praise warmed her more successfully than either the fire or the heavy buffalo robe. "Maybe I'll work for the Pony Express, then, after we've reached California," she teased.

"I hope not."

Delsie frowned. "But you just said—"

"I know." His low chuckle made her pulse quicken. "I figure the rest of us will be out of a job if they hire you."

She joined in his quiet laughter, smiling to herself at the implied compliment. "What would you do instead? If you weren't an Express rider?"

Myles shifted onto his back again. "I'd be a horse rancher." Delsie recalled his words from the other day about needing money to buy property. "Someday I'm going to own a big spread of land." His earnest tone reached out and held her captive, painting images in her mind as he spoke. "I'll build a nice big house on it with stables large enough to hold dozens of horses. Horses I'll breed and sell. I've even got the name of the ranch."

"What is it?"

"The B and P."

Delsie pulled the robe higher. "I imagine the *P* stands for Patton. But what does the *B* stand for?"

"Brown. It was my parents' last name."

"But you took Charles's name?"

Myles murmured agreement.

"He must a have been a wonderful father."

"He was." Both pride and pain colored his answer.

A strong urge to reach out and hold his hand swept through her. She understood the intense grief of losing a parent, and yet, Myles had lost three. Afraid he might not welcome her touch, though, she kept her hands buried beneath the robe and instead infused her next question with an empathetic tone. "What was he like?"

"Happy," Myles said with another chuckle. "Always an optimist, no matter how bad things seemed. He was honest and kind, too." He paused as if weighing whether to add something else to the list. "He was also God-fearing. Like you."

She sensed what he didn't add—Myles had been the same, at one time. It was easy to tell how much he admired Charles Patton. But did he see that he, too, was as trustworthy and caring as his stepfather had obviously been?

Before Delsie could give voice to her thoughts, a loud snore from Amos filled the dugout. She and Myles both laughed. With a grunt, Amos rolled onto his side. Quiet descended over the room once more.

"Tell me another story," she prompted. She wasn't ready to have their conversation over yet—Myles had talked more to her today than he had the past five days combined.

"About what?"

She thought a moment. "About Charles. What are your favorite memories of him?"

When Myles didn't respond for a moment, she feared he would retreat back behind his typical gruffness. Then he cleared his throat. "All right. I can still remember the first time I met him…"

Delsie burrowed deeper beneath the buffalo robe as she listened. His deep voice soothed her exhaustion. She no longer felt bone-tired or cold but perfectly comfortable.

Sometime later the creak of the stove door startled her awake. She hadn't realized she'd fallen asleep. "What time is it?"

Myles lay back down on his makeshift bed. "Late."

"I didn't mean to fall—"

"Delsie," he said cutting her off.

"Yes?" Was he upset that she hadn't stayed awake?

"Go to sleep," he said in a firm but kind tone.

"I can?" Even as she asked it, her eyelids refused to remain open.

"Yes, sleeping beauty." His unseen smile permeated each word. "You'll be fine now."

You'll be fine. Peace blanketed her at the heartfelt reassurance, as effectively as the heat from the stove. How long had it been since she'd felt such peace?

Rather ironic, she thought with a smile, as she snuggled deeper into the lumpy mattress. That peace would find her in a dirt house in the middle of Nebraska.

Chapter Eight

To Myles's keen eye, his horse's steady gallop had begun to lag. Time for another rest. "Amos?" he called. The older man, acting as lead today, twisted in the saddle to look at Myles. "Know where you want to rest?"

Amos pointed at the rock formation that had been in their sights the past thirty miles or so. "I heard there's a spring near Chimney Rock. We can stop and water the horses there."

Myles eyed the rock, which had grown increasingly taller the closer they came to it. It wasn't the first unusual formation they'd seen today—they'd passed by two others that Amos had informed them were called Courthouse Rock and Jail Rock.

Judging by the surrounding terrain, Myles knew the flatness of the plains would soon be a distant memory. Not that he minded. The thought of the mountainous landscape Amos had explained lay ahead filled him with as much excitement as it did trepidation. There was so much of the West, and this country, he hadn't expected to see. But now that he had a taste of what lay beyond his own Express run and Saint Joe, he couldn't help wanting to experience more and more. In a way, traveling farther than he ever had before made his dream of a horse ranch feel a little more within reach.

"Are we stopping?" Delsie rode up beside him.

Myles nodded and pointed at Chimney Rock. "Amos says there's a spring near the rock."

"Oh good," she said, turning to gaze at the formation. "I was hoping we might get close to it."

Myles studied her profile, analyzing those beautiful features for any signs of fatigue. After their ordeal in the rain the night before, he had purposely slowed the pace of the horses on the first two stretches of their ride today to ensure she wouldn't tire too easily. Once she figured out what he was doing, though, she'd insisted on returning to their normal speed.

If anything she looked more radiant this afternoon, her blue eyes bright as she took in the passing scenery, her lips curved in a slight smile. Or perhaps riding close with her last night and telling her stories from his life had addled his brain. Myles could almost believe it. Some of those stories he'd never told anyone, not even Cynthia, whom he'd known for years. But it was more than that. Despite his best efforts, Delsie was slowly picking her way through his defenses.

The fear he'd suffered last night when he thought she might not make it had felt as frigid and paralyzing as a snowstorm on the prairie. He would have done anything to help her. The last time he'd felt that way was when he'd watched Charles's life slip away. Thankfully, Delsie had survived. The relief he'd experienced, knowing she would be all right, had been every bit as sweet as his anxiety had been bitter.

There was no doubt in his mind Delsie was a fighter. If he could find a woman like that, strong and determined, then perhaps he wouldn't mind sharing his name and his dream of a ranch with someone else.

The thought brought a ripple of surprise running through him. Did he really want to meet and court another woman after experiencing Cynthia's treachery? Of its own volition, his mind filled with the memories of the last time he'd seen her.

Myles waited in the moonlight by the gardenia bush. The heady scent of the flowers always reminded him of Cynthia's perfume. Music and laughter floated on the warm evening air from the nearby three-story house. The Grovers' party was in full swing. Would Cynthia be able to sneak away as her note had promised?

The swish of full skirts preceded her. Myles smiled and stepped forward. He'd always thought Cynthia looked like a porcelain doll with her white face, red lips and blond hair.

"Myles," she said, her voice breathless as if she'd raced across the lawn. As eager to see him as he was to see her, he hoped.

He took both her gloved hands in his. "Hello, darling."

She turned her cheek to allow him to press a quick kiss to her smooth skin. "I couldn't get away from the captain a moment sooner. Have you been waiting long?"

"Not long." The thought of that army gentleman

dancing with Cynthia made Myles frown. It should be him whirling her around the Grovers' fancy parlor. But try as he might he couldn't quite picture himself there— dressed in something nicer than his church clothes, talk-ing with Cynthia's father about politics and the state of the world.

"I only have a few minutes." She heaved a sigh, then brightened just as rapidly. "Do you like my new ball gown?"

He twirled her around. "You look as pretty as ever. Did you speak with your mother and father?"

Cynthia shifted her weight, throwing a glance at the house behind them. "I did."

"And?" Some of his impatience leaked into his tone, making it sharper than Myles had intended. But he'd waited six long years for this day—the day Cynthia would finally be twenty-one. Old enough to decide for herself whom she wanted to marry.

"Myles, I love you. You know that."

Why did the words set off a loud clang of warning in-side his head? He gave her hands a gentle squeeze. "I love you, too, Cindy, and that's why I want to marry you."

"I—I know. It's just... Mother and Father..."

Myles ground his teeth as irritation washed over him. "They still don't approve of me, do they?"

Cynthia dipped her head in a nod, sending her blond curls bobbing. "I don't think they've forgiven you for turning down the position of livery stable overseer this winter. I told them that your job with the Pony Express is a good one, but my father said the venture's too new to know for certain. He says you can't provide for me."

"I can—I will." Myles rubbed his thumb over the fine fabric of her gloves. "I can make good money as an Express rider, but I don't plan on doing that forever. You know I want to have a horse ranch someday."

"I told my parents as much."

Myles pushed out his breath. "You're old enough to decide for yourself, Cynthia." He tugged her closer "I may not be able to give you ball gowns or servants, but I promise to be a loving and honorable husband."

She broke free from his hold to cover her face with her hands. A quiet sob escaped her fingers. "Oh, Myles." He drew her head to his shoulder. "I don't want this to end... I don't want to say goodbye."

Goodbye? He released her, his gut twisting into a knot. "What are you saying?"

"I can't marry you. Father forbade it."

"But...but we love each other. We could go right now and wake the pastor. Start our life together like we've always wanted. Even without your parents' permission."

Cynthia brushed at her cheeks. "I want to, I do. But I can't defy my mother and father. I'm the only child they have and they want me to marry well."

"To someone like the captain?" Myles didn't bother to hide his bitterness.

"Oh, see. You do understand. I knew you would."

His jaw went slack. Did Cynthia care for him at all? Had their courtship only been a way for her to rebel against her parents' demands? He'd waited all this time for her to choose and now she had, but it wasn't him she'd chosen.

As he stared into her half-smiling face, something hardened inside Myles. She was like every other debutante he'd seen come into the livery stable—spoiled, frightened of poverty and in love with wealth. At least he'd discovered the truth now, rather than several years into their marriage.

"Goodbye, Cynthia." The words tasted ripe with rejection.

"Will I see you again?" All traces of her earlier distress had disappeared.

Myles shook his head. "Give your mother and father my best."

"Myles, are you angry?"

He didn't respond. Instead he spun around and marched down the street, toward the river. He'd been a fool, thinking he—an orphan and Express rider— could woo and marry one of the town's most eligible young ladies.

Moses suddenly danced to the side and halted, jerking Myles from his thoughts. He looked up to see he'd nearly plowed them into Amos's horse. "Sorry," he grumbled as he and the older man dismounted. They'd reached Chimney Rock and the spring while Myles had been lost in his memories.

Amos shot him an amused look but kept blessedly silent.

"Want to explore the rock?" Delsie asked, her face etched with wonder.

Myles glanced at Amos, but the man was already

leading the horses toward the water. "You two go on. I'll see to the animals."

Delsie led out, holding her skirt in one hand as she picked her way across the grass. The pant legs of her trousers showed beneath her hem, calling to mind Myles's brief glimpse at her shapely calf that first day. A smile worked his mouth at the memory of how proper she'd tried to be, even without a sidesaddle.

Now look at her, he thought with a wry shake of his head, *traipsing through the brush without a care for her dress and wearing that hat like a real rider*. He could hardly believe they'd only met less than a week ago. It seemed more like a month after all they'd been through.

At the base of the rock spire, Delsie stopped. Myles came up beside her. Instead of the lofty height of the formation, her attention seemed riveted on the names and initials carved into the soft rock. There were dozens and dozens of them, some fresh, others growing faint from the effects of the sun, rain and wind.

"Just think how many people have passed by this very spot." She reached out and traced a name with her finger. "All looking for a new life out West." Her voice held the same wistfulness it did whenever she spoke of her sister. Did Delsie hold out hope of possibly carving a new life out here, too?

Myles reached into his boot and withdrew his knife. "I say we add our names to theirs."

She looked from the knife to him, then smiled fully. "All right." She accepted the blade then began chiseling her name into the stone. He let his gaze wander up the towering rock. Had God made it this way? As a beacon for those coming West?

"There." Delsie brushed dust from the letters with her hand and passed him the knife. She'd carved only her first name.

Myles went to work, scoring his full name—Myles Brown Patton—into the rock. When he'd finished, he stepped back in satisfaction. Let all the world know he'd come this way, and the next time he passed by this rock, he'd see how well his name had weathered the elements.

Delsie had walked a short distance away as he'd been carving. He found her staring east, her arms clasped tight, her expression pensive. The reason she hadn't chiseled her full name into the rock suddenly hit him.

"Your father doesn't know you're doing this, does he?"

Pressing her lips together, she shook her head.

"Don't you think he's sick with worry?" He might not be a parent himself, but he couldn't imagine a father being anything less than panicked over the disappearance of his daughter.

Delsie kicked at a clump of grass. "No...he thinks I'm still at my aunt Cissy's in Saint Louis. At least for another few weeks."

"Where does your aunt think you are?"

A half-rueful smile appeared on her lips. "Heading back home, by way of a friend's."

Myles followed her gaze across the prairie to the eastern horizon. What would Mr. Radford do if he found out his daughter was not in Missouri as he'd supposed but halfway across the country? "Why not just tell him what you were doing?"

"He would have refused to let me come." Her voice held such melancholy that it twisted Myles's heart. "Papa told Lillie if she went after Clay that he would never contact her again. It would be as if she no longer existed." She blew out a breath as if repeating the words caused her fresh pain. "He wasn't trying to be cruel—he may be stern and rigid sometimes but never cruel. I think he honestly thought such an ultimatum would make Lillie change her mind. But she's as stubborn as him." An embittered laugh escaped her mouth.

"Then why risk his anger yourself?"

Delsie turned to look at him, her gaze full of the same raw resolution he'd seen time and again these past six days. "Because I made a promise to my mother, when she was dying. She pleaded with me to keep my family together. When Lillie left, I thought I'd failed."

She removed her hat and brushed a lock of dark hair from her forehead. "Then I found the letters she'd written me—letters Papa had hidden. In her last one Lillie told me if she didn't hear from me by the time she married, she would not attempt to contact me again. Our family…" Delsie visibly swallowed as if gathering courage to finish. "Our family would be dead to her, as she'd been to our father this last year."

Admiration burned warm inside Myles. For the first time since agreeing to come along, he could see what this journey could cost Delsie, especially if she didn't make it to her sister in time. She was willing to sacrifice physical discomfort, her father's potential wrath and possibly her own life in an effort to hold her small family together. That was something Charles had understood and lived, up until the day he'd died.

A sudden longing for a noble cause, for a family of his own, filled Myles to distraction. He'd told himself he was content living alone with only Elijah for company and visiting with Amos during his Express runs. But maybe it wasn't enough.

He reached out his hand, motioning her toward him. She hesitated only a moment before she moved into his arms. "We'll get you there, Delsie," he murmured. "Don't you worry. We'll help you keep your promise."

She nodded against his shoulder, while he stroked her hair as if she were a frightened child or the sister he'd never had. Nothing could be further from the truth, though. The same perfection he'd felt riding with her on Moses and carrying her into the dugout yesterday rose up within him as he held her.

Too bad the one girl he could easily picture being at his side forever would never be free to choose him. She'd witnessed the pain her sister's choice in beaus had inflicted on their father—and Myles knew as sure as she was standing here that Delsie would never do the same.

The beginning notes of a fiddle drew Delsie from the station porch where she'd been sitting with Amos and Myles. They'd left Chimney Rock behind hours ago.

"Do you hear that?" she asked, her toe tapping beneath her skirt.

A short distance to the west a large wagon train had encamped for the night. It was the first wagon company

Delsie had seen. She'd wanted to wander over and talk to the emigrants, but her dusty, dirt-covered traveling dress made her hesitate. Not that the wagon occupants would be faring significantly better. Now the lure of the music called at her to abandon her embarrassment.

While she appreciated Amos's occasional harmonica concert, Delsie still missed the music she'd experienced nearly every day back at home. Playing music on the piano, listening to it at the opera and especially, dancing to it.

"Do you think they're going to have a dance?"

Myles shrugged at her question, even as the song changed from a lively ditty to a polka.

Delsie returned to the porch and motioned for the two men to stand. "Come on, gentlemen. I need a partner."

Amos laughed but shook his head. "Don't know if these old bones can handle dancing after another hard day's ride." Delsie couldn't help thinking his words contradicted his usual agility, which sometimes seemed to rival even hers and Myles's. The older man cut a glance at Myles—one that looked rather calculated to Delsie. "Why don't you go on, Myles?"

"Me?" Myles removed his hat and wiped at his brow with his sleeve. "You know I'm not much of a dancer, Amos."

"I'll teach you," Deslie volunteered. Even if Amos was scheming to give her and Myles more time to themselves, she didn't care. Right now she only wanted to dance and forget for a few blissful moments the hard task ahead of her and her father's irate response when he eventually found out about it. "Please, Myles."

He eyed her sternly, but she gave him a sweet smile in return. Finally he pushed out a sigh and climbed to his feet. "Fine."

"Thank you." She resisted the urge to kiss his bearded cheek in gratitude. Instead she clasped her hands together and fell into step beside him as they headed toward the wagon train. The music grew louder the closer they came. Delsie did a little skip at the thought of dancing.

Myles's low rumble of a laugh sounded beside her. "I don't think I've seen you this excited since I told you I'd take you on my run that first day."

Her cheeks warmed with a blush, but she ignored it. "I love dancing nearly as much as I do my sister." He rewarded her joke with a full smile, making her heart skip right along with her feet.

At the edge of the circled wagons, he stopped her. "Why don't you teach me here?"

Between two of the wagons, she could see a group, young and old, dancing to the fiddle's lively music. Their energy begged her to come closer, but she feared she'd lose her partner if she insisted. At least they were close enough to easily follow along to the tune.

"All right." She turned to face Myles and lifted her right hand in the air. "You'll hold this hand here and your other will go on my waist."

He complied, taking her hand in his. He placed his right hand on her waist as she rested her left one on his shoulder. Flurries erupted in Delsie's middle at his touch and the way he gazed intently at her. Being in his arms, in this way, felt different than when he'd comforted her earlier that afternoon.

"You…uh…might want to take off your hat," she said, the words sticking in her dry throat.

Without breaking eye contact, Myles pulled off his hat and tossed it onto the grass nearby. Delsie couldn't help chuckling.

"You're going to do fine. Just follow my lead."

"Sounds like business as usual." His lips worked up into a teasing smile, drawing her attention to them. What would it be like to kiss those masculine lips? Flynn had given her several chaste pecks on the cheek, though he hadn't attempted to kiss her mouth yet. She'd harbored a slight disappointment over that fact, but now she felt secretly glad. Perhaps Flynn wasn't the man she wanted to share her first real kiss with after all. "So what do we do?"

Myles's inquiry broke through her thoughts, eliciting another blush. She'd be mortified if he could guess at what she'd been thinking.

Lifting her chin, she did her best to school her chaotic feelings. "The polka is quite simple. It's basically a skip step and a turn." She demonstrated with her feet, tugging Myles with her. "One and two, one and two."

After a few steps, he caught the gist. They whirled around across the ground, in time with the music.

"You're doing good," Delsie declared with a smile. "Now that you have those steps, we can try to add something fancier—"

Myles interrupted her by spinning her out and back to him, all the while keeping time with the polka beat.

Delsie stared at him in astonishment. "I thought you said you didn't dance."

"No. I said I wasn't much of a dancer." He spun her out again as he added, "Charles taught me more than how to work with horses. It's just been a few years since I made use of his lessons."

"Did you never dance with your girl back in Missouri?"

It was the wrong thing to say. Myles slowed to a stop, his expression one of hardened pain. "Not in her fancy parlor. I was never invited to those parties."

Delsie sensed he didn't want her pity, so she kept silent. But that didn't stop memories marching through her mind of parties at home in Pennsylvania, parties Lillie's beau had never been invited to. "Well, I think that's a real shame." She tipped her head up to look him in the eye. "Because you're quite adept on your feet."

The guarded quality faded from his dark eyes, replaced by an appreciative gleam. "I've had two good teachers."

She laughed as he led her through another of the fiddler's polka numbers. They moved in perfect time with each other, his hand holding her waist with gentle pressure. The longer they danced the more his normal gruff exterior dropped away. Without his hat, she was able to peruse his face unencumbered. She could easily imagine him turning many female heads back at home with his bristled jaw, strong shoulders and unfathomable dark eyes.

Those eyes studied her with equal abandon, setting Delsie's pulse galloping along with their feet and renewing the flurry of sensations in her stomach. Wasn't this how Lillie had described her feelings for Clay when Delsie asked if her sister loved the poor farmer?

I love him very much, Lillie had answered.

But how do you know it's love? she'd countered.

Lillie had smiled. *You know it in the way your heart pounds every time you see him. Or how butterflies alight in your stomach when he touches your hand.* She had drawn her knees up to her chin and wrapped her arms around them. *But most of all, you know it when he fills your thoughts. When your heart wells up with peace and joy at the idea of being with him forever.*

Delsie had never felt anything even remotely similar when it came to Flynn. Myles on the other hand… Her breath caught in her throat. Could she possibly be feeling more than friendship for this Express rider? It seemed ridiculous, having only known him a mere six days, and yet, she'd experienced many of those same emotions in regard to Myles that Lillie felt for Clay.

"Are you all right?" he asked.

Delsie realized she'd slowed and was no longer following his lead. "I'm sorry. I think I just need to…to sit down." He didn't look convinced until she added in a light tone, "All that twirling around."

Myles finally released her. Taking a seat on the ground, she took in deep breaths of the summer air to slow her rapidly beating heart. He dropped down beside her. They listened in silence to the dance music.

When the song ended, the fiddler struck up a different sort of number. Instead of dancing, the emigrants began to sing. She couldn't decipher the words, but the melody rang with conviction and hope.

"My father has a man at home he wants me to marry." The admission was out before she even considered why she was saying it. Something about Myles's comforting presence and the music pulled it from her. "His name is Flynn Coppell. He manages my father's bank."

Myles didn't respond right away. Instead he leaned back on his elbows, his gaze on the emigrants. "Do you care for him?"

"I don't know. He's Papa's choice." She ripped up a piece of prairie grass and twisted it around her finger. "Did you care for…?"

"Cynthia?" he supplied.

"Yes, Cynthia." She knew she was being overly bold by asking, but she couldn't dismiss her curiosity about this woman who'd clearly captured Myles's attention.

Myles sat up and rested his arms on his knees. "I did care for her. Thought she felt the same, too. But she didn't."

"What happened?" she asked quietly, fearing he wouldn't answer.

A heavy sigh drifted toward her before he spoke again. "I guess you could say she was a lot like your sister. Except instead of choosing me, she chose the man her parents wanted."

Sadness filled Delsie at his story along with a measure of irony at the similarities to Lillie's. "How long had you known her?"

"Six years." Picking up his hat off the grass, he fingered the brim. "She came into the livery stable three times in a matter of days. Charles finally told me it wasn't because she had a real need of a horse. We saw each other at least twice a week after that."

"Did her parents know?"

"Not for a few years." His regretful tone wasn't lost on Delsie. "Maybe if they had, things might have gone differently." He shrugged. "Then again, I don't know that she and I would have been happy together. Cynthia would have hated all this."

She felt relief to hear his voice no longer held bitterness but resignation. "You mean the dirt and the weather and the scanty food?" She swept her arm in an arc to take in the Express station, the distant bluffs and the wagons. "Why, this is a palatial palace, Myles Patton."

He chuckled, as she'd hoped. "Then that makes you the queen, Delsie Radford."

Rather than teasing, the words sounded more like an endearment. One that filled her heart with warm pleasure. She busied herself with the grass she'd plucked up.

"We'd better head back," he said, disrupting the quiet between them. "Early start again tomorrow."

She dipped her head in a nod. Before she could climb to her feet, though, he offered her his hand. Delsie allowed him to help her up, though it meant she stood rather close to him again.

"Thank you for the dance lesson." He brushed an errant hair from her face, her hand still gently gripped in his.

"You're welcome," she managed to get out over the pounding of her heartbeat in her throat. "Thank you for dancing with me."

He smiled and released her hand. But even as they started back across the grass toward the home station, Delsie couldn't quell her racing pulse. Why in the world had she let herself develop feelings for a man her father would never condone as a suitable husband? A man who, if she chose, would only further divide her splintered family?

Chapter Nine

After witnessing the distant bustle of Fort Laramie, Wyoming, as they'd ridden past, Delsie found the present hills almost too quiet, devoid of people or movement. She shifted in the saddle, tugging her hat farther down on her head against the incessant sun. Though she hadn't wanted to stop at the fort after her last encounter near Fort Kearney, she couldn't entirely squelch her curiosity at seeing a place that teemed with more life than she'd seen in several days. They'd been riding for a solid week now.

"Which means today is Sunday." She'd forgotten until this moment. At home she would have been attending church with her father, but out here, there was no house of worship. That didn't mean she couldn't hold her own little service, though. Amos would certainly join her, but Delsie wasn't sure about Myles. "No harm in asking."

At the next stop, Delsie broached the subject as soon as she'd dismounted. "Gentlemen, I've realized it's the

Sabbath and I would like to hold a little service." She caught the sudden rigidness of Myles's shoulders even before she'd finished. "If you don't wish to take part, that's perfectly fine. I'll be…" She motioned to a spot along the banks of the North Platte. "Over there."

"I'll join you." Amos removed his hat. "It's been far too long since I've had someone else to worship with."

Delsie smiled her pleasure. "Wonderful. And you, Myles?" A strong hope stirred within her, but it was dashed the moment he spoke.

"I'll tend to the horses," he muttered.

"We'll be over there should you change your mind," she said with forced cheerfulness. She kept her chin up as she walked to the spot she'd indicated, Amos trailing her. But inside she felt like crying. Why should she care if Myles didn't want to participate? Why couldn't she be content with him asking her to bless their meal the other night and not hope for more?

Because I like him—very much, her heart admitted.

She pushed the thought aside. No good would come from exploring it. Her father would never approve of her choice, just as he hadn't Lillie's.

Once she was settled on the grass, Delsie watched the flow of the river for a moment. Too bad she didn't have a Bible. "What shall we do first?" she asked Amos when he sat down next to her. She wasn't entirely sure the best way to proceed.

He rubbed at his gray beard. "How about we start with prayer?"

"Yes." She managed another smile. "That would be lovely. Would you say it, Amos?"

With a nod, he bowed his head and verbalized their gratitude for a safe journey and for God's blessings in their lives. He prayed for her family, for her and Myles, and for continued protection and guidance. By the time he murmured "Amen," there were tears swimming in Delsie's eyes.

No matter her worries or unconventional situation, she felt certain she would be all right. God was looking out for her. *And Myles, too*, something whispered inside her. *Don't give up on him.* The words echoed those Amos had said to her.

Brushing at her wet eyes, she smiled at the older man. "Thank you. Now how about we share our favorite Bible verses?"

The sound of singing reached Myles's ears, even though he was trying hard to ignore the two figures seated by the river's edge. Amos's tenor mixed perfectly with Delsie's sweet soprano. Against his better judgment, Myles found himself listening.

For the beauty of the earth,
For the glory of the skies,
For the love which from our birth
Over and around us lies:
Lord of all, to Thee we raise
This our hymn of grateful praise.

For the beauty of each hour,
Of the day and of the night,
Hill and vale, and tree and flower,

Sun and moon, and stars of light:
Lord of all, to Thee we raise
This our hymn of grateful praise.

Could there be more perfect words to describe their
journey West this past week? Try as he might he couldn't
resist the pull and harmony of the music, even if he didn't
know the words. He began to hum baritone, quietly, as he
walked toward them. On the now-familiar chorus, Myles
finally joined his voice full force with theirs.

Delsie whirled around, her eyes wide with uncon-
cealed surprise. She kept right on singing to the end of
the chorus, though, as Myles lowered himself to the
ground at her left.

The final harmonious notes floated crystal clear
across the river. "That," Delsie said, clearing her throat,
"was lovely. Thank you, both."

He couldn't quite work up the nerve to look at her
fully—not after refusing to join them earlier. But he was
spared having to do so when Amos suggested they end
with another prayer. Delsie offered it.

He'd grown accustomed to her simple, heartfelt
prayers, ones that sounded more like a conversation
than a list of blessings or needs. *Perhaps if I could talk
to God that way.* The thought startled Myles enough
that he opened his eyes. When had he started thinking
he needed the Lord in his life again?

Probably about the time this dark-haired female sitting next to him had showed up at the Express stables,
with her double measure of determination and faith.

After Delsie's prayer, Amos volunteered to check

on the horses. Myles let the not-so-subtle excuse go; he found he wasn't ready yet to disrupt the peace he felt sitting here beside the river with Delsie. Though he might have to corner the older man later and ask what Amos was doing by constantly trying to give them time together. Nothing would come of it. They were both aware of that. Amos was wasting his time trying to create something that would never be.

"Did you like that hymn?" Delsie asked. Her tone sounded innocent enough, but he guessed what she was really asking. Why had he decided to join them at the end?

"It sounded like a good one." He bit back a smile when his noncommittal answer brought a frown to her lips.

She started to rise. "Yes, well, I suppose it's time to go."

"I haven't sung a hymn in years," Myles admitted, keeping his gaze on the river. From the corner of his eye, he saw her slowly sit back down. "Haven't been in a church, either." He fingered his hat. "Not since before Charles died."

Delsie drew her knees up to her chest and rested her chin there. "The death of a parent is very difficult, at any age."

"I didn't think I fit in after that," Myles added. A part of him wanted to stop talking, to rebury the hurt, but a greater part of him wanted to share the burden weighing him down. "I had no family, no wife. What use did God have for me? He started to feel about as unobtainable and distant as Cynthia and her rich society life."

Momentary silence met his words. Myles stared at his hat, embarrassment creeping over him. He'd gone and said too much. Delsie was likely to pity or condemn him, and he had no use for either.

"Why did you name your bird Elijah?"

The question caught him off guard. "What?"

"Elijah? Where did his name come from?"

Myles glanced up to see that determined glint in her dark blue eyes. He'd underestimated her—again. She wasn't going to heap judgment on him; she was going to root around until she found even a single seed of faith still sprouting inside him.

"His name comes from the Bible," Myles answered over a rueful smile. "But you knew that, didn't you?"

She shrugged, but not without smiling herself. "I suspected as much. Which story inspired you to pick Elijah?"

He couldn't help a grin. "The one when he and the pagan priests square off to call down fire from above. I always liked how he teases them to cry louder because he says maybe their god is sleeping." He chuckled, remembering the animated way Charles would tell the story. "But my favorite part is how he douses the entire altar with water before praying. And then the fire comes, lots of it."

Delsie remained silent, listening. Resting his hat on his knee, Myles found a pebble among the grass. "Elijah had no doubts God would hear him. Only faith and confidence." He lobbed the small rock into the river. "Of course, I also like the story about the ravens feeding him. I guess both of those influenced the bird's name."

"Maybe influenced you, too." She didn't pose it as a question, but Myles nodded just the same. "I think those are excellent reasons for naming him Elijah. Especially since it looks like God sent you a little fire, too. In the form of the bird, I mean."

Myles frowned in confusion. "Come again?"

Delsie twisted on the grass to face him, "When did you find Elijah?"

"About four months ago."

"Before everything ended with Cynthia, right?"

He rubbed at his chin, trying to figure out her line of reasoning. "Well, yes."

"See?" She sounded as if she'd just presented him with his horse ranch. "God knew you'd need someone. Someone who needed you, too." Her face radiated confidence in a way that enhanced her natural beauty.

Myles turned to stare at the river again. Uncertainty clouded his mind. What did Delsie know of real hardship or real faith? She'd never been challenged before this week, living in her fancy house with every possible need provided for.

But she did lose her mother, a quiet voice inside reminded. Along with her sister. And now she's caught in a tug-o-war with her father over her family, with very little freedom to choose her own life.

Tasting regret at his harsh judgment, he honestly considered her theory. Had God really sent Elijah to him, knowing Myles might need something in his life to care for if things didn't work out with Cynthia? The idea seemed far-fetched, and yet, something deep within him stirred at the possibility. Were there other evidences that God hadn't abandoned him like Cynthia had?

He catalogued his friendship with Amos and how the older man had stepped in after Charles's death to be as much a father figure as a friend. Then there was the freedom Myles enjoyed, being able to give up the livery stable for the Pony Express without the worry of having to support a family yet.

A glance at Delsie plucking up grass beside him brought another revolutionary thought. Maybe their paths had crossed for more reasons than him helping her reach California on time. Maybe she was here to help him, as well.

Myles had no doubt God was watching over her—the experience near Fort Kearney had solidified that. And if He cared enough for Delsie to help her keep her family together, then perhaps He cared enough for Myles to bring her into his life.

"Time to go, you two," Amos called from behind.

Myles plunked on his hat and stood, offering Delsie his hand and helping her to her feet. "Thank you for joining us, even if it was at the end." The sincerity in her gaze and her feminine nearness brought a familiar jolt to his heart.

"You're welcome." He rubbed his thumb over the smooth skin on the back of her palm. She'd abandoned her gloves somewhere along the trail. "Thanks for your words."

He led her back to the horses, her hand firmly gripped in his, though he knew he probably ought to let go. There was no sense meddling in things that weren't meant to be. Still, he ignored the argument. Only when Delsie reached her mare did Myles finally release her.

But long afterward, he could still feel the coolness of her fingers against his and the heat of her faith in his heart.

Delsie dismounted in the shadow of Fort Bridger's adobe wall. This fort and the other landmarks they'd passed in the past four days—Devil's Gate, Independence Rock, Pacific Springs—were no longer mere names told to her by Amos. Each one now held a mental picture inside her mind.

"Why are we resting here?" A frisson of concern ran up her spine at being so near another fort. She wouldn't soon forget the terror she'd experienced outside Fort Kearney—and she hadn't even been close to the structure itself.

"Moses slipped a shoe," Myles replied evenly as he gathered his horse's reins.

Delsie pushed up her hat. "Moses?" *Another Bible name*, she thought with a smile. She'd sensed Myles's faith during their impromptu church service, even if he'd insisted it was weak.

"Didn't you name your horse?" he countered, his black eyes showing more mirth than irritation.

"Yes. It's Horse."

He barked a laugh. "Not very creative. What do you call your horse back home?"

"Gabriel," she said, blushing. Lillie had teased her about the name, but Delsie refused to change it. The young foal had been given to her shortly after their mother's death, and to Delsie, the horse was a comfort.

Myles's teasing expression softened. "That's a good one. I'll have to keep it in mind." He started for the fort entrance, calling over his shoulder, "Do you want to come?"

She pressed her lips together in indecision. She wanted to see the inside of a real fort, but what if something happened again?

"You'll be fine," Amos reassured as though he could read her mind. Perhaps the old man could. "This fort is quite safe. Just stick with Myles. I'll watch out for the horses."

On impulse, Delsie went up on tiptoe and pressed a quick kiss to the man's whiskered cheek. "Thank you, Amos. For everything." He would have made some boy or girl a wonderful father.

Amos shrugged and turned away, but not before she caught sight of his happy grin and tear-filled eyes. She would miss him when she reached Lillie—he and Myles both. Picking up her skirt in one hand, she hurried after Myles.

The fort teemed with noise and people. Trappers, Indians, horses and pioneers created a moving sea of color and conversation. Delsie paused to take it in, her gaze sweeping from the wooden and adobe structures of the fort to the different occupants. A dark-haired Indian dressed in leather leggings and shirt stared intently back at her with eyes as dark as coal. He wore round earrings and a number of beaded necklaces draped his neck.

Delsie turned to ask Myles about the Indian, but he

was no longer nearby. A worm of alarm uncurled inside her. Where had he gone? She pushed through the crowd, searching frantically. At last she spied him heading toward the stables, leading Moses behind him.

Pushing out a breath of relief, she rushed after them. She wanted no reoccurrence of what had happened the last time she'd ventured off on her own near a fort.

"There you are," Myles said before leading Moses into the stable. "Wasn't sure if you preferred looking over the things to buy."

Delsie shook her head. "I don't mind waiting here with you…" She blushed as she realized how her words might sound to him. "And Moses, too, of course," she added with a forced laugh.

Myles, thankfully, made no comment. Instead he spoke to the smithy about Moses's shoe.

She glanced around and found a barrel to sit on. Taking off her hat, she fanned herself with it, relishing even a moment to sit without moving.

Riding wasn't as trying anymore, but she would be glad when her days no longer consisted of hours and hours in a saddle. Or would she? She allowed her gaze to sweep the fort beyond the stable's overhang. While she didn't have much taste for fort life, she'd grown so used to the open sky and the endless miles to think, to pray and to simply breathe. Her beloved home back in Pennsylvania had grown increasingly more confining in memory—a place to be seen and conform.

She couldn't go back and expect things to be the same because she was no longer the same. Learning new skills, besting the elements and pushing herself through one difficulty after another had succeeded in peeling away nearly all of her former shyness and uncertainty. She was stronger than she'd imagined and longed for greater freedom than she'd once thought. But she had no other choice. Home was where she was needed, where she'd promised to be.

For the first time in years, that promise felt as weighty as a buffalo robe upon her shoulders instead of a tenuous thread of connection to her mother. "Is this truly what you had in mind, Mother?" she whispered, her lips barely moving, as her eyes sought the blue sky above. "To find Lillie and return home to life unchanged? To someone like Flynn?"

A sudden hard pinch to her arm made her yelp as much from pain as surprise. She twisted on the barrel to find the Indian she'd seen earlier towering over her. Delsie's heart pounded with panic as the man released her arm and fingered her hair.

"Myles," she managed to squeak out of her dry throat as she plunked her hat back on her head.

The Indian proceeded to pull at her lower lip and examine her teeth as if she were a horse on display. Delsie lifted a trembling hand and firmly pushed his away. "Myles?" she called, louder.

"What?" he grumbled. From the corner of her eye, she caught sight of him moving toward her, but he froze when he saw the Indian standing there.

"Squaw very beautiful," the Indian said, his tone languid and deep.

"Yes, she is." Myles stepped closer, not taking his gaze off the man. He might stand several inches taller than her companion, but the fierce protection in Myles's black eyes eased Delsie's panicked pulse a little.

"You need new horse?" The Indian gestured to Moses behind them.

"Not new horse, just new horseshoe," Myles answered evenly.

The Indian sized up Moses as he had Delsie earlier. "Horse look old and tired. Ride too hard. I have new horse. Young and full of energy." He waved his hand toward the fort entrance.

Myles darted a glance in that direction, then back at the Indian. "What do you want for your young horse?"

Delsie held her breath as she waited for the Indian's reply. Something in his unemotional face made her shiver.

"I give you horse," he answered matter-of-factly. "You give me squaw."

A soft gasp escaped her and she started to rise, intent on refusing the man. But Myles pressed a firm hand onto her shoulder, indicating she stay seated.

When he seemed satisfied she wouldn't move, he let go and rubbed at his chin as if actually contemplating the offer. Delsie gripped the sides of the barrel with both hands, irritation replacing some of her fear. Would Myles really consider trading her for a horse? After all they'd gone through? She tightened her fists. He wouldn't get one cent from her if he handed her over to this Indian now. Not one single…

Myles slowly shook his head, his expression almost apologetic. "It's a good trade—for me. But not for you." He motioned to Delsie. "Squaw is trouble."

She gave a squeal of protest, then pressed her lips together when he shot her a warning look.

"This squaw doesn't cook and she can't sit a horse too well." She felt her whole body tremble at his words, but it wasn't with fright this time. Now it was anger coursing through her. "She knows nothing about skinning an animal, either, or how to tan a hide. And she never, never stops talking."

The Indian glanced with obvious skepticism at the silent Delsie.

"She's quiet now," Myles explained, "but the moment you're out of earshot, I can guarantee you that I'll get an earful."

"But you keep squaw?" Confusion clouded the man's bronzed features.

Myles lifted his shoulders in a lazy shrug. "Her father owns a very accurate shotgun."

The Indian sniffed with dismissiveness. "I keep horse, then, and you keep troubling squaw."

"Only if you're sure."

Spinning on his heel, the Indian marched away, his back erect.

Delsie scrambled off the barrel, her hands clenched at her sides. Anger made her skin itch and her collar too tight. "Why would you—"

Myles clapped his hand over her mouth, his face mere inches from her own. "Shh," he hissed, throwing a glance at the retreating Indian. "I had to be convincing. Otherwise he and his friends might have followed us once we left here and simply taken you. We might not have stood a chance if he found you…" He visibly swallowed as he lowered his hand. "If he found you pleasing."

He'd said all those things to protect her—once again. Delsie reached out and touched his arm, the firm muscle almost familiar beneath her fingers. "Thank you." She folded her arms as a sudden shiver ran through her. "For a moment there, I thought you might actually give in. Of course your arguments to the contrary were very believable, as well."

Myles grinned. "There was only one thing on that list that was true."

"Yes, I can't tan a hide," she said with a laugh.

But he shook his head. "Not that one. I've no doubt you could do it if you had a mind to." He started back toward Moses and the smithy.

Delsie stepped quickly after him. "Then what?"

He paused long enough to throw her a look over his shoulder. A look that held a mixture of amusement, appreciation and regret—all rolled into one. "The part about being trouble," he murmured in a voice that sent a tingle racing down her spine. Not one of anger but wild hope.

She ducked out of the way as he paid the smithy and gathered Moses's reins. But even as they wound their way back toward the fort entrance, Delsie knew she wouldn't soon forget the husky tone of Myles's voice as he'd said those words or the caring in his dark eyes. One day, soon, when she was no longer riding at his side day in and day out, she would pull out this memory to savor again and again.

Chapter Ten

Myles pushed his empty plate aside and rested his elbows on the smooth wood table as he leaned forward to better hear the Express rider seated across from him and Amos. The dining room at Porter Rockwell's Hot Springs Brewery Hotel, south of Salt Lake City, remained full of people and conversation, despite the late evening hour.

"You'll probably fare all right," the rider named Tucker stated matter-of-factly as he lifted his mug to his mouth and took a drink. "It's the stations what's in real trouble."

"How many have been attacked?" Amos asked, his voice tight with seriousness. Myles sensed the older man was every bit on edge as himself tonight. As of tomorrow, they were riding straight into the lion's den, so to speak, with little knowledge on how bad things might be.

Tucker set his mug down. "Can't say for certain. My run's been fairly quiet, except for a scrimmage between one station owner and the Indians. But I have heard of other stations being burned, stock driven off and owners killed."

Amos shot Myles a look. It was the same dire rumblings they'd heard before leaving Nebraska behind. Would the rumors prove true? Would they be able to find sufficient food or shelter in the middle of a warpath?

"I'd get new horses, if I was you," Tucker said. "Especially since you've been riding the same ones for nearly two weeks. Those Indian ponies have a harder time outrunning Express horses. That might be your greatest weapon."

Myles ran a hand over his beard. He hated the idea of parting with Moses—the horse had been as faithful a companion as Elijah. But if acquiring new mounts might save their lives, he would let Moses go. That was if Delsie was in agreement about funding the purchase of three new horses.

Looking past Amos, he found her seat at their table was empty. At some point during the conversation with Tucker, she must have slipped away. A tremor of unease flitted through Myles. While there were a number of women here tonight, the male occupants of the hotel far outnumbered the female ones.

"Where'd Delsie go?" he asked Amos quietly.

Amos shrugged. "Not sure. She said she needed some air."

His agitation increased, especially given the popularity of the nearby brewery. "I'm going to look for her. Tell her what we found out." He nodded at Tucker, snagged some meat to give to Elijah and stood. "Excuse me, gentlemen."

He made his way out of the dining room. Outside Myles paused in the dying light. Delsie wasn't milling about the hotel like several of the other guests. Should he knock on her door? His gaze settled on the adobe barn near the hotel, and an inner nudge guided his feet in that direction.

Horse-scented air filled his nostrils as he stepped through the open doors of the large building. Sure enough he spied Delsie beside one of the stalls, stroking Moses's nose. The anxiety churning in his gut dissipated at the sight. Elijah swooped down from a rafter to land on Myles's shoulder. The bird had obviously followed Delsie. The thought pleased him, though he knew it shouldn't matter if the sparrow hawk had taken a liking to her, as well.

She turned as he approached, her smile less vibrant than normal. "Hello."

He came to a stop beside her. "Didn't see you slip out."

"I couldn't listen to that sort of talk anymore." She stated the words simply, but Myles didn't miss the melancholy that seeped into her tone.

"We'll make it, Delsie."

He placed his hand over hers where it rested on the stall door. Without a word, she entwined her fingers with his. They stood that way for at least a minute, neither one speaking. The solace of the barn and her presence eased some of the tension from Myles's shoulders.

He meant what he'd told her—somehow, some way, he would get her to her sister.

"You're a good horse, aren't you?" Delsie rubbed the animal's nose again.

"He's been more than willing to do what we've asked him to." He released her hand to pull some hay from a nearby bale and feed it to Moses. "I've only known a couple of horses like that, even after twenty years of working with them."

Elijah hopped onto the stall door and ruffled his feathers in indignation when Moses blew air in the bird's direction. Myles smiled. Too bad he couldn't keep the beast. "That man Tucker suggested we buy new horses."

Delsie sighed and let her hand fall to her side. "Is that what you think we should do?"

He leaned against the stall post and offered Elijah some of the meat from his pocket. "I do, given what might lie ahead. And the sooner the better. I hate to part with a perfectly decent horse, but we need ones that haven't been ridden hard for eleven days straight."

Her mouth pressed into a hesitant line.

"If it's about the money…"

She shook her head. "It isn't that. I've got enough to buy new horses and still pay you and Amos what I promised."

"You just hate to say goodbye," he murmured, his eyes fastened on her profile. Would he ever meet another woman as beautiful, strong and compassionate as Delsie Radford? He was beginning to have his doubts.

She twisted to face him. "Yes, I don't want to say

goodbye." Myles had the sudden impression she, too, was talking about more than the horse. Then the hesitancy in her expression transformed into familiar determination. "I want you to have him, Myles."

"What?" he said, laughing quietly.

"I'm serious." She took a step toward him, filling his senses with the momentary scent of lavender. "You said he was a good animal. The best."

"Well, yes, but…"

Her dark blue eyes pleaded with him. "I don't want him left behind. Not after all he's done for me…for us. Please. I'll pay to have him boarded here until you and Amos return. Then he's yours. You can sell your new horse, too, on your return trip." She laid her hand against his arm. "Consider both an investment in your future ranch."

Myles stared at her, hardly daring to believe she meant it. He'd never owned his own horse. Charles had, but Myles had left the aging Jedidiah behind when he quit the livery stable. Could he afford to keep a mount on what he was paid for Express riding? The logistics paled in comparison, though, to the sight of Delsie's expectant face and the possibility of being one step closer to his dreams for the future.

"Why?" He couldn't help the question. Other than Amos, no one else had taken an interest in what he did or where he went in a very long time.

She lowered her gaze and fingered his sleeve. The gentle touch sent shoots of feeling up his arm. "Because Amos…and you…have come to mean a great deal to me."

And yet she wasn't giving Amos a horse. Was it possible that she'd come to care for him as much as he did for her? He decided to test his theory, despite the voice of reason in his head telling him he was foolish to give his heart to another rich female. One who wasn't free to give her heart in return.

With his finger, he tipped her chin upward. Unshed tears glistened in her eyes as they met his. "Then I accept," he replied huskily.

"I'm glad," she whispered with a faint trace of a smile, pulling his attention to her lips. It wasn't the first time he'd contemplated kissing her—he had the night they'd danced by the wagon train and the day the Indian had tried bartering for her. But those moments had felt too public, unlike this one.

"Thank you, Delsie," he murmured.

He didn't know which of them moved first or if they moved in tandem. But one moment he was staring into those beautiful eyes and the next he felt her lips beneath his own. The kiss was featherlight. Her hand came to rest alongside his bearded jaw as Myles poured his hopes—however blighted—for a future together into this one kiss.

When Delsie stepped back, several long heartbeats later, there were tears on her cheeks. "I'd better go."

She hesitated a moment, then reached out once more and trailed her fingers down the side of his face, as if memorizing the lines and features. Pain filled her eyes—a pain Myles couldn't erase this time no matter how badly he wanted to.

"Good night, Myles."

She lowered her hand and moved slowly past him. The words hit him with all the force of a hoof to his gut. She wasn't simply bidding him good-night. She was saying an early goodbye. Myles watched, with irritating helplessness, as she exited the barn.

When he could no longer see her, he rammed a fist against the stall post, disrupting Elijah and sending the bird flying to an overhead rafter. The ache inside him felt too reminiscent of what he'd felt as a four-year-old boy when he'd lost both his parents to illness within two days of each other. His grief at losing Charles, too, nearly paled to the pain lancing through him now.

Why had he allowed himself to fall for Delsie? A woman he couldn't have, no matter how much she clearly cared for him in return. She wouldn't divide her family further by accepting a life with him, and Myles could no longer blame her. Riding with her and Amos day after day had given him the closest thing to family that he'd had in years. He wouldn't want to give that up, no matter how attractive another avenue. Delsie had come too far and endured too much to break her father's heart a second time.

So it would be Myles's heart that took the beating. But if it meant Delsie was happy, if it meant she got what she ultimately wanted, he would do it again—a thousand times over.

He hung his head at the realization, and a weight as heavy as cast iron settled over his shoulders. The unknowns before them faded in consequence to the thought of her slipping out of his life for good in seven short days. The woman he'd spent nearly every minute of every day with for the past two weeks, the woman he'd enjoyed kissing a hundred times more than he'd ever liked kissing Cynthia, the woman who'd bolstered his faith and given him a reason to smile would be gone—and he was powerless to stop that final goodbye.

"Please, God," he found himself whispering, his hands gripping the ledge of the stall in earnestness. He hadn't really prayed in years, but he couldn't face this last portion of their journey on his own. "Help me endure the next week and see her, safely, to the end."

Delsie bit her lip as she eyed the mountains from beneath her hat. The sunbaked land they'd ridden through today boasted little in color or leafy vegetation. A patch of light rain earlier had turned the desert into a watery beauty and filled the air with the smell of damp earth and sagebrush. But now, the unrelenting sun had burned away the last of the moisture.

A deep feeling of melancholy welled within her, bringing the threat of tears. She sniffed hard to will them back. She'd never been prone to tears like Lillie was, and yet, she'd been moved to crying twice in no time at all. First in the barn with Myles, and now at the barrenness surrounding her, in a place so unlike home she felt as if she were moving through a dream world.

The memory of kissing Myles filled her thoughts as it had countless times since last night. She'd never felt so cherished as she had in that moment. Her first kiss had proven to be more wonderful than she'd imagined it would be. And yet, she'd also felt a strong measure of heartbreak intermingled with the joy. It had taken every ounce of her will to walk away from Myles and not beg him to stay with her—always. Was this what Lillie had experienced at the thought of being parted forever from Clay?

Instead of compassion, though, an ember of anger filled her heart. Why should Lillie have her greatest desire, a life as the wife of the man she adored, and Delsie must uproot her wishes for the sake of their family? Immediate shame accompanied the angry question. Lillie had followed her heart, but it hadn't come without a heavy price. And no matter how Delsie ached to remain at the side of the man riding stoically in front of her, she wouldn't exact such a price from her father a second time.

Myles had clearly drawn the same conclusion. While he'd remained solicitous as they'd purchased new horses at Camp Floyd and along the ride since, she'd sensed the partial return of the reticence he'd worn like a shield in the beginning. His gaze no longer lingered in her direction as it once had, and his gentle grip fell from her elbow quicker than before.

Delsie hated knowing she was the cause of his hidden grief, but she felt incapable of changing any of it. Better to concentrate on reaching Lillie, as she had so many times on this journey, than to dwell on the painful reminders of what might have been between her and Myles.

That didn't stop the single tear from dripping down her cheek, though. She hastily brushed it away, hoping Amos hadn't noticed it from his spot to her right. The older man had been quieter than usual today, casting troubled looks between her and Myles more than once. She didn't have the heart to explain the source of the unspoken tension radiating among the three of them.

"I think we ought to rest on the other side of that riverbed," Amos called to Myles. The announcement sounded loud in Delsie's ears after a long stretch of relative silence.

Myles twisted in the saddle. "Will do. The horses are starting to slow."

Delsie searched the opposite bank of the river for something that might provide shade and was relieved to see several short trees. The temperature felt much hotter here than it had on the prairies or among the mountains. Hopefully, she'd be able to fill her nearly empty canteen at the river, as well.

They reached the bank and she peered down at the trickle of water running along the riverbed. Not much of a river, but enough water for them and the horses to drink. She followed Myles and his mount down the sloping incline and held her breath until her horse's hooves struck the bottom. Her mare dropped her nose and began to drink from the gurgling brook.

"When they're done drinking," Myles directed, "let's get them up on the opposite bank. It looks like there's a little grass near those trees."

Delsie nodded. Once her mare lifted its head again, she dug her heels into its flanks and guided the horse up the other bank. At the top, she slipped from the saddle and led the animal to the trees she'd seen earlier. She looped the reins around a nearby branch and turned to see Amos and Myles coming toward her.

"I need to fill my canteen," she said over her shoulder as she removed the object from around the saddle horn.

"Me, too." Myles tied up his mount and grabbed his canteen.

"What about you, Amos?" she asked. "Can I fill yours?"

Amos shook his head from where he'd spread out in the shade. "Mine's nearly full. But thank you."

Delsie didn't know how he did it, drinking so little but never getting overly thirsty as far as she could tell. "All right. Enjoy your nap, then." She coaxed a smile from him, as she'd hoped, and trailed Myles back down the bank to the river bottom.

Kneeling, she scooped up a handful of the cool liquid and drank. Droplets escaped her grip and slid down her chin and dress front, but she didn't mind. She wet her hand again and rubbed it across the back of her neck and forehead.

"It's hot, isn't it?" she mused as Myles filled his canteen.

He eyed the sun from under his hat and gave a wordless nod.

Strained quiet filled the air between them, depressing her further. She wanted to go back to the banter and friendliness. Perhaps kissing him had been a mistake—though Delsie couldn't wish away the moment altogether.

"About last night…" She stared at the water flowing into her canteen instead of at Myles's dark eyes. "I didn't mean for us to…" She licked her dry lips, the words clogging in her throat. "If I offended you, Myles…"

The sudden pressure of his finger beneath her chin made her heart sputter, both with happiness and trepidation. What would he say in response to her bumbling apology?

"Delsie."

She lifted her gaze to his handsome face.

"Don't be sorry." His intense look held her captive. Emotions shifted across his features—hope, regret, acceptance. He moved his finger from her chin to her lower lip. Her pulse beat harder, filling her ears with the sound of rushing wind. "But we can't change…"

Myles lowered his hand and cocked his head, as if listening. "Do you hear that?"

Could he hear the pounding of her heartbeat? "No," she said, shaking her head.

"It sounds like wind, but nothing's moving."

Wind? Wasn't that her pulse? Delsie took a deep breath to steady her drumming heart rate, but even as she calmed, the sound grew louder. "Wait. I do hear it."

Myles tossed his canteen on the bank above them, then stood and jerked her to her feet. "Come on."

"But my canteen…"

"Leave it." With his hand still gripping her arm, he rushed her toward the bank at a jog.

"Myles? What's going on? What's that sound?" A movement to her right pulled her attention in that direction. To her horror, she saw a wall of churning water at least ten feet high racing along the river bottom straight toward them. "Myles!" she screamed.

He glanced over her head at the flood and his face hardened. With quick, strong movements, he yanked her to his side and tried to help her scramble up the bank. The dirt slid beneath their shoes, slowing their progress.

Delsie froze with fear. She could hardly breathe through the terror engulfing her as she watched the water coming closer and closer. If it hit them, she knew instinctively that they'd be swept away and drowned.

"Come on," Myles yelled, pulling on her arm again. "We can make it, Delsie."

His confidence snapped her out of her horrified trance. She clawed at the river bank with both hands. The roar of the water filled her ears, as loud and awful as any nightmare creature. The first droplets of angry spray smacked her face just as Amos appeared above them and hauled them both onto safe ground.

Delsie dropped onto her back, knocking her hat from her head and breathing heavily. If they hadn't moved when they did, if Amos hadn't come to their rescue… She squeezed her eyes shut against the thought.

"Delsie? Are you all right?"

She opened her eyes to find Myles leaning over her, his expression haggard. "I'm…" She swallowed hard, trying to push back the sob racing up her throat. But it leaked out in a strangled cry.

He lifted her carefully from the ground and cradled her against his chest. "It's all right," he murmured. "You're all right."

"B-but I lost my canteen," she said in between shaking, sobbing breaths.

His soft laughter eased the trembling in her body. "Is that what you're most upset about?"

She shrugged, inciting another chuckle from him,

right before he pressed a tender kiss to her forehead. Flutters of delight filled her stomach and eased any lingering dread.

"You darling, little soldier."

Delsie tipped her chin upward to find him smiling down at her. His earlier reserve had disappeared, replaced by amused adoration. She wiped at her wet cheeks, her gaze shifting from his dark eyes to his mouth. As if Myles sensed her longing, he rubbed his thumb against her lips once more, then placed another kiss to her hairline. Slowly he helped her onto her feet.

"Let's get you some water and a little food."

Even when Amos passed her his own canteen, his eyes full of questions, she didn't feel embarrassed at Myles's show of affection. No matter what happened between them now, she knew from the top of her head to the toes of her shoes that he cared for her—perhaps even loved her. And that was enough. At least she prayed it would be.

Chapter Eleven

"Another empty station," Myles announced as he ducked out the door to where Delsie and Amos sat in their saddles waiting.

Her somber expression matched the gravity stirring within him and mirrored the lines of concern pinching Amos's weathered face. Myles eyed the nearby corrals. "No stock, either."

The horses and cattle had likely been run off by the same Indians who'd driven the workers from the station. He moved to his horse and scanned the surrounding clumps of brush for any sign of movement, though he guessed the station had been emptied several days ago.

A feeling in his gut last night had told him yesterday's ride through the desert—and their near drowning in the flash flood—might be considered easy. At least when compared with what lay ahead of them now.

Several of the stations they'd passed by today weren't simply empty like this one—they'd been burned to the ground. The little food they'd procured from one diligent owner had been eaten, and from the looks of things, they weren't likely to find a home station to eat or board at tonight.

The sun was already dropping toward the western horizon. Both he and Amos had agreed to ride longer than normal, in hopes of finding a post that hadn't been on the receiving end of an Indian ambush.

"What you do think?" he asked Amos.

Amos's sharp gaze swept across the desert, his mouth a thin line. "I say we water the horses at the well there, then ride south a few miles. We can camp under the open for the night."

If Delsie feared the departure from their typical evening routine, she didn't say. Instead she simply slid off the saddle and led her mare toward the well. Amos followed suit, pulling his gun from his waistband. Myles located a broken bucket—one of the few things that hadn't been taken from inside the station. While Amos stood guard, he managed to get enough water in the bucket for all three horses to drink. After that, he filled his and Amos's canteens. Who knew when they'd find another water source?

Amos kept his gun at the ready as they saddled up and turned their mounts south, to skirt the nearby canyon. They picked their way among the sagebrush for several miles before the older man stopped them beside a clump of trees he called pinyon pines.

"I'll see what I can hunt up in the way of food," he said, dismounting. "Start the fire now, so we can be through with it before dark. Don't need anyone else knowing we're here."

Myles tied up the horses as Delsie began gathering sticks. "I suppose it's a good thing I learned how to cook when I did," she said with a trace of amusement. "Do you think it will be like this the rest of the way to California?"

"It might be," Myles answered honestly, taking the sticks from her. He set about starting the small fire, while she settled onto the ground nearby.

"Is Elijah off hunting, too?" She glanced up at the sky.

Myles nodded and coaxed the tiny flames to life with some dry grass and more twigs. "I suppose if Amos can't find anything, we could share whatever rodent Elijah catches." He meant the comment to be humorous, but Delsie didn't laugh.

"Thank you, again, for doing this, Myles. You didn't have to." She drew a circle in the dirt with her finger. "And now I've landed us in the middle of the desert with marauding Indians and little food. Just to reach Lillie." She lifted her chin to reveal raw anguish in her deep blue eyes. "If anything happened to you...or Amos..."

"We chose to come." It was as simple as that. Or maybe, it wasn't them who'd chosen, but rather Someone else choosing *them* instead. Either way he no longer had any doubts about the validity of their journey. He might have agreed in the beginning for the sake of his future, but he'd stumbled onto two things far more precious than even his dreams of a horse ranch—his friendship with Delsie and a renewed seed of faith. Charles would be proud.

"Besides," he continued, "this isn't just about reaching your sister. It's about your family, Delsie."

"And that's something you can understand?" Her words were nearly identical to something she'd said that first day in Saint Joseph. Something he'd thought of over and over since.

He dipped his head in a nod, his eyes locked on hers. "That's something I can understand—now."

The smile she rewarded him with brought the distinct memory of kissing her to Myles's mind. Not the chaste kiss of yesterday after they'd been rescued from near drowning, but the kiss they'd shared in the quiet barn. But giving in to his wish now would only increase the inevitable pain of goodbye later—for both of them. So he busied himself with the fire and with talking over what details Delsie knew about Lillie's whereabouts until Amos came back.

"He's a bit scrawny," Amos said, hoisting the jackrabbit in his hand, "but he'll do."

Delsie insisted on skinning the creature herself, even when Myles volunteered to do it for her. He couldn't help admiring her all the more as she set about the gruesome task without complaint or outward show of disgust. She'd changed a lot in the past two weeks. Or had she always possessed these qualities but hadn't been given opportunity to cultivate them? He couldn't help wondering if she would be content to return to her rich house and easy life after all she'd been through.

Once he'd thought her too pampered to survive in his world, but he'd been forced to reassess his opinion somewhere along the trail. Delsie would make any horse rider or rancher a fine wife. But it wouldn't be him. The hard truth cut deep as Myles focused on making a spit from sticks to cook the rabbit.

Elijah returned soon afterward with a mouse and settled outside their little circle to eat. The horses picked at the few patches of grass nearby. For tonight, at least, they would all have something to eat, despite the less-than-optimal situation—Myles felt gratitude for that.

When the rabbit had been thoroughly cooked, Amos divided up the meat between the three of them. Myles noticed the older man took a slightly smaller portion for himself than what he handed Myles or Delsie. The feeling of thankfulness inside Myles grew larger at the gesture. Amos was not only a good man but a true friend. Myles vowed he wouldn't take the man's companionship for granted anymore.

After all the meat had been consumed, Myles doused the fire. The sun had set minutes before, taking the heat of the day with it. Delsie visibly shivered at the drop in temperature.

"It'll be cold tonight," Amos told them. "Better use the saddle blankets."

Myles gathered the blankets and passed one to Delsie and to Amos. His own he spread out on the ground on the other side of Delsie. Amos quietly regaled them with a few stories from his youth and answered Delsie's questions about his wife. Though he tried hard to listen, sleepiness stole over Myles and he drifted off.

Sometime later he jerked awake at the sound of something rustling nearby. He sat up, his hand on the revolver at his side, but it was only one of the horses

shifting beside the trees. Taking a deep breath to calm
his thudding heartbeat, he shot a look at Delsie. She'd
curled into a ball beneath her blanket, and yet, Myles
could see she was still shivering. Amos slept soundly
on her other side, oblivious to her cold or the horse's
movements.

Myles hated the thought of her freezing and getting little sleep because of it. If he gave her his blanket, though, he'd end up just as cold and sleepless. He
rubbed a hand over his jaw, considering what to do. In
the moonlight he spied the sturdy trunk of the closest
pinyon pine. The branches began high enough on the
tree that it formed an easy shelter to climb under.

Removing his blanket, he set it over Delsie and gathered her into his arms. She startled awake and blinked
up at him.

"You're quaking like an aspen tree, sleeping beauty,"
he murmured, "but I've got an idea to keep you warm."

He carried her to the pine and ducked beneath its
branches. Resting his back against the trunk, he settled
Delsie at his side and draped his blanket over them both.

"What will my father think?" Delsie said sleepily,
even as she nestled beneath his arm. Warmth spread
through him, as much from her nearness as from the
contentment that filled him at holding her again.

Myles smoothed her hair and tucked her tighter
against him. "Just tell him I promised to get you back
in one piece, and that's what I'm doing."

"Thank…you…Myles."

Shutting his eyes, Myles let his breathing even out
and his body relax. Sleeping sitting up would likely

mean a less than restful night and a kink in his neck by morning. But he didn't care. If he couldn't embrace Delsie forever—and he couldn't—then he'd simply be grateful for this moment. This moment watching over the woman he'd come to care for more than Elijah or horse ranching or himself. A moment he would cherish for the rest of his life.

Delsie kept her eyes shut, even as she slowly began to wake. She'd never felt so content or comfortable—even more so than in that dugout, with its thick buffalo robes. Her hand loosely gripped soft fabric and warm air fanned her hair. A steady heartbeat thrummed in her ears. She pressed her cheek more snugly into the solid warmth beneath it. Until she heard a deep rumbling chuckle that vibrated through her chest.

"Would've thought you'd be warmed up by now."

Reality doused Delsie with all the shock of ice water. She was dozing beside Myles and had been all night. She scrambled up, her face hot. What would her father do if he could see her? Any amount of freedom she'd enjoyed would be gone. She would likely be foisted off on Flynn to save her reputation.

"I— I'm sorry. I didn't mean…" She let her apology fade out when he chuckled again. "It's not funny, Myles. If my father…"

He shook out his blanket. "Like I told you last night, I intend for you to reach your father in one piece, Delsie. And that means not letting you lie on the cold ground all night and catching sick." He bent forward to peer directly into her eyes. "Besides, nothing untoward happened. I promise."

"Well, that's good to know." Amos watched them from beneath the branches.

Myles stiffened beside her, red creeping up his neck. "Amos. Morning." He ran a hand over the bristles of his jaw without looking at Delsie. "Delsie was shivering something fierce. I wasn't sure what else…to do."

It was her turn to laugh softly. "Apparently Myles was being gentlemanly."

A smile worked at Amos's mouth as though he, too, was trying not to chuckle. "Good to hear. I'm going to see if I can't rummage up some breakfast."

Delsie maneuvered out from under the pinyon pine and brushed bits of dirt and twigs from her dress. Myles offered her some water from his canteen. The water tasted good, but her stomach still rumbled with hunger.

While he saw to the horses, Delsie started making a fire. By the time she had some good-sized flames built up, Amos returned. "What's on the menu for this morning?" she asked teasingly.

"Snake." Amos held the long reptile aloft. Delsie fought a cringe by reminding herself it was food, and possibly the only meal they'd get until tonight.

Amos helped her prepare the snake, then the three of them ate the meat. She certainly wouldn't put it down as a delicacy or even something she wished to have on a regular basis, but she had to admit it wasn't all bad.

After washing down the snake meat with a little more water, each of them climbed back into their saddles. Amos led the way through the sagebrush to the main trail, where they headed due west again. The sun had fully risen in the east, and with it, the temperature. Delsie could hardly believe she'd been shivering violently with cold last night, when the day felt warm and pleasant now.

The memory of being cold sparked the recollection of waking with her cheek pressed to Myles's shirt and his arm resting loosely against her shoulders. She ought to be mortified, but he'd done nothing improper. He'd just been concerned for her.

Not for the first time, she offered a silent prayer of gratitude for Myles's presence in her life and for his and Amos's help. God had truly been looking out for her to lead her to two such competent and kind men. She wished there was more she could do to repay them, beyond the money she'd promised them at the end of their journey and the horse waiting for Myles. If undying thankfulness could be converted into wealth, these two men riding silently ahead and beside her would live like kings the rest of their lives.

Delsie smiled at the thought of either Amos or Myles sporting a crown and strutting around a palace. While they had both insisted they'd chosen to come on this journey and would see it through fully, she was still grateful they had all made it so far unscathed. In light of all she'd experienced—a runaway horse, nearly freezing to death, an unwelcome marriage proposal, a flash flood and a night out in the open with only rabbit and snake to eat—Delsie couldn't imagine anything worse ahead. A seed of optimism sprang up inside her and she fueled it with thoughts of Lillie and the rapidly narrowing distance between her and her sister. Lillie would be married in five days, and Delsie had every intention and belief she would be at the blessed event.

The first station they came upon that morning stood as empty as the one they'd encountered the night before. Thankfully, this one also had a well. Amos suggested taking a rest earlier than normal to water the horses and let them feed on the surrounding grass, and Myles agreed.

Delsie dismounted and accepted another drink from Myles's canteen. Wiping her mouth, she eyed the nearby cabin. Could there possibly be any food left inside? Something they might take with them? She left the men and moved with purposeful steps to the door, which had been left ajar. A quick peek through the gap showed the place was devoid of its former occupants. She pushed through and smiled when she spotted the cupboard across the room. Perhaps there was a little flour inside it.

She started forward but stumbled over something on the floor. Righting herself, Delsie glanced down to see the offending object. It was a boot and not an empty one, either. Her gaze shifted from the boot, to the pant leg, to the dead man's vacant eyes and finally to his bloodied forehead. A panicked scream fled her mouth as she stumbled blindly back out the door.

"Delsie?" Myles rushed toward her, Amos right behind him, his gun in his hand.

"Th-that man in there. He's been…" The horror washed over her anew, sickening her stomach. She clamped a hand over her lips and fled to the nearby corral, where she dropped to her knees beside the fence. In a matter of minutes, she'd emptied her meager breakfast into the dust. Her body trembled with shock as if cold, though a clammy feeling made her sweaty, too. She sank against one of the fence posts and wrapped her arms around her knees.

"It's all right," she whispered to herself. "It's all right."

From the corner of her eye, she watched Myles slowly approach her as if she were a skittish colt. "Delsie? You all right, darling?"

She shook her head and rocked her body back and forth.

"You've had a shock, but you're going to be fine. Do you hear me?" He squatted next to her and placed his hand on her shoulder. The human contact released some of the numbness inside her.

"I wish I hadn't seen... I'll never forget..." She stifled a cry with her hand to her mouth.

"Amos is burying the man now." Sure enough she heard the scrape of a shovel against the dirt. Where Amos had procured a shovel, she didn't know.

"Do you want to sit some more or do you think you can stand?"

"I... I'll stand."

Myles gently helped her onto her feet, then pulled her to his chest. Delsie wrapped her arms around his waist and allowed the steady beat of his heart to soothe her shock.

"What have I done, Myles?"

He rested his chin on top of her hair—she'd hung

her hat on the saddle horn before going into the cabin. "You didn't do anything. That man was dead long before we came along."

"No. I mean having us come all this way, in the middle of a warpath." She bit her lip to keep from sobbing. "I knew we might encounter things, but I foolishly let my desire to reach Lillie outweigh the dangers."

Myles eased back and tipped her face upward. "It wasn't foolish. God knew you'd be here—now—on this very trail, fighting to restore your family."

"Do you really believe that?"

A faint smile creased his mouth. "Do you?" he countered.

Delsie thought back to the night Myles had told her the journey wouldn't work, at least not in the way she'd planned in the beginning. She'd been full of doubt and despair until she'd read that verse of scripture. *Cast not away therefore your confidence.* She'd tossed aside some of her confidence since then, but she still had some remaining. This was what God wanted her to do and He'd provided everything she'd needed to make it happen.

"Whatever comes, Delsie, He's with us." His words so closely mirrored the ones in her own head that she wondered if he could somehow read her thoughts. "Isn't that what He wanted Elijah and those priests to understand?"

She nodded, grateful for the reminder.

"Don't give up on Him or Lillie. Not yet. Not when we're so close."

His assurances restored some of her own, but doubts

still loomed large in her mind. "But the worst might lie ahead. We could end up like that…" She swallowed the taste of bile in her throat. "Like that man."

His expression hardened with resolve, deepening the black of his eyes. "Then we'll do so, knowing we followed God's will and didn't let fear rule our lives."

Embracing him, she cleared her throat enough to say, "You're a good man, Myles Patton."

"And you're a strong woman, Delsie Radford. Don't let anyone tell you otherwise."

She let his courage and compliment seep into her troubled heart and thoughts.

"You ready to keep on?"

She took a deep breath and stepped back to see his face—this handsome face she'd come to know nearly as well as her own. "As long as you're keeping on with me."

He tucked a curl behind her ear and smiled, though the gesture held a trace of sadness. "Until the last inch of the trail."

Chapter Twelve

Where had those faith-filled words come from? Myles thought ruefully. Fifteen days ago he would have scoffed at the idea of spouting off religious sentiments, especially to a beautiful woman. He and God had parted ways after Charles's death and both of them had seemed fine with it. Today, though, he'd known exactly what needed to be said to bolster Delsie's shattered confidence. But more than that, he believed every word he'd spoken, too.

Whether it was God working through him or Myles's own desire to be the man Delsie clearly saw in him or perhaps both, he wasn't sure. All he knew for certain in this moment was that this journey was no longer some foolhardy venture.

God was aware of him—even as lonely and embittered as Myles had been—and He'd placed something directly into his path that he couldn't ignore or run from. A little soldier with eyes of deep blue, a smile that brought him pure delight and a faith as large as the prairie sky. He'd been dodging God, but God hadn't let that bother Him. Instead He'd dropped Delsie right in front of Myles and let her work her charm and kindness, a compassion Myles guessed had held her family together for so long after her mother's death.

However deep her strength and confidence ran, though, he still wished she hadn't been the one to discover the scalped station owner earlier. If only he could have protected her from such a gruesome sight. He darted a glance to his left. She rode with her back erect, her face trained forward, but he sensed the sadness lingering around her.

A few more days, he reassured himself. *Then the worst will be over.*

At least in terms of the trail dangers. His biggest obstacle still lay ahead—saying goodbye, indefinitely, to Delsie. He didn't want to think about not seeing her lovely face every day or hearing her laughter or feeling her gentle touch that had a far greater effect on him than all the hazards they'd faced so far.

He drove such depressing thoughts from his mind by studying the surrounding desert, looking for signs of possible ambush. Sometime later he spotted buildings and movement up ahead that had him reining in his horse and placing a hand on one of his guns.

Amos and Delsie drew to a stop beside him. "What is it?" she asked quietly, her hands clenching her mare's reins tighter than normal.

Myles shook his head. "Not sure. Looks like a bunch of horses and people."

Amos squinted. "I don't think they're foes. But let's ride in slow just the same."

"Suits me." Myles nudged his mount forward, but he removed one of his revolvers and set it across his lap, just in case.

He led the way, slowly, toward the station and the group ahead. The closer he came, though, the more the details came into focus. It wasn't Indians. A group of what appeared to be Express riders and workers milled about the station. Myles hadn't seen this many men in one spot for several days.

"Howdy," he called out as he, Amos and Delsie stopped at the edge of the station yard.

"Howdy back," a man with sandy blond hair answered. He and a few other riders strode over to the trio.

Myles dismounted before helping Delsie to the ground. He knew full well she could get off her mare unassisted, but he didn't particularly like the wide-eyed looks from the men watching her. "Got some sort of rendezvous going on?"

The sandy-haired man chuckled. "Not by choice." He turned his attention to Delsie. "What brings you to this fair desert, miss?"

She glanced at Myles, then smiled at the man. "We're traveling to California as quickly as we can. For my sister's wedding." She removed her hat and studied the group of men. "We'd be very much obliged if we could purchase some food from you, gentlemen. We didn't have a home station to lodge in last night, which meant little to eat for dinner or breakfast."

"Sorry to say but you won't find any posts open

from here to Carson Valley, Nevada," a short man replied. "Indians have attacked them all and driven off the livestock."

The sandy-haired rider spoke up again. "That's why we riders and station keepers met here. We're waiting for soldiers to come and help us reopen them."

Myles looked at Delsie. The color had drained from her face, but she held her chin aloft.

"We can certainly feed you," the same rider added. "Come on."

Myles trailed Delsie and Amos to the nearby cabin. They were introduced to the owner, then invited to sit for a meal of flapjacks. Myles and Amos ate three helpings each, and even Delsie had seconds.

Once they'd eaten their fill, the owner explained the current situation with the Indians. Myles grew more and more discouraged as he talked. Without home stations, or any stations at all, they'd be forced to find their own food and water again. Then there was the very real possibility of meeting up with some of the Indians themselves. Their safest option was to wait for the soldiers, too, but that would mean Delsie would miss her sister's wedding.

Delsie excused herself when the talk turned to those who'd been killed, though Myles remained behind. If they were to continue, and everything in him told him they would, he wanted to know exactly what sort of fight they were riding into.

After a time the conversation turned to geography and landmarks. Myles left Amos to find Delsie. She'd been outside, alone, for at least a half an hour. Was she safe? Had any of the riders tried taking advantage of his absence?

Relief coursed through him when he found her, standing alone, feeding grass to several of the station horses on the other side of the corral fence. She turned at his approach and threw him a tight smile.

"Sounds rather…dire…doesn't it?" She fed the last bits of grass to one of the animals, then brushed off her hands.

"Yes." He couldn't deny it. "But you knew it might be. *We* knew it might be."

Resting her hands on the highest rung of the fence, she stared at something across the corral. "It all sounded so simple two weeks ago. Ride as far and as long as we can, purchase food, sleep, do it again the next day."

"And it has been." Myles placed his hand atop hers. "Apparently now is where it gets more complicated, but it's not impossible. Do you want to keep going?"

She twisted to face him, her back to the fence. Her gaze was full of equal parts uncertainty and determination. "I have to try, Myles. But I understand if you and Amos don't want to…"

"I'm not leaving," he practically growled.

He planted himself in front of her, encroaching on her space. She tipped her chin up to look at him. The undisguised trust shining in her blue eyes, the warmth of her breath against his jaw and the nearness of this beautiful woman stole his words.

He loved her. The realization washed over him as soft as a whisper and as brash as a thunderstorm. And because he loved her he would accompany her through one danger after another before letting her go at the end of the trail. Her happiness and desire for a complete family meant more to him than a thousand horse ranches.

With great effort, he stepped back. A hint of what might have been disappointment flitted across her somber expression, making him wonder if she might love him back. Myles pushed aside the hope such a thought inspired. It didn't matter.

"So what will it be, Miss Radford?" His voice sounded husky with emotion, even to his own ears. "Are you ready to finish this, no matter what lies in our path?"

She glanced past him in the direction of the station, her shoulders rising and falling with a soft sigh. He wanted to reassure her, as he'd done earlier after the incident with the dead man. But this time, with the knowledge of the new perils they might face, she needed to make the decision herself, whether to go or stay.

When she met his level look straight on a few moments later, every lovely feature was etched with resolve. "I'm ready."

Delsie shifted in the saddle and licked her dry lips. *Don't think about food or water,* she chided herself for surely the hundredth time, even as visions of roasted lamb, mashed potatoes, meringues and pitchers of ice-cold lemonade rose into her mind.

What she wouldn't give to feel the same burning tenacity she had two days earlier when she'd told Myles she was ready to keep going. That determination, while still smoldering deep within her, had cooled considerably after forty-eight hours of little to eat or drink.

That Express rider had been right—none of the stations they'd passed were occupied. Out of sheer necessity they'd lingered at those with working wells or nearby springs, but both Amos and Myles were reluctant to stay in one place for long.

The lack of real sustenance for them and their horses was beginning to show in their slower pace. They'd been forced to ride until well after dark the night before to cover the needed distance. That also meant no fire, so they'd divided the small amount of jerky they'd procured at the rendezvous Express station among the three of them. Delsie was grateful for even that little bit, but she'd still gone to bed more hungry than not. Amos had managed to kill another snake this morning, which meant some breakfast. But that had been hours ago.

She pressed a hand to her grumbling stomach and tried to focus on something else. Like the way Myles had looked at her beside the corral—his intense gaze capturing hers. Their shared kiss in the barn seemed like months ago now and the start of her journey back in Missouri felt like another lifetime.

What if she didn't make it to Lillie's wedding in two days? What if she expired from thirst or hunger instead? Her sister would never know what Delsie had endured to reach her. Or their father, either.

"You all right?" Myles nudged his horse closer to hers. He'd asked the same question nearly every hour or whenever her pace started to lag behind his and Amos's.

She nodded, too tired and thirsty to form a reply.

As if sensing her need, which Delsie was starting

to think he could, he passed her his canteen. "Here. Drink."

"But…" She swallowed to bring moisture to her parched mouth. "We aren't supposed to drink until we rest."

Myles continued to hold the canteen out to her, his mouth a grim line.

With a sigh of acceptance, she took the canteen. The tepid liquid still felt glorious sliding down her throat. She allowed herself one more swallow, then passed the container back. Instead of taking a drink himself, Myles put the water away. The sight brought the sting of tears to Delsie's eyes. Never in her wildest dreams would she have imagined she'd find a man so loyal and good-hearted and so far from home to be her dearest friend.

He's more than a friend, her heart argued. The press of tears increased. Yes, she cared for Myles—loved him, even—in a way that went well beyond mere friendship.

I love him.

The truth hit her with such force that Delsie sucked in a sharp breath, the moisture in her eyes gone as quickly as it had come.

"Something wrong?" Myles asked, peering closely at her.

She gulped and shook her head. She loved him, this ornery, wonderful, handsome Express rider sticking close to her side. The pure joy and giddiness of her re-alization was short-lived, though. Loving Myles didn't change the fact that she had to return to her father after Lillie's wedding. The only way she knew to fully mend the rift in her family was to return home. But when she did, she couldn't marry Flynn—not anymore. Not when she knew what it felt like to love a man. She glanced at Myles and saw him watching her. *And be loved in return.*

Perhaps she would find someone else back in Pennsylvania. But she guessed it would be a very long time before she had any room in her heart for anyone but Myles.

Wiping sweat from her forehead with her sleeve, she set her jaw, determined to think of something other than food or Myles. Two things she couldn't have. A soft prick of claws near her collarbone alerted her to Elijah's sudden perch on her shoulder. Stunned, she twisted to face Myles.

"Well, I'll be," he said with a chuckle. "He's never done that before. Not even with Amos."

A ripple of pride wound through Delsie. A few short weeks ago she hadn't ridden anything but sidesaddle or known how to cook or even understood her own strength. Now she easily sat on her horse with a sparrow hawk on her shoulder.

She released one hand from the reins to brush her finger over Elijah's soft feathers. No wonder Myles loved the bird so much. The cloud of despair she'd been riding beneath for almost two straight days evaporated under the hawk's calming presence. She could do this—they could do this.

Myles eyed the distant station with relief. Even the missing roof and charred adobe were a somewhat welcome sight, a chance to rest and hopefully find some food and water. He hadn't liked the weariness lining

Delsie's face earlier. She'd been wilting before his eyes
the past two days and it scared him. On occasion he still
saw that spark of life and optimism flare in her expression, as it had when Elijah chose to ride on her shoulder, but it faded all too quickly. The burden of riding
so far without regular meals and water was taking its
toll on her and the horses. He'd had to slow their pace
to compensate.

When they reached the burned station, Myles cau-
tiously slid from his saddle. He moved slowly, a revolver
in each hand, to the cabin and pushed the door in with
his boot. There was no one, alive or otherwise, inside.
He blew out the breath he'd been holding. While there
didn't appear to be anything in the way of food, either,
Amos had told them of a nearby spring.

"It's empty," he announced as he stepped back outside.

Amos nodded. "Figured as much. The spring's back
that way."

Delsie dropped to the dirt beside her mare, while
Elijah flew off to hunt. "I can taste the water already."

The spring sat several hundred yards from the station. The horses eagerly drank, then Myles, Amos and
Delsie knelt down to scoop up water for themselves.
Myles removed his hat and dumped handfuls of the cool
water onto his head and warm face. Delsie followed suit,
laughing as tiny rivers ran down her hair and cheeks.

"How much farther will we go tonight?" she asked
Amos.

Amos rubbed at his bristled chin. "I figure another

twenty miles will put us just sixty more from Placerville, where your sister lives."

Delsie's face lit brighter than Myles had seen it in hours. "We're that close?"

The older man nodded, a pleased smile on his face. Myles guessed the reason had more to do with Delsie's enthusiasm than being so close to the end of their journey. "We can try and hunt up something to eat around here, then keep going before we stop for the ni—"

A bloodcurdling yell pierced the air, cutting off Amos's explanation and sending ice-cold shivers up Myles's spine. The horses shifted nervously, their eyes wide. Myles jumped to his feet, but he couldn't see the source of the war cry.

"Take one of the guns and get into the brush," he hollered at Delsie. "We'll get the horses in the corral."

Her face devoid of color, she accepted the gun he thrust into her hand and scrambled into the bushes to lie down on her stomach. Satisfied, Myles grabbed the reins of her mount and his and sprinted toward the corral. He sensed more than saw Amos and the other horse coming right behind him.

He pushed open the gate, grateful the fence had survived the earlier attack on the station, and led the horses inside. The moment Amos had the gate closed, Myles released the reins. "You guard the horses," he told the older man. "I'll take a position by the cabin."

Amos gave a quick nod, his expression grim.

After vaulting the corral fence, Myles moved half-hunched-over until he reached the cabin. His heart beat double time within his chest and his mouth felt full of sand, as though he hadn't just drunk his fill at the spring.

The Indians still hadn't shown themselves, but he wouldn't be fooled into thinking they'd left. He crept forward along the cabin wall until he reached the front corner. Five Indians on ponies were riding hard toward the station from the east, bows drawn. Had they been trailing them for some time, waiting for them to stop? Either way, they would have to ride past Myles before they reached the corral at his back.

Taking aim at the lead rider, he offered a quick prayer of forgiveness. He'd never shot a man before, but he wouldn't let harm come to Delsie or Amos. He cocked the gun and squeezed the trigger. The blast was nearly as loud as his own heartbeat in his ears. He watched as the Indian fell to the ground.

The other men jerked away from the dead man and continued forward. Myles fired the gun again, hitting one rider in the leg. The man screamed in pain and wheeled his horse to the side, but the other three didn't slow. Sweat dripped into Myles's eyes, obscuring his view for a moment. He shot at one rider attempting to go around the cabin the opposite way from where he crouched, knocking the man off his pony.

Myles emptied his gun on the remaining two Indians, but they weaved out of range each time. Shots from the corral confirmed Amos, too, was trying to stop their advance.

It was time to load the extra cylinder he'd grabbed. He tried to hurry, but his hands fumbled through the task as if it was his first time. Memories of teaching Delsie to shoot filled his thoughts, but he gritted his teeth and pushed them aside. If he focused on her or his fear of something happening to her, he wouldn't be able to protect her.

He'd just finished with the cylinder when a sudden thought filled his mind. *Look up.* Jerking his head up, Myles saw the Indian he'd shot to the ground earlier was back on his feet. Even worse, he had a bow and arrow trained at Myles's heart. Myles cocked the hammer, took quick aim and fired his gun, but the Indian had done the same with his weapon. He'd released his arrow with deadly precision, straight at Myles.

Within a single heartbeat, Myles fired a second time, then twisted to shelter his chest. He heard the Indian's death cry right before a searing pain below his shoulder tore a similar cry from his own mouth.

Red-and-white dots covered his vision as he slumped to the ground. Where were the other three Indians? He couldn't see them.

"Myles!" Delsie screamed.

"Stay back," he cried, his voice hardly more than a whisper. "Don't come out."

He crawled forward, intent on reaching her, the sounds around him growing more and more distant. He thought he heard Amos call his name from behind, thought he caught sight of the other two Indians leading the injured one away. But he couldn't be sure over the roar of the pain in his head, his back, his lungs. He only knew he had to reach Delsie, had to be sure she wasn't hurt. But he only managed to drag himself another few feet before the agony reared up to claim him and he pitched forward into darkness.

Chapter Thirteen

"Myles!"

The scream left Delsie's throat raw. She'd watched in horror as the Indian had released his arrow toward the spot where she knew Myles was crouched, then the man had fallen, unmoving, to the ground. But she couldn't see or hear Myles. Fear pulsed icy in her veins at the thought of him hurt, or worse… She bit her lip against her rising panic. Branches scratched at her face and dress, but she waited, her eyes trained on the cabin. *Please be safe. Please be safe.*

Movement to her left pulled her attention in that direction. The other Indians were leaving. Relief coursed through her, but it was fleeting. She heard Amos yell Myles's name as well, but there was no response. Where was he? She climbed slowly to her knees, her body trembling with worry. Not even the sight of their pursuers had inspired as much fear in her as the thought of losing Myles did.

Then suddenly he was there, crawling in front of the

cabin. Delsie rushed to her feet, a smile working the corners of her mouth. Until she saw the arrow sticking out of his back, below his shoulder. Fresh terror washed over her as she stumbled from the shelter of the brush, the revolver still gripped in her hand.

"Myles," she screamed again, but he slumped to the ground, his eyes shut. "No, no, no, no." She rushed across the station yard, doing her best to ignore the dead Indian still lying there. This couldn't be happening.

Amos reached his side right before her. Delsie dropped herself and the gun to the ground, her hands hovering over Myles's still body. Blood wet his shirt around the arrow.

"He's not…" She couldn't even voice the word.

Bending down, Amos glanced at her and shook his head. "He's not dead—just unconscious from the pain. That arrow's gonna need to come out. Go see what they've got in that cabin by way of supplies."

She willed back the tears pressing hard against her eyes and nodded. Climbing to her feet, she hurried into the cabin. What would help Myles? She turned in a helpless circle, her mind too cloudy with fear to think. "Come on, Delsie," she chided herself.

She found a blanket under the bed that had been singed but still had plenty of workable material left to it. There was also a tin cup and a chipped china bowl. She added them both to the blanket in her arms. Her search of the rest of the cabin produced nothing else of value, so she ran back outside.

Amos glanced up as she came near him. "What have you got?"

"A blanket we could use as bandage material and a cup and bowl for carrying some of the spring water."

"That's all?"

"Yes," she said, nodding.

The gravity of the situation had etched itself onto every line of Amos's face. Still, he set his jaw and turned to face Myles again. "Will you go get some water from the spring?"

Setting the blanket next to him, Delsie obeyed. She filled the cup and bowl with as much water as they could hold, then she moved carefully but quickly back to Amos and Myles.

Amos took the filled dishes from her and placed them on the ground. "Now I need you to go over by the horses, Delsie."

"What for?" She didn't want to leave Myles.

The older man released a breath of resignation. "I've got to pull this arrow out, and I know he wouldn't want you around when I do it."

Delsie gazed down at Myles. His handsome face blurred with renewed tears. "All right."

"Good girl."

She set her sights on the corral and forced her feet to move in that direction, away from Myles's prone figure. When she reached the horses, she walked the fence line until the cabin obscured her view of the two men. What would happen when Amos pulled out the arrow? She didn't have to wait long to find out.

A cry so loud and full of pain it made her gasp shattered the quiet evening air. The horses even skittered at the sound. No longer checking the tears coursing down her cheeks, she wrapped her arms around the nearest fence post and hung on. Another agonized shout filled her ears. "Please don't let him die, Lord. Please don't let him die."

After several long minutes, she heard Amos call for her. Delsie rushed back. The arrow no longer protruded from Myles's back, but he was no longer unconscious, either. Hard lines of pain creased his face, and his chest rose and fell with labored breaths. Amos had tied a portion of the blanket over his wound, though the blood still seeped through.

"We need to get him inside but moving him is going to hurt something fierce." Amos knelt in front of Myles's head. "I'll take his upper body, but I need you to get his legs."

Delsie pressed her mouth over a fresh sob. "I can do that." She positioned herself below Myles's boots, praying she would have the strength to carry him and not injure him further.

"All right," Amos said. "On the count of three, we'll lift him together. Ready?"

She managed a nod, even as her heart beat faster against her ribs.

"One…two…three!"

She lifted Myles's legs as Amos raised his head and shoulders. Myles cried out in agony as they slowly turned him toward the cabin. The cry tore at her heart, but she made herself focus on walking one step after the other. Once inside she helped Amos lay him, stomach down, on the tick mattress.

When she stepped back, she saw that he'd passed out

again. Perhaps that was better, for now. "I'll get more water," she volunteered. At least it was something she could do.

She collected the bowl and cup, which had both been emptied of nearly all their liquid, and returned to the spring. Had it only been a short time ago when they'd all been sitting here happy? Delsie filled the vessels and carried them back to the cabin. Amos had pulled a chair up to the bed and was once again examining Myles's wound.

"Is it very bad?" She hated not knowing, but at the same time, she feared his answer.

"It's not good," Amos replied honestly. "But we would have lost him for sure if it had struck his chest or stomach." He stood and headed for the door. "Since it looks like we'll be here for some time, I'm going to see what I can find for supper and get to work burying those two men outside."

Delsie sat in the chair next to Myles. A minute or two later, Amos ducked back inside, both of Myles's guns in hand.

"You keep one of these with you," he said, handing her one of the guns. "I doubt those Indians are coming back tonight, but you know how to use this if they do."

She gave a wooden nod, her eyes trained on Myles.

"Delsie?"

She turned toward Amos, standing in the doorway. "Yes?"

"I'm praying for him, too."

His words infused her with renewed hope.

"I'll be back." He shut the door behind him.

She set the gun on the floor, within easy reach, beside her chair, then she took Myles's hand in hers. How many times had these strong, masculine hands provided comfort to her over the past few weeks? She gave his fingers a gentle squeeze, willing all her strength and hope and love to reach him through her touch.

Shutting her watery eyes, she bent her head and began her silent prayers for help.

Bright light and immense pain registered simultaneously in Myles's mind. He jerked awake, opening his eyes, and regretted the movement at once. The back of his shoulder roared in agony. Sucking his breath in through clenched teeth, he did his best to relax his body.

"Myles? Are you awake?" The scent of lavender wafted over him as Delsie leaned near. Carefully he turned his head to look at her. She sat on a chair at his bedside, her eyes wide with concern, her hands twisting and untwisting a handkerchief in her lap. The sight of her alive and unharmed brought him a moment of peace.

"Where's Amos? Is he all right?"

A sheen of tears graced her long lashes, but she managed a tentative smile. "Amos is fine. He went to find some breakfast. Are you hungry? You didn't want anything last night."

"Last night?" Myles ran a hand over his tried eyes, trying to recall the last thing he remembered. Amos had pulled the arrow from his back—that was something he wouldn't soon forget—then he'd been carried into the cabin. After that, he could vaguely recall Amos rebandaging his wound once or twice. "What time is it?"

Delsie glanced at the roofless ceiling of the cabin. "Probably nearing eight o'clock or so."

"Eight o'clock?" he echoed. Normally they would have been two hours or more into their journey by now. Delsie couldn't afford a late start—not when her sister was getting married tomorrow. "Can you help me sit up?"

"I don't think that's such a good—"

"Please, Delsie. Help me up." He'd vowed to get her to the end of the trail, no matter what, and he wouldn't go back on his word.

She hesitated a moment longer, then set her jaw and sat forward. "It's probably best if you roll onto your good side first."

He nodded. Gently he moved his left arm under his body and rolled onto that side. Pain screamed at him to keep still, but he fought it by gritting his teeth. "All right. Now help me sit up."

Biting her lip, she reached out and gingerly took hold of his right arm. Even the reluctant tug she gave his arm aggravated his injury. He clenched his jaw over the ache and sat up. Immediately the cabin began to spin and tilt. Myles lowered his head, nearly to his chest, and gripped his knees until the dizziness subsided.

Would he be able to sit on his horse? Anxiety churned his empty stomach at the thought of not being able to continue on for Delsie. He loved her and he'd promised to protect her—he had to keep going.

When he could see straight again, he tipped his chin up, his left hand curling into a tight fist against his thigh. "All right. Now I want you to help me stand."

"What?" Delsie shook her head. "Myles, you were shot with an arrow last night. You've either been passed out or restless with the pain since then."

He met her determined gaze with one of his own. "We were supposed to go another twenty miles last night before we stopped. That would've put us only sixty miles from your sister. She gets married tomorrow, Delsie."

She visibly swallowed, but the firmness in her expression didn't waver. "I'll just have to miss it. Because I'm not leaving you behind."

She'd give up her chance to reconcile with her family, for him? He studied her beautiful face, an unfamiliar lump filling his throat. He coughed it away. "You don't know what you're saying. I'm not going to let you quit."

"And you can't ride today."

"Stubborn woman," he muttered, shaking his head.

The tiniest smile lifted her lips. "Pigheaded man."

Her fortitude would be the death of them both, he thought wryly. How could he convince her that he would do anything for her, even if that meant they had to tie him to the saddle? But already, the room was beginning to tip again and he felt as if he might vomit from sitting up even this long. With a groan of defeat, he dropped to his side.

"Are you all right? Can I get you anything?"

"I'll take some water," he said, more to give her something to do while he took the few minutes to himself to think. Or try to think. The pain messed with his normally clearheaded mind. That, and the concern and sacrifice of the woman he loved.

"I'll be right back." She picked up a cup and exited the cabin.

Myles forced a few deep breaths, though his chest protested it as much as his shoulder did. If he couldn't ride, then what? He would not lie here and watch Delsie miss the very event she'd come nearly eighteen hundred miles to be at.

Could Amos go with her? Possibly. But without the older man's help, Myles might not survive long enough to climb back into a saddle. As much as he hated to admit it, he needed someone here to help him get food, water and fresh bandages.

That left only one solution, and the more Myles pondered it, the more he felt the rightness of it deep down. Delsie could go on. The lessons he'd given her on the trail hadn't been just happenstance. Surely God had seen what might happen, and He'd inspired Myles to help her learn to fend for herself.

Did he dare let her go, though? He hated the idea of not being at her side, protecting her, as she ventured on her own in an unfamiliar desert.

But she's not alone.

The thought reminded him of the one he'd had right before the Indian had shot him. The recollection filled him with awe, temporarily numbing his pain. If he hadn't looked up when he did, he wouldn't have turned away from the arrow. It would have struck him in the chest or abdomen, and that would have meant a sure and agonizing death.

God wasn't just aware of Delsie. He was looking out for Myles, too. The man who'd bitterly told himself he'd been abandoned, that God had no need of him and his lowly station in life, had been wrong. If anything, God had stepped up His efforts to help Myles since Charles's death, giving him a friend in Cynthia, and Elijah and Amos. And now Delsie.

The lump returned to his throat and this time tears pricked his eyes as a feeling of warmth and peace settled like a blanket over his entire body. His shoulder still throbbed with pain, but he would be all right.

And so would Delsie.

She stepped back into the cabin, carefully carrying the full cup. "Here you go."

Myles willed back the moisture in his eyes and lifted his head as she brought the cup to his mouth. "Thank you."

She smiled, a real smile. "You're welcome. Amos should be back soon, and then you can have a little meat."

He reached out and took her free hand in his. She threw him a questioning glance. "After he comes back, I want you to have him saddle up your mare."

"Myles, we went over this." She glanced away. "I'm not leaving—"

"Delsie?" He waited for her to face him again. "I need you to do this. Your sister needs you to do this." He turned her hand over and ran his thumb over the hardened blisters of her palm. "I think God needs you to do this, too."

Her brow knit in disbelief. "I don't know when to stop or what to feed my horse."

Was she relenting? "Amos can give you his watch

or you can simply stop at every other station and pay them to feed you and the mare."

"What about the Indians?"

"We're close enough to Carson Valley that there shouldn't be any more trouble like that. The Express stations should be open from this point on." He motioned to the gun on the table. "Just in case, you can take one of my revolvers with you. You'll be fine. Your horse can outrun those ponies we saw yesterday."

She pressed her lips together. "I don't know."

"You can do this, darling." The endearment rolled effortlessly off his tongue. Would he say it as easily again, to some other woman, someday? "We practiced how to saddle and unsaddle your mare, if you need to do that. You also know how to shoot and how to cook. It's only eighty miles. Slightly less than a typical day for us on the trail."

Delsie released a heavy sigh and dropped her chin. A single tear rolled down her face.

"It wasn't just coincidence that we met," Myles said, using his other hand, despite the pain it caused, to brush the tear from her skin. Skin that was no longer creamy white but slightly brown and freckled. And he loved it. "God put you and me there together by the stables that day. And He helped me teach you everything you need to finish this, Delsie. You can set everything right with your family. You can keep your promise."

When she lifted her head, her chin was trembling. "But I don't want to say goodbye." Her words were perfect echoes of those she'd voiced right before their kiss in the barn all those days ago.

Was that the real reason for her reluctance? He didn't want to say goodbye, either, especially not now, like this. "It was coming eventually," Myles replied, if only to mask the ache near his heart at the thought of not seeing her again.

She frowned. Was she hoping he'd say more? The words pushed toward his mouth and made his heart pound in his chest. He wanted to tell her how much she meant to him, that he loved her more than he'd ever loved anyone. But he couldn't. It wasn't fair to her, to claim her heart when neither of them could make good on such a claim. She had to return to her father and her life in Pennsylvania and he had to return to his job and his tiny room back in Saint Joe.

"I'll never ever forget you, Myles." She clasped his hand between both of hers. "You have become..." Her voice hitched with a sob. "My dearest, dearest friend."

"And you mine," he murmured so low he wasn't sure if she heard him. "Does this mean you're going?" he asked more loudly.

She laughed, in spite of her tears. "I suppose it does."

"Then I'll say farewell, Miss Delsie Radford..." Foolish or not, he lifted one of her hands and kissed her knuckles, enjoying the feel of her skin beneath his lips for the last time.

"Goodbye, Myles Patton." That steely spark had returned to her dark blue eyes. "Promise me you will get better?"

"I promise."

With a decisive nod, she stood and went to the table where her valise sat beside his gun. "Here's the money for you and Amos." She set the stacks of bills on the chair beside his bed.

"That's too much," Myles protested. "We didn't get you all the way there."

She glared down at him. "It's my money and I'll do with it as I want."

Amos appeared in the doorway, a limp coyote hanging from one hand. "Myles, you're awake." He took in Delsie and the money and cocked his head. "What's going on?"

She shot Myles a look, then raised her chin. Her bravery was better medicine than anything he could think of. "I'm going on, alone."

"You certain?" Amos asked.

This time she didn't hesitate. "Yes."

Amos shot her a sad smile, reminding Myles that he wasn't the only one regretting Delsie's approaching absence. "Then we'd best draw you up a map."

Chapter Fourteen

Delsie hadn't felt this weary since her first full day of riding, almost three weeks ago. Or this lonely since Lillie had left. While Amos and Myles hadn't been real conversationalists most of the time, she'd realized after only a few miles on her own that she missed their steady company.

After adjusting her grip on the reins, she checked the pocket watch Amos had insisted she take with her. *A gift*, he told her, *for a woman I would have been proud to have as a daughter.* The face of the clock became distorted from her tears, but she sniffed them back. Another thirty minutes or so before she needed to rest the mare.

She released the watch to dangle from where she'd pinned it to her waistband and gazed at the landscape around her. Unlike the desolate desert landscape, now there were trees and green hills. But even the lovely scenery couldn't keep her thoughts from returning— once again—to Myles.

Saying goodbye to him had left her feeling more hollow inside than seeing her sister leave. At least she would be reunited with Lillie tonight. She was likely to never see Myles again.

She pressed a hand to her heart, wishing she could relieve the pain throbbing there. No wonder people talked about dying of a broken heart. Would time eventually ease the ache or would she carry this soreness for the rest of her life?

She'd wanted so much to tell Myles that she loved him and couldn't bear to have him gone from her life, and for him to say the same. But she knew it would've only made leaving him that much harder.

"What am I to do, girl?" she murmured to the mare. The mount flicked her ears back as though listening. "I don't know that I can ever truly forget him."

Memories of Myles were tightly, and wonderfully, woven through every part of her journey West. And though her pain was acute at separating from him, she wouldn't trade the experience of knowing him. A traitorous tear slid down her cheek, but she quickly swiped it away. She'd cried enough the past few days. Recalling Myles's words of confidence, that she could make this last stretch alone, renewed her usual optimism and faith.

Lowering her chin, she shut her eyes. "Bless me to make it to Lillie," she quietly prayed aloud. "And bless Myles that he'll fully recover. Help him get the horse ranch he desires. Bless Amos, too. They are both good men. The best I've ever met." Her voice wobbled with emotion, but she swallowed it back. "I'll be forever grateful for the chance to know them."

When she opened her eyes, Delsie lifted her head and nudged her horse to move a little faster. She had nearly eighty miles to go before she could once again embrace her sister. And nothing would stop her from getting there.

Fire streaked the western sky as the sun disappeared. Delsie removed her hat and allowed the nice evening breeze to ruffle her sweat-dampened hair. Her muscles felt unusually sore tonight, especially considering she'd been riding every day for weeks. But she'd had to perform all their daily tasks alone these past fifty-five miles or so. Getting in and out of the saddle, talking to the Express station owners, watering her horse, procuring food for both of them. She hadn't realized how much Amos and Myles had helped, or the company they'd provided, until they were no longer with her.

Blowing out a tired sigh, she plopped her hat back on and patted her mare's neck. "We're so close, girl. Only twenty-five miles to go."

She'd already decided to keep riding, even after dark. Stopping now was unthinkable when she was so close to reaching Lillie. Thankfully, she and her horse had been well fed at the last station where they'd rested. With a full belly, she figured she could easily keep going, especially if the moon were bright enough to see by.

With no one to talk to, she began to hum a song. It was the one she and Amos had sung before Myles had finally joined in. A smile lifted her lips at the recollection. She'd had her suspicions early on that Myles's faith had only been shaken and not completely erased.

And that had proven true. She hoped he would continue to nourish it, though she couldn't help thinking a handsome, God-fearing man like him would surely be snatched up sooner than later by some young lady.

The possibility made her smile slip, so she hurried to replace it with thoughts of Lillie. What would her sister say when Delsie knocked on her door at the boardinghouse in a few more hours? She couldn't wait to see the surprise in her sister's green eyes and to throw her arms around her. Why, she'd even be able to help her dress for the wedding tomorrow.

Sunset soon gave way to dusk, lengthening the shadows around her. She checked her watch. It was about time to stop and rest the mare, but she'd wait until she found some water.

The light was fast fading from the sky. Delsie peered up at the crescent-shaped moon. It wasn't nearly as bright as she'd hoped, though it would surely provide enough visibility to keep riding.

The sound of water reached her ears before she found the stream. She slid from the saddle and took a moment to let her legs adjust to being on the ground again. Then she led the mare toward the water.

Darkness shrouded the brush and trees along the stream's bank. A shiver of concern slid up her spine, but Delsie squelched it with the knowledge that she had Myles's gun in its holster on her saddle.

"Everything's going to be fine," she murmured as she let the mare drink its fill from the stream. Once the horse had finished, she looped the reins, more by feel than sight, around a nearby branch. Thirsty, too, she knelt beside the gurgling water and scooped some into her hand to drink. When her immediate thirst had been satisfied, she set the canteen Myles had given her into the water to fill it.

The stirring of the horse in the brush caused her to jump, then laugh at her own foolishness. "Hang on," she called out to it. "I'm almost done."

Sticking her finger into the canteen, she determined she had enough water. Delsie climbed to her feet. The shadows had deepened even in the few minutes she'd been by the stream. Which tree had she tied the mare to?

"Here, girl. Where are you?" A knot of worry began to tighten her stomach and made her pulse trip faster in concern.

Hearing a noise ahead, she moved in that direction. Branches scraped at her face and arms until she finally stepped out from under their shelter. Where was her horse? The worry churned to full panic as Delsie scanned the trail. A movement jerked her attention to her right. In the faint light of the moon, she finally caught sight of the mare, moving at a trot in the opposite direction.

"Wait. Come back." She dropped the canteen to the ground and hiked up her skirt in order to run. Her rapid footfalls matched her heartbeat as she raced after the horse. "Come back."

The animal continued to move at a steady clip, indifferent to Delsie's repeated cries and frantic sprint. Before long she could no longer see the mare in front of her. She tripped over something in the semidarkness and stumbled to the ground. Her breath came in great heaves, made worse by the sobs she tried to hold back.

Anger, at the horse and herself, had her pounding her fist against the dirt with a choked cry. The loss of her mare was unthinkable. How would she ever reach Lillie now? She couldn't purchase another animal. All her remaining money had been stowed in a knapsack on the saddle, along with Myles's gun. Everything she'd owned and needed had just disappeared into the night.

Her frustration soon gave way to hopelessness and fear. She pulled herself into a sitting position and shivered. What was she to do now? She still had more than twenty miles to go to reach Lillie in Placerville and nothing but her own two feet to get her there. Had she come so far, and endured so much, only to be thwarted in this moment, nearly within sight of her goal?

You're a strong woman, Delsie Radford. Don't let anyone tell you otherwise.

Myles's voice filled her head and heart and warmed her trembling body. He had never given up on her, not once. And neither had God.

Rising to her feet, she moved purposely back the way she'd come. While she no longer had her map, either, she knew they'd been heading more or less in a westerly direction all day. And that was the way she'd keep going.

Her foot struck something hard. Kneeling down, she realized she'd kicked the canteen. Not only would it give her needed water but it also oriented her in the darkness. This was where she'd veered off the trail to reach the stream. She whispered a prayer of gratitude and a petition for protection, then continued forward.

Once she located the trail, Delsie turned west and began walking as quickly as she could. It didn't take her long to realize how cumbersome her long skirt was to moving on the ground instead of on a horse. Stopping, she sat down and tore several inches from the hem. The fabric, trail-worn as it was, ripped easily. Delsie tossed the strip of cloth away, hoisted her canteen again and took a few steps.

Much better.

She picked up her pace to make up for the few stolen minutes. The creaking of branches and the whoosh of wings overhead sounded louder than normal, making her clutch the canteen tightly to her chest like a shield. But she didn't let the nocturnal noises slow her down.

Thankfully, she still had Amos's pocket watch. Every ten minutes, she allowed herself a drink to help keep her strength up. Soon she was taking sips every five minutes, though, to keep herself awake. Her feet ached in her shoes, and her tired eyelids longed to fall shut.

Biting her lip against the sleepiness, Delsie forged ahead. She passed the time by doing calculations in her head. If she averaged a walking speed of twelve minutes per mile, she could walk five miles in an hour. At that rate, she would be to Lillie's in…five hours. Plenty of time before the wedding, though she wasn't sure if the boardinghouse proprietress would admit her inside in the middle of the night.

She would figure something out—

"Oomph." She suddenly found herself sprawled on hands and knees. What had she stumbled over this time? Feeling along the dirt with her hands, Delsie discovered a hole, most likely a burrow of some sort, that she must have stepped into. "No harm done," she muttered to herself as she rose to her feet, but a sharp pain in her left ankle had her crying out in protest.

Fighting panic, she straightened to her full height and gingerly set her left foot down. "All right. Let's try this again." She tried to take a step forward, but painful shoots of feeling radiated from her injured ankle.

"No!"

She hobbled forward, determined to keep going, but the throbbing made walking painfully slow. How was she supposed to reach Lillie on a sprained ankle? Was it time to admit defeat? She didn't have a horse, and now she couldn't walk…

Despair, every bit as raw and stabbing as her ankle, drove her to the ground, where she sat, clutching her injured foot. There was no way she would make Lillie's wedding now. The thought of breaking her promise to their mother and never seeing her sister again had her hanging her head in defeat.

And what of Myles…? Were he and Amos safe or had the Indians come back? She wasn't likely to see either of her companions ever again. The thought filled her throat with the bitter taste of pain and regret.

"What do I do now?" she whispered through the heartache tightening her lungs.

After allowing herself another moment or two of self-pity, Delsie lifted her head and set her jaw. The next station had to be close by, given the miles she'd ridden before stopping the mare at the stream. If she could reach the Express station, she might just find a way to make it to Lillie after all. Rising to her feet, she began a painful shuffle forward. She had a wedding to get to.

The light spilling from the window up ahead infused Delsie with needed energy. Had she ever seen anything more beautiful? She quickened her limping pace. Crossing the empty yard, she hobbled up onto the porch and knocked at the door. A tall man, probably in his midthirties, answered.

"Can I help you, miss?" He glanced past her into the shadowed yard.

"Yes," she gasped out over the pain of her ankle. "I've lost my horse, you see. And then I sprained my ankle. But I need to be at my sister's wedding tomorrow…" The room behind him had begun to shift and Delsie felt herself falling forward.

"Whoa there." He reached out and grasped her elbow. "Let's you get off that foot and then you can tell me where you're from and where you're going."

Delsie allowed him to lead her into a tidy parlor, where she sank into one of the armchairs.

"Now, which ankle is hurt?"

She pointed to her left. The man nodded, then gently lifted her foot and placed it on a cushioned footrest. Clearly she'd arrived at a place much nicer than a simple remounting station for Express riders.

"Let me go get my wife. I'm sure she'll want to help." He gave her a friendly smile.

"Thank you."

The man slipped from the room, leaving Delsie alone again. She took off her hat, rested her head against the back of the chair and shut her eyes. When was the last time she'd felt this tired?

"What do we have here?"

Delsie opened her eyes and sat up. A blond-haired woman, pulling a shawl over her nightgown, was coming down the stairs.

"I'm sorry to disturb you," she started to say, but the woman shook her head.

"We're rather used to strangers coming here at all hours of the night. What with the stagecoaches and teamsters stopping all the time." She came to stand next to Delsie's chair and smiled. "Never had a woman here on her own, though. What's your name?"

Her kind manner was nearly Delsie's undoing. Willing back useless tears, she gave the woman a tentative smile. "My name is Delsie Radford. I lost my horse about five miles back and then twisted my ankle walking in the dark."

The woman took a seat on the nearby settee. "And what were you doing riding alone, Miss Radford?"

Delsie swallowed. "My companions were waylaid about sixty miles back when one of them was injured by Indians."

The woman's green eyes widened and she gave a startled laugh. "I think you'd best start at the beginning of your tale. But first, if you'll follow me into the kitchen, we'll see what we can do for you in the way of food and something for that ankle."

"Thank you…" Delsie waited for the woman to supply her name.

"Please, call me Edith."

With Edith's help, she stood and limped down the hall to the kitchen at the back of the house. She took a seat at the table, her left leg propped up on the bench next to her. Edith sliced some bread and brought it to the table for Delsie to eat before sitting down in a nearby chair. While she nibbled on the bread and jam, she told Edith her entire story—from finding the letters from Lillie in her father's desk to leaving Myles and Amos this morning.

"And that is how I ended up here," Delsie finished, "and why I must be at Lillie's wedding tomorrow."

"What time is the wedding?"

Delsie shook her head. "I don't know. Morning, I assume."

"Placerville is a good twenty miles from here," Edith said, drumming her fingers on the chair arm, "but I'm sure one of the teamsters headed in that direction could drive you."

A flicker of hope filled Delsie until she remembered she had nothing with which to pay for a ride. "I'm afraid I can't pay someone to take me or afford lodging tonight. But if I could sleep in your stable..." That solved one problem, though it didn't solve how she would get to Placerville on a sprained ankle.

"Nonsense." Edith reached out and patted Delsie's hand. "You will stay in one of our rooms tonight and I'll talk with the teamsters in the morning at breakfast. Ol' Ike is a regular here and a man to be trusted. He could probably drive you."

Delsie's chin wobbled with emotion. Edith's genuine compassion reminded her so much of her own mother that a keen sense of loss swept through her. "I don't even know what to say." Myles would laugh at that.

Edith chuckled and stood. "Then don't worry about saying anything. Now let's get that ankle wrapped up."

In no time at all her ankle had been securely wrapped with a bandage and Edith was helping her up the stairs to a vacant room. After dressing in a borrowed nightgown, Delsie slipped into bed. She would allow herself to sleep for a few hours, then she'd be up before the sun and back on her way to Lillie.

Chapter Fifteen

Warm rays of sunshine nudged Delsie awake. She blinked at the unfamiliar surroundings and sat up, trying to orient herself. Her torn dress and Amos's pocket watch brought instant remembering. Throwing off her blankets, she limped across the room to pick up the watch. It was already seven o'clock. Had the teamsters left? Her heart beat wildly at the thought. But no, Edith would have come to wake her.

Pacified, she quickly changed out of the nightgown and back into her dress. Dirt marred the material and the once vibrant color had faded after days in the sun. Not the most proper thing to wear to a wedding, but it couldn't be helped.

Delsie raked her fingers through her hair and settled for a simple braid. Her gaze fell onto her hat and trousers. Did she dare part with them? The trousers she didn't mind leaving behind. But as uncomely as the wide-brimmed hat might be on her, she couldn't part with it. It represented her only token, beyond memories, from her time with Myles.

Placing the hat on her head, she shuffled out of the room and down the stairs. Edith met her at the bottom.

"I was just coming up to see if you were awake. How did you sleep?"

"Very well." Delsie steadied herself against the wall. "Did Ike agree to drive me?"

Edith nodded, smiling. "He's leaving now, though. So you'll have to take these biscuits with you." She handed Delsie several biscuits wrapped in a napkin. "I would have had you join us for breakfast earlier, but I figured you needed the rest."

"Thank you, Edith." On impulse she gave the woman a quick hug.

"You are more than welcome, Delsie. I wish you all the best." She helped Delsie out the door and down the porch steps, where a large wagon sat waiting. "I'll be praying you make it."

Delsie thanked her again, then allowed Ike, a wiry man with gentle eyes, to help her onto the seat. As the wagon rolled forward, she waved goodbye to Edith.

Ike spoke little, reminding Delsie a bit of Myles, but he wasn't unfriendly. She even coaxed a smile from him after offering him one of the biscuits. The sky overhead was a perfect arc of blue, bringing recollections of the prairie to her mind. She could hardly believe she'd come almost eighteen hundred miles in nineteen days.

The creak of the wagon and the thud of the team's hooves filled the quiet between her and Ike. He kept the horses moving at a steady pace, but it still felt slow compared to what Delsie was used to. She checked the pocket watch again. It was eight o'clock now. Would she make it on time?

She shifted on the hard seat, almost wishing for her saddle. How strange it felt not to be on the back of a horse as she'd been every day these past few weeks.

Each turn of the wheels brought her closer to Lillie, but Delsie willed them to spin faster. She couldn't miss her sister, not when she was so very close.

I'm coming, Lillie, she thought, her foot tapping out a rhythm of its own. *I'm coming.*

If Ike sensed her fretting energy, he didn't comment. Instead he kept his gaze ahead and the reins gripped securely in his sun-spotted hands. Delsie wished her own hands were as occupied. Instead she rubbed at the watch face with her thumb, fiddled with her dress cuffs, and adjusted and readjusted her hat.

At the moment she thought she would either scream with nerves or throw up her hastily eaten breakfast, she spied buildings in the distance.

"Is that Placerville?"

"Yep," Ike intoned in a calm voice.

Her heart began to thud double time. Her journey's end was in sight. She only prayed she wasn't too late.

"Where do you need to go, miss?"

She told him the name of the boardinghouse.

"I know it. I'll take you there, but I can't stay. Got to keep on schedule."

"I understand. Thank you, Ike."

He nodded in acknowledgment. Delsie gripped her hands in her lap as he slowed the horses at the edge of the town. Once they reached what she guessed must be Main Street, Ike turned the huge wagon onto a side street and stopped. "This is it."

Her hands shook so badly, she could hardly climb down. "Thank you again, Ike," she called over her shoulder as she hurried at a painful hop to the door. She tried the handle, but it was locked. Behind her she could hear Ike and the wagon driving away. Delsie knocked once, twice.

"Coming," a voice hollered from inside. At last the door opened and a short woman with a severe bun glowered down at her. "You need a room?"

"No. I need to see Miss Lillian Radford."

"Miss Lillie?" the woman echoed. "She's up and gone. Left first thing this morning."

Gone? Deep regret pulsed through Delsie's veins and she sagged against the door in despair. Lillie wasn't supposed to leave for Oregon until tomorrow. "Thank you." She turned away and stared unseeing down the street. Where was she to go now?

"If you need to speak to her, she's likely still at the church. Gettin' herself hitched to that handsome Clay Weeks." The woman gave a low whistle and chuckled. "I would've been there myself but couldn't find no one to watch the place…"

Delsie whirled around, hope burning strong in her throat and eyes. "She's still at the church?"

"I reckon so."

"Which church?"

The woman pointed down the street. "Right there. On the other side of Main."

She took off at a shuffling run. Her ankle ached with the effort, but she ignored it. When she reached Main Street, she hurried across, dodging several wagons. There was the church, a white clapboard building with a bell tower and spire. She hobbled down the dusty street to the bottom of the steps. There she paused to catch her breath. She couldn't hear anything from inside, but several wagons were still sitting out front.

Gripping the banister, she hopped up the stairs to the front door. She gripped the handle and pulled it open. Cooler air greeted her as she limped inside and stopped. There at the front of the church, before the preacher, stood Lillie dressed in a simple ivory gown and veil. She held hands with Clay, who was looking tall and handsome in a nice brown suit.

The sight of her sister after so many months apart ripped a sudden cry of longing from Delsie's mouth. The sound echoed in the quiet church. Delsie pressed her hand to her lips as the few people in the congregation turned around. Lillie and Clay twisted to face her, too. Delsie's eyes met her sister's beneath the lacy veil.

"Delsie?" Her name came out as a gasp.

"Yes, Lillie." She took a step forward. "It's me."

Within seconds, Lillie was hurrying up the aisle, Clay right behind her. Delsie met them halfway and threw her arms around Lillie. She held her sister for a long moment, her tears wetting the shoulder of Lillie's gown.

When Lillie drew back, she was smiling, in spite of the tears on her own cheeks. "I can't believe you're here." She took in the sight of Delsie's hat and disheveled dress. "What happened to you?"

Delsie clasped her sister's hand and squeezed it. "That, dear Lillie, is a very long story."

"Perhaps it can wait until after your sister and I are married," Clay said, his smile teasing.

"Yes, of course." Embarrassment washed over her anew as Delsie glanced at the preacher and the guests, all staring with curiosity at her and her sister.

Lillie tugged her toward the front of the church. "Now that you're here, you must sit right in front."

She started to protest given her unsightly attire, but Clay murmured good-naturedly, "I wouldn't cross her if I were you."

Delsie chuckled. "A fact I know all too well. All right." She took a seat on the front pew.

"Are we ready now?" the preacher asked, his gaze inquisitive but not unkind.

Lillie and Clay nodded as one and turned to face each other once more. The love emanating from their glowing faces brought another surge of joy to Delsie's heart.

"Dearly beloved," the preacher began.

I made it, Myles. Delsie wished so badly she could tell him. She glanced in the direction of the window, but instead of buildings, she saw the handsome face and dark eyes of the man she loved watching her from astride his horse. *I made it.*

"Do you think Delsie made it, to her sister?" Myles said as he rotated his shoulder, trying to stretch the stiff muscles from lying on his side or stomach, despite the aggravated pain. He and Amos had just finished supper. It had only been a day and a half since Delsie had left them to continue on alone, but it felt twice that long to him. "I guess we'll never know," he murmured more to himself than to Amos.

The older man sat at the table, cleaning his gun. Myles owed his healing, however slow, to Amos. Even without a doctor or proper medical supplies, his friend had so far kept Myles's wound from festering and becoming worse. He had God to thank for that, too.

"I think she made it," Amos said quietly.

"What if something happened, though?"

He felt the familiar apprehension churning inside him, souring the food in his belly. Typically he fought the worry with reassurances that he'd done the right thing. But every now and then, especially since they'd had no word and probably wouldn't, the doubts crept in and robbed his peace of mind over Delsie.

He lifted his head to find Amos watching him intently. "I think she made it," he repeated, "because something deep in here says she did." He tapped his chest. "Something that goes beyond sight and knowledge to tell me everything will be all right. With Delsie." He raised his graying eyebrows at Myles. "And with you."

The words hit Myles with as much force as the Indian's arrow. If he searched his heart, really and truly searched, he sensed a calmness there, confirming what Amos said. Delsie would be all right, and so would they. Though Myles still couldn't help wishing he'd been able to see her reach her sister, been able to kiss her once more, been able to tell her that she was the best thing to come into his life in a long time.

"Think we'll have our jobs waiting for us?" he asked, changing the subject. He let his gaze move from Amos to where Elijah sat on the nearby cupboard eating some of the leftover supper meat.

"Sure hope so," Amos said with a chuckle. "The Pony Express hasn't been going long enough to get kicked out yet."

Myles cracked a smile. "Do you like working at the station?"

"I like working with the stock and visiting with the riders." He glanced up from his gun. "What about you? You thinkin' of being an Express rider for much longer?"

Myles's answer came easy. "Just long enough to make a little money."

"And start your ranch?" He'd told Amos more than once about his dream.

Myles nodded and propped his good shoulder against the headboard. "I reckon another six months, a year maybe, of Express riding and I should have enough to buy a little land. I've already got me a horse."

Amos shot him a surprised look. "Have you, now?"

"Delsie gave me Moses."

"Moses?" Amos laughed.

Myles feigned a scowl. "Don't you start on the name, too."

"So she gave you a horse, huh?" Something in the other man's tone had Myles on edge.

"And?" Myles pressed, though he wasn't sure he wanted to hear the rest.

Amos gave a nonchalant shrug, his hands still working over his gun. "That's a rather generous gift." He paused to throw a meaningful glance at Myles. "Don't know that I'd let a horse-giving lady with a spine of iron slip away from me that easily."

Myles sniffed. Delsie wasn't here anymore, and Amos was still playing matchmaker. "I shouldn't have to spell out why that's impossible."

"No," Amos said, giving a thoughtful shake of his head. "But you might get closer to having what you want if you start pondering over ways to make it possible."

With a noncommittal grunt, Myles rested his head back and looked up toward the absent ceiling. Thank goodness it hadn't rained yet. It wasn't as if he hadn't thought through the scenarios over and over since Delsie had left. But she wouldn't leave her father to marry a lowly Express rider and Myles didn't have any way to make more money unless he kept riding.

His chances of winning her, and her father, over were likely to decrease with every passing month, too. Even if he did eventually acquire his horse ranch and made it successful, there was no guarantee she wouldn't already be married to someone else by then. And he wouldn't ask her to wait, months or years, for him. It wouldn't be fair to someone as lovely and remarkable as Delsie.

"Nope." He dropped his chin and glared at Amos. "Still doesn't change things. She has to return to her father, who already has someone picked out for her, I might add. And Delsie would sooner be hung than split her family a second time by running off with a poor horse rider."

Amos's continued calm in the face of Myles's impassioned speech irked him. But Myles could at least appreciate his friend's efforts to see him and Delsie happy and together, however unlikely.

"You ever heard the verse about the Lord working in mysterious ways?"

The question surprised Myles. "I reckon so, yes."

The older man lifted his gaze to Myles's, those blue-gray eyes filled with quiet confidence. "I suggest you remember that verse from time to time, Myles Patton. And instead of ruminating about it in your finite way, why not turn the matter over to the Lord?"

Myles twisted his head to peer out the window. Charles would have likely said something similar. And while every part of him balked at the impossibility of he and Delsie finding their way back to each other, he wouldn't give over to the bitterness and mistrust that had filled his old life. His life before meeting her.

Hope had been awakened inside him, and whatever his fear at believing too much, he couldn't wrestle the idea from his mind. *All right, Lord*, he finally prayed in silence. *You know I love her. And whether it's meant to be between us or not...* Myles swallowed and brushed at his eyes with his thumb. *I turn the outcome over to You.*

"Oh, Delsie. I'm going to miss you so much." Lillie hugged her once again, crushing the small hat she'd given Delsie to keep. Along with the dress she wore, a nightgown, an extra change of clothes and enough money to travel home. Lillie and Clay wouldn't hear of her taking anything less. "I wish you could stay longer."

Delsie eased back and squeezed her sister's hands. While they'd enjoyed several hours talking after the wedding yesterday, their time together still felt too brief. "I do, too. But you and Clay are pulling out in a few hours," she gently reminded. "And I need to return home. To Papa."

Lillie nodded, though tears still shone in her eyes. "You will write, won't you?"

"Of course. Once a week, at least."

"Maybe someday you could even come visit us in Oregon." She glanced up at Clay with an adoring smile. "It's going to be beautiful there. Lots of trees, just like back home. But with almost no winter."

"I will try."

"Try?" Lillie laughed and kissed Delsie's cheek. "That doesn't sound like the girl who stumbled into my wedding yesterday with a sprained ankle and eighteen hundred miles worth of dust and dirt on her clothes."

Delsie chuckled. How she'd missed Lillie. And now she had to say goodbye all over again. This time, though, she told herself, she would be able to write her sister and receive letters in return. She would make certain their father understood that.

"Time to go, miss," the stagecoach driver said. "Where's your luggage?"

She lifted the borrowed valise from Lillie. "This is it."

The driver's eyes widened and he shook his head.

"Never seen a lady come through with something so small."

Delsie wanted to tell him she'd learned to travel quite light, and if needed, could skin and cook a rabbit for supper, as well. But she held her tongue.

"Goodbye, Delsie." Lillie crushed her in another tight hug. "Tell Papa…I love him."

Surprised, she drew back to search her sister's face. "Do you mean that, Lillie? Have you forgiven him?"

Her sister released her to clasp Clay's hand. "It's me I hope he's forgiven. I was angry and stubborn. But I understand now the lengths we'll go to keep those we love safe and happy. Look at what you did, Delsie, for us."

It was Delsie's turn to pull Lillie close for one last embrace. She'd been right, all along, in coming. "I love you, Lillie."

"I love you, too."

Delsie went up on tiptoe and gave Clay a quick kiss on the cheek. "Welcome to the family."

"Thank you." He looked down at her sister and beamed. They would be happy together. A tremor of melancholy passed through her at the thought of not finding that herself.

"Let's go, miss." She heeded the driver's call this time and allowed him to help her into the stagecoach. An older woman and her husband sat on the cushioned seat opposite hers. Delsie leaned out the open window and waved to Lillie and Clay as the stagecoach jerked forward.

"Oh dear, close that window, child," the woman protested, waving a handkerchief at her. "That dreadful dust will come in."

Delsie bit back a smile at the thought of how harmless dust truly was and shut the window. She kept the curtain up, though. Now that she was inside the stagecoach, she felt suddenly confined. She longed for the open sky and sun overhead and the chance to ride side by side with Myles again.

Shutting her eyes, she let herself drift through the memories of the past several weeks—meeting Myles that first day, how he'd saved her from the runaway horse and later from the trappers, his care when she'd taken sick with cold, his kiss in the barn, his strong embrace. Each recollection brought vivid sweetness for their time together. Until she recalled the moment she'd told him goodbye. Bitter sadness swept through her then. This time the roll of the wheels was taking her farther and farther from the one she loved.

"Do you think we'll be set upon by highwaymen or Indians, my dear?" the woman asked her husband in a loud whisper. "I can't think of anything more horrid."

Delsie opened her eyes and stared at the passing scenery. Indians or highwayman no longer elicited the same fear in her that they once had. She'd experienced the former and lived to tell the tale. Besides, there were more horrible things to encounter in life than dust or an attack on the stage. Leaving behind the man she loved, forever, now ranked highest in Delsie's mind.

Chapter Sixteen

"Lookee there. Patton's back!" someone yelled as Myles climbed from his saddle and took Moses by the reins. He glanced up at the sign hung over the Pony Express Stables. Had it really been seven weeks since he'd last stood here, talking to Delsie? It felt more like seven months.

He passed his horse off to one of the stock hands. "Take care of him for a bit, will you? I'll be back." Hopefully, with his job still intact.

"Nice-looking horse. Is he yours?" the man asked.

"He is." The first smile he'd felt in days worked at Myles's mouth. This was the first of what he hoped would be many of his own horses.

Thinking of Delsie's gift didn't come without a price, though. It brought to mind the giver, too. As if Myles needed any more reason to remember her. She might have been physically absent on his and Amos's long trek home, but every inch of the trail held some tender recollection of her.

He'd come to accept, long before he'd sold his other mount and collected Moses near Salt Lake City, that he missed Delsie, intensely. He missed her smile, her determination, her strength, her beauty, her goodness. The trail held none of the same excitement or interest for him without her alongside him to talk to, or tease or watch over.

While he went through the motions of rising, riding, eating and sleeping every day, deep down Myles felt a dull ache that couldn't be completely ignored. Only in his nightly prayers, a habit he'd taken up on their way back East, did he find some relief from the gnawing inside him.

Setting his jaw, Myles walked to the Express office at the hotel. Express riding had lost some of its luster, too, but he still needed this job. His absence had been twice as long as he'd originally thought. Had they given his job to another eager rider by now?

His gaze wandered over the familiar streets and buildings of Saint Joseph. But Myles no longer found them as appealing as he once had. He missed the wide-openness of the West and the lure of its new possibilities.

As soon as I have the money I need, he vowed, *I'm heading back to California.*

It would mean being even farther away from Delsie, but maybe then he could find the peace that had eluded him since she'd ridden off the day before her sister's wedding. Besides, he'd turned all of that over to the Lord, as Amos had suggested. It was in His hands now.

After a rather short stop at the Express office, Myles had to admit his unrealistic hopes for him and Delsie weren't the only things God was looking out for. His fears over his employment had been unfounded. He still had a job as an Express rider, though his superior did admit to considering giving the job to someone else if Myles hadn't shown up by the following week.

He offered a silent prayer of gratitude as he retraced his steps back to the stables. He needed to see about boarding Moses for a while, using some of the money he'd got from selling the other horse.

Grateful to find Moses had been brushed and fed, Myles led him on foot to the livery stable. Memories of working with Charles filled his thoughts as the welcome scent of hay and horses permeated his nose. He hadn't been here in months.

"Myles," the new owner said, smiling. "What can I do for you?"

"I need to board my horse for at least a month." He rubbed a hand down Moses's nose. "Maybe longer."

The livery owner nodded. "This isn't an Express horse, is it?"

"No, sir. This horse is mine."

"Well, we would be more than happy to board him for you."

After settling the arrangements and paying the man, Myles returned to the stables. Elijah was waiting for him on a corner of the roofline. The bird alighted onto his shoulder as Myles strode up. He wanted to see if any of the other riders had a hankering for something other than boardinghouse fare for dinner. Not that he relished the idea of company, but he'd realized after parting ways with Amos a day and a half earlier that he was tired of living so isolated.

"There's a lady here to see you," another rider announced when Myles entered the stables. "Just outside, near the corral."

"A lady?" Myles threw a glance over his shoulder, though he knew he couldn't see whoever was waiting for him from here. "Did she give you a name?"

"Nope."

"All right." Myles headed back outside, his heart beating faster in his chest. It couldn't be Delsie, but telling himself so didn't stop the wild hope from taking root inside him nonetheless. She was likely still traveling back to Pennsylvania. But had she decided to stop and see him? The possibility had him moving faster with anticipation.

He forced a slower pace as he neared the corral, not wanting to appear too eager to whoever waited. Sure enough a woman stood with her back to him, but right away, Myles noticed the coil of hair at her neck wasn't dark. It was blond. Bitter disappointment scalded his tongue as he swallowed. Whoever the woman might be, he wasn't going to transport someone else across the country. Delsie would remain his first and only human parcel.

"Can I help you?" he asked as he came to a stop several feet away from the lady. Elijah flew off, leaving him alone.

The woman turned and smiled, but her friendly reaction did nothing to ease the sudden wariness roiling in Myles's gut.

"Cynthia? What are you doing here?"

"Myles." She moved with purpose toward him, though her whole demeanor radiated nervousness instead of her usual carefree manner.

He folded his arms and regarded her silently. What did she possibly have to say?

"You look...well."

"As do you," he replied evenly. She was still a beauty, but he'd found someone else who exhibited beauty both inside and out. Even if he couldn't be with Delsie, he would seek someone like her—at least someday.

Cynthia glanced at the ground, her lips pulled into a frown. "I don't blame you for still being angry, Myles. I've had a lot of time to ponder over that night."

"I'm not angry, not anymore." Myles lowered his arms to his sides. The words seemed to echo through him and he recognized their truth. When had he forgiven Cynthia? *Somewhere along the trail with Delsie*, he thought wryly.

Hope lit Cynthia's green eyes. "Oh, good. Because things haven't been the same without you." She sidled up next to him and put her gloved hand on his arm. "I've missed you. The captain has become such a bore."

Her touch did nothing to him. He felt no regret or bitterness but no thrilling joy, either. "That's too bad, Cynthia." He gently extracted his arm from her clutch. "I hope you find someone who truly makes you happy, someone who you'll make happy, too."

Her brow knit together in a familiar look of confusion. "Whatever do you mean, Myles? I came here today to tell you that I'm sorry for the way things ended. I want you back."

He couldn't help a laugh. "And don't I get a say in this?"

"Well, yes, of course. But I assumed you'd be a little happier to see me, to know I've missed you…" Her voice trailed off and her eyes widened. "You've met someone else, haven't you?"

He wouldn't tell her all about Delsie or how his feelings for the woman before him had paled to mere infatuation when compared to what he felt for Delsie. "There is someone," he stated simply.

Cynthia drew herself up as though truly offended. "Aha. I knew it. Does she care for you as much as I do? Can she give you a sizable fortune, like I can?"

Her mouth curved up into another smile, but this one struck Myles as more calculating than anything else. "Father and I reached a little negotiation a few weeks back. Because I'm of age now, he agreed to give me a share of my inheritance. A large portion, to use for whatever, or whomever, I wish. You wouldn't have to ride these smelly horses anymore. You could have your ranch, Myles. Right now."

So that was how she thought she could ensnare him. She was cleverer than he may have given her credit for in the past. But while the thought of having his ranch much sooner than he'd planned sounded attractive, it wasn't worth a lifetime as Cynthia's husband. Accepting her offer wouldn't be fair, to either of them.

"Look, Cynthia, I'll always appreciate your friendship." And he meant it. Her presence in his life had stoked within him the desire to push himself, to achieve more than he might have thought possible. "But there isn't anything more between us. I'm sorry."

She looked momentarily stunned, as if she couldn't fathom anyone refusing her—and maybe she couldn't. Her reaction was short-lived, though. With a lift of her chin, she shot him a haughty look. "I suppose it is your loss, then. Goodbye, Myles. This time it's final."

"Goodbye, Cynthia. I wish you all the best." He clasped her hand between his, hoping she sensed his sincerity.

"I intend to have the best," she said with an over-confident laugh as she pulled her hand back. "Adieu." She sauntered away, a handkerchief pressed to her nose.

He blew out his breath, then whistled for Elijah. The bird appeared a few moments later and landed on his shoulder. "What'd you fly off for?"

Elijah cocked his head.

"It's safe now," Myles said, chuckling. Ironically his earlier melancholy had faded during his encounter with Cynthia.

What if he hadn't met Delsie all those weeks ago? He likely would have accepted Cynthia's offer today. A shudder ran through him at the thought. Neither of them would have been truly happy.

It was one more thing to be grateful for regarding his time with Delsie. Being with her had changed him and what he'd once thought he wanted. If nothing else, he'd try to be content with that.

Taking a deep breath, Delsie entered the house. "Papa? I'm home." She unpinned her traveling hat and hung it on the hall tree, her gaze sweeping the beautifully carved banister and gas-lit chandelier overhead.

She was home. And yet, standing here among the opulence, she felt as if she were a guest herself. Nothing around her had changed, but she had.

"Delsie!" Her father strode forward and embraced her tightly, bringing a rush of happiness to her. Whatever his faults, she'd missed him. "You are home at last. How was the journey?"

She stepped back, hoping he wouldn't yet notice her fading brown skin or the healing blisters beneath her gloves. "Long," she answered truthfully. Riding on the back of the horse at express speed had felt infinitely faster than the tiring ride in a jostling stagecoach that she'd endured the past several weeks.

"I received your telegram from Missouri. Who is this friend you detoured to visit?"

Delsie tucked an errant curl back into her chignon in a casual manner that belied the rapid thumping of her heart. "I'll tell you all about it later. But first, I want to hear all the news of home." She linked her arm through his.

"Not much in the way of news, but I do have a surprise." He led her into the parlor, where a tall figure with dark hair stood with his back to the doorway. Backlit by the bright evening light, Delsie couldn't tell who waited for her. Could it be Myles? Her pulse tripped faster and faster with hope. Had he learned her address from Amos and beaten her home?

Then the person turned and her hope shattered like glass.

"Flynn," she said more brightly than she felt.

"Welcome home, Delsie." He crossed the room to place a quick kiss on her cheek. She waited for the

smattering of flurries in her middle or for some reaction at all. But she felt nothing. Worse, Flynn's kiss
succeeded in stirring memories in her mind of kissing
Myles. "We've missed you," he said, smiling fully at her.

"Have you?"

He chuckled as if she'd said something truly clever.
"Of course. Two months is a long time to be away."

Yes, she thought, *it is*. Long enough that she no longer felt at ease in her old life.

"Let us adjourn to the dining room for dinner," Mr.
Radford announced, patting her hand where it still held
his arm.

Delsie nodded and woodenly followed him into the
next room, where she took a seat beside him at the table,
across from Flynn. She'd hoped her first evening back
would include time alone with her father, to tell him everything simmering in her conscience. But it appeared
she would have to wait until their guest left for the night.

The food tasted delicious. After weeks of stagecoach
fare, the roast mutton and greens were better than anything she'd eaten since that first home station in Nebraska. Delsie ate every bite, including two helpings of
Mrs. Kipling's custard. Her appearance wasn't the only
thing to change during her journey West; her appetite
had increased, too.

"You seem rather famished, my dear," Mr. Radford
remarked with a touch of censure and teasing. "Don't
they feed you on those coaches?"

Delsie blushed. "Yes, of course. It's just that…I've
missed Mrs. Kipling's food." Which was largely true.
She would never take food, whatever its source, for

granted again. "Did any correspondence come while I was away?"

He dabbed his mouth with his napkin. "Actually, there is. One from your aunt, though I can't imagine what she'd have to say when you only just saw her. And another from someone named…Allan?" He shook his head. "No…it was.. Amos."

"Amos?" Delsie scrambled up from her chair and went to the buffet table, where the letters were kept on a silver platter. A letter from Amos lay on top of the stack. She picked it up and pressed it to her heart, suddenly able to breathe for the first time since entering the house. "If you'll excuse me, I'll read it in my room."

"Now?" Mr. Radford frowned. "Can't it wait, Delsie? Flynn is here. And who's this Amos person anyway?"

She placed a kiss on his cheek. "Don't worry, Papa. I'll explain everything soon. But I must read this letter. Please excuse me, Flynn."

Flynn gave an obviously forced smile, but he dipped his head in acquiescence.

"Good night." With that she hurried from the room and up the stairs, anxious for news of her friends. Once inside her bedroom, she flopped onto her stomach across the waist-high bed and tore open the letter.

The date was from a week earlier, from Guittard's Station in Kansas.

Dearest Delsie,

I hope this letter finds you well and safely back home, after seeing your sister. Myles and I made the return trip a bit more slowly than the three of

us did West. His injury has healed well, though
he will likely bear a scar for the rest of his life.
We both hope the reunion with your sister was all
you'd hoped it would be.

I can't say we didn't miss your presence riding east. Moses was anxiously waiting for Myles
when we returned to Rockwell's. You'll be pleased
to know, too, that Myles and I still had our jobs
with the Pony Express awaiting our return. I hope
you'll write when you're able.

Your faithful servant,

Hank Amos

Delsie had forgotten his first name—to her, he would
always be simply Amos. She read the letter through
again, relieved to hear Myles was healthy once more
and that she hadn't cost either of them their jobs.

Taking a seat at her desk, she pulled out a clean stack
of paper and began writing a letter back to Amos. She
detailed her experiences that last day and night before
finally reaching Lillie, the long travel back to Pennsylvania and how much she dearly missed her friends.

When she finished, she set the letter aside and stared
at the next blank page. Should she write Myles? Amos
hadn't said that Myles wanted to correspond, as well.
She picked up her pen, then set it down once more. Better to leave what had passed between them behind. No
good could come from trying to continue something
that would never come to fruition, as long as her father held to his stubborn opinions. But there was one

thing she was determined to change his mind about—her marrying Flynn.

An hour or so later, Delsie waited unseen at the top of the stairs while her father walked Flynn to the door. Once the man had departed and her father had retired to the parlor, she finally descended. Cheery lamplight lit the parlor and reflected off the beveled glass of her father's book cupboard. He glanced up from his reading as she entered the room and took a seat in the armchair opposite his.

"Flynn departed." He stuck his finger in his book. "I think you may have disappointed him by scurrying off to your room so quickly after dinner."

Delsie leaned back against the familiar softness of the chair. "If I offended him in any way, I am truly sorry."

Mr. Radford nodded and opened his book again. "I'll invite him for dinner tomorrow night and you can apologize to him then."

"Actually…" Delsie licked her lips, her heart racing. It was her moment to be strong. "I'd rather you didn't invite him."

The book closed with a sudden *clap*. "Why ever not?"

She straightened in her chair. "Because I don't love Flynn. And I will never love him." She tucked her shaking hands demurely in her lap. "I know that now."

"But it's an excellent match," he protested. "With your beauty and inheritance and his business sense, he can take over the bank for me. You would be set up very comfortably for life, Delsie."

"That may be true, but I won't trade my happiness for it. I can't marry where I feel no love."

His brows lowered in consternation. "Is that what all these weeks at your aunt's has done? Turned you as rebellious as…" He visibly swallowed and glanced away, unwilling or unable to say Lillie's name.

"I will not defy you as Lillie did," Delsie said in a gentle tone. "But I will not marry Flynn, either."

"Aren't they one in the same?" he countered, his voice more weary than angry.

She shook her head. "No, because I won't leave you, either." She reached forward and rested her hand against his where it gripped his knee. "We will simply have to find another suitor who can provide for me, but one whom I love, too."

He blew out his breath in a resigned sigh. "Very well. You know I've never been good at refusing you anything or staying angry at you for long."

A lump of emotion filled her throat. Her father was a good man, even if he and Lillie had both reacted badly to her choice to follow Clay. "I'm glad to hear I still have some sway." She threw him a teasing smile that made him laugh lightly. "Because I have something else to confess."

He chuckled once more and ran a hand over his eyes. "I don't know that I can take any more revelations tonight, dear daughter."

"Just one more." Though it was likely to upset him far more than her announcement about Flynn.

He finally nodded for her to continue.

Delsie's heart resumed its harried pace as she sat back and clasped her hands together. "I've been to see Lillie, Papa."

"Lillie?" He smirked with disbelief. "That's impossible. Your sister is, who knows where, in California."

"I know where she is. I found her letters. In your desk."

The startled merriment drained from his face, leaving it looking haggard. "When did you find them?"

Delsie kept her chin up. "Right before I went to Aunt Cissy's." Stony silence met her words. "Please don't be angry at me for discovering them. I've been so anxious to hear from her, to know she's all right."

Mr. Radford glanced away, staring into the light of the lamp. "I probably shouldn't have kept them from you. But I worried that you…you might wish to leave, too, if your sister put it into your head to follow after her." She could tell the words cost him to say.

Delsie waited for him to look at her again. "I am not like Lillie, or you," she added tenderly. "I told you I would never leave you to go live far away, and I intend to keep my word. But it isn't right to keep Lillie from me. Or from us. She is sorry for the way she handled things. She loves you, and I'm sure she would welcome your blessing on her marriage to Clay."

"So she finally up and married that farmer, did she?" He sniffed. "Did she write and tell you that? About her and the Weeks boy and about being sorry?"

"No." Delsie shook her head. "She told me in person about her being sorry and that she loves you. And as far as the wedding…" She swallowed her dry throat and plunged on. "I was there. That's what I meant when I said I'd been to see Lillie."

His jaw went slack as he gaped at her, his expression one of confusion. "That's where you've been all these weeks?"

"Actually, no." She gave a nervous laugh. "I stayed with Aunt Cissy for two weeks, then traveled to California over the course of nineteen days, where I witnessed Lillie and Clay's wedding. Then the next day I boarded the stage to return here. So theoretically, I was only with Lillie for a day."

He bent forward, frowning, his forearms on his knees. "I don't understand."

She released a shaky breath. "I should probably start at the beginning."

"That would be preferred."

In a voice that became stronger the more she confided, Delsie shared the details of Lillie's last letter and about her plan to reach her sister in time by using the Pony Express as escort.

"Alone?" Mr. Radford bellowed. "Without a chaperone? Were you out of your mind, Delsie?"

She calmly shook her head—she'd known there would be many parts to this story he would not like. "I was in my right mind. Only anxious to get to Lillie and let her know I cared before she left for Oregon." She gave him a patient smile. "And I was not alone. I was in the company of two gentlemen. An Express rider and a guide."

He muttered something inaudible beneath his breath and lumbered to his feet.

"Please, Papa. Sit down. There's more to tell."

"I prefer to stand, thank you." He began pacing the

rug in front of her. "Or rather…walk. Especially if all your exposés prove to be as distressing as this first one."

Doing her best to ignore his agitation, Delsie explained the necessary changes to her plan in order to arrive in California on time. She told him about soliciting Amos's help and Myles's agreement to continue on, as well. She shared the things she'd seen on her way Westward, the daily routine, the purchasing of the new horses and the change in landscape from prairies to mountains to desert.

There were things she left off mentioning, though, especially her feelings for Myles. When she got to the part about needing to continue on alone, she simply shared that an injury to one of her party meant she had to ride the rest of the way to Lillie's by herself. She did tell her father about losing her horse and spraining her ankle, but how in spite of such challenges, she was still able to make it on time to the wedding.

"Lillie looked so beautiful and happy. I wish you could have seen her." Delsie blinked back the sheen of tears the memories brought to her tired eyes. "Clay will take care of her, I can promise you that, and she will care for him. It was wonderful to see them both."

He'd quit his pacing to come stand beside her chair, his hands clasped behind his back. "Thank you for detailing your experience. However…"

Delsie lifted her chin to look at him. "However?"

"You mean to tell me you traveled across the entire country without incident, beyond losing a horse and twisting your ankle?" He narrowed his gaze. "You suffered no other risk to life or limb?"

"No." The word came out no louder than a whisper, but it carried the weight of all the incidences when she might have been killed. Delsie glanced away.

"Ah, I see. So I am right." Mr. Radford marched away from her chair again. "I need to know everything, Delsie. Please."

She studied her hands. Most of the blisters had long since faded, as had the freckles on her skin from days in the sun, but they looked different from the way they had before she'd left all those weeks ago. They were hands capable of hard work and comfort. Hands that had held those of the man she loved, hands that had been protected by him, as well.

"I nearly fell to my death on a runaway horse," she said, her voice low. "And later, was almost assaulted by a group of trappers. Myles…Mr. Patton…came to my aid both times."

"Is that all?" His tone, though firm, couldn't hide the heartbreak she sensed in him at hearing she'd come so close to being hurt.

Delsie shook her head and gave a humorless laugh. "I took very ill riding through a storm one night and we barely escaped a flash flood in the desert." Telling these accounts, independent of the overall story of her journey, brought home their seriousness in a way she hadn't felt quite as keenly when going through them. "We were also attacked by Indians."

"What?" he barked. "Is that what happened to the rider?"

Memories of that day raced through her mind and

Delsie shivered. "Mr. Patton held them off, but he was struck with an arrow in his shoulder."

"And did he…"

Delsie blew out a breath, sharp relief coursing through her once again. "No, he's recovered. Amos told me so in the letter I read tonight."

He returned to his seat, his hands draped loosely between his knees. "Anything else?"

"That's all." Except for her realization that she loved Myles, but there was little point in sharing such news. "And I'm here now—safe and well."

Silence accompanied her words for nearly a minute. Finally her father stirred from his statue-like position to run a hand over his face. Delsie hadn't seen him look so full of despair since the death of her mother.

"What is it?" she asked, kneeling beside him.

He lifted his hands in a helpless gesture. "I had no idea my stubbornness would drive you to do something…so…so dangerous. You might have been killed, Delsie."

She rested her arm on his knee. "But I wasn't. I wouldn't have gone, especially without your permission, if I hadn't felt it was right and that I would somehow make it."

"There's that rock-solid faith again," he murmured, shooting her a patronizing smile.

"Yes, but not just in God. I have faith in you and Lillie, too."

He took her hand inside his and squeezed it. "I was wrong about Lillie. I shouldn't have driven her away like that. But I…" He pressed his mouth into a tight line before continuing, "I feared what might happen to her. If she stayed close by, and married who I thought she should, then I could protect her, keep her safe. Unlike your mother."

"Oh, Papa." She gave his hand a squeeze in return. "You can't keep anything and everything bad from happening, even to those you love. But we can pray and trust in the Lord that He will make all things right in the end. Just as things have been made right this time."

"Have they all been made right?" His searching gaze made Delsie wonder if he could read what she hadn't shared.

She pulled her hand back and turned to rest her back against the settee. "I'm not sure what you mean."

"What happened to those two men?" he asked as he sat back.

"They…um…returned to their jobs at the different Express stations. The one in Kansas and the other in Missouri." She didn't dare look at him, afraid he'd see the longing on her face at the thought of Myles.

"And will you be writing to them?"

The conversation had taken a disastrous turn. Delsie couldn't bear the idea of hearing him say out loud that he didn't approve of Myles, that a marriage to an Express rider from Missouri would mean leaving him without any family nearby.

"I believe I shall correspond with Amos," she said brightly. "He's rather lonely with his wife gone and no children." She stood and shook out her skirt. "I believe I'll retire now. It's been a long day."

Pretending she didn't see his questioning look, she

bent and placed a kiss on his cheek. "Good night, Papa. It's wonderful to be home."

"Good night, Delsie." He picked up his neglected book and rubbed at the cover. "Thank you for telling me your story. And for doing what you felt you must to keep the family together."

"You're welcome." She moved toward the door, but she turned when he called her back, her heart jolting with sudden dread.

His attention had returned to the open page. "With all that traveling, are you sure you're content to be home now?" The question sounded innocent enough, though Delsie couldn't help feeling as if he were really asking something else. Something she wasn't ready to voice—perhaps she never would be.

She dipped her head in a decisive nod. "I am here to stay."

Chapter Seventeen

The hot, sticky days of July melted into August and still Delsie couldn't find relief from the incessant heat. She often took to spending time beneath the giant shade tree in the yard, hoping for a breeze, as she helped their gardener with weeding and planting.

She longed for the dry warmth of the West and for more to fill her time than gardening and social calls. A feeling of uselessness permeated nearly every hour of her day. The only bright spots since returning home were exchanging letters with Amos and with Lillie. Her father had even penned a postscript in Delsie's last letter to her sister. A full reconciliation between them not only appeared to be inevitable but likely to happen much sooner than Delsie had thought possible.

Dabbing at her damp forehead with her handkerchief, she stepped into her father's study, where he sat working at his desk. "Here are the household accounts." She'd been keeping them since the death of her mother, when her father had discovered her skill for numbers.

She set the ledgers on his desk, then dropped into one of the chairs opposite his. "I'm so ready for this heat to be over."

He glanced up from writing, his brow furrowed. "You've never been bothered by the summers before."

"No, you're right. But it somehow feels more humid this year."

She glanced out the nearest window at the flowers resting against the glass. The blossoms she'd seen heading West weren't so manicured, but they were no less beautiful. She felt a bit like a wildflower herself these days—transplanted from the open prairie to the confines of a stately garden.

"Is something wrong, Delsie?"

"Hmm?" She turned to look at him.

He sat back in his chair and studied her. "You seem a bit restless, my dear."

She forced a reassuring smile to her lips. "I'll be fine. Truly." Her gaze dropped to the account books. "Though it might be nice to have more to occupy my time than household numbers and gardening and paying visits to our friends."

To her surprise she heard him chuckle. "I thought as much. You've been wandering through the house for weeks like a seaman banished to land."

"I'm sorry." She twisted her handkerchief around her finger, afraid to say more.

"Or maybe," Mr. Radford continued, "like a woman who's lost her heart?"

Delsie jerked her head up. "Whatever do you mean?"

He gave another chuckle and waved away her shock.

"Never mind that now. I have something I'd like you to help me with. A project to occupy your time."

Interest thrummed through Delsie as she scooted her chair closer to his desk. "What sort of project?"

"I would like to open another bank." He shifted some papers on his desk, and thankfully, didn't see the expression of disappointment she felt creep onto her face. "With Flynn doing such an excellent job managing the one here, I'll admit I, too, have felt a bit like a horse put out to pasture."

"Where would you open a new one?" she asked, more out of politeness than genuine curiosity now.

He grinned as he placed a map before her. Delsie studied it, surprised to see the town didn't look exceedingly large. Then she read the name scrawled in the top left corner of the map—Stockton, California. A soft gasp escaped her lips, prompting more laughter from her father.

"You want to build a bank in California? But whatever for?"

"Because I can," he stated simply. "And because my dear, youngest daughter seems to have left her vitality for life somewhere out West." He lifted his hands in mock surrender. "I figured it might be worth discovering what some of the appeal is out there."

Delsie looked at the map again and shook her head in disbelief. "But how would you oversee a bank in California from here?"

Mr. Radford nodded thoughtfully. "An excellent question, one I considered quite a bit when I first conceived the idea. Then I started to think there was nothing still holding you and me here, now that you and Flynn are no longer a possibility."

Her heart began to race as Delsie anticipated what he meant to say next.

"While we have this lovely home and all its memories of your wonderful mother, it doesn't seem to make much sense to remain so far from the rest of our family." He glanced around the study, his expression wistful. "I have carved out a good life here, but perhaps, it's time for both of us to carve a new life somewhere else."

"Do you really mean that, Papa?" Hope beat so wildly inside her it almost hurt. The thought of being closer to Lillie and Clay in a new and exciting place, a place that meant being in closer proximity to the memories Delsie had made with Myles, brought a lump to her throat. While she might not be able to be with him, she could bravely take the path her time with him had opened up for her.

"Of course I mean to go through with this—and quite soon. I'd like the bank built and functional by October. And that's where I need your help, dear daughter." He picked up another large paper. This one appeared to be a drawing of a building instead of a map. "I would like you to oversee the expenditures and plans...of our new home in California."

Twilight filled the sky as Myles dismounted near the stables at Guittard's Station. After passing off the mail to the next rider, he entered the familiar kitchen, but his appetite hadn't been the same since Amos had taken sick. "Evening, Mrs. Guittard," he said to the woman working at the stove.

She turned and smiled at him. "Bonjour, Myles. Supper is almost ready."

"How is he?"

Her face immediately changed from welcome to worry. "He is worse since last week." She stepped closer as she added in a hushed tone, "I don't know that you would have seen him, to say goodbye, if you had come even a day later."

Though he'd suspected as much, the news still hit Myles hard like a punch to the gut. He'd hated seeing Amos waste away these past few weeks. The alert guide who'd traveled with him and Delsie months ago had been reduced to a shell of a man, confined solely to bed.

"Can I see him, before supper?"

"Of course, of course."

Myles nodded his appreciation and slipped back out the door. Elijah had been waiting for him and dropped to his shoulder as Myles walked past the stable to a lone, small cabin. Knocking softly, he didn't wait for Amos's reply but simply entered. A good fire burned in the fireplace, blocking out the October chill that sharpened the air outside.

Myles placed the single chair next to the bed where Amos slept. Elijah alighted on a peg near the door. The similarities between this moment and Myles's time in the desert after being shot with the arrow struck him sharply with its irony. Only this time it was him keeping a vigil at Amos's bedside, instead of the other way around.

Raspy breathing filled the quiet cabin. Myles studied his friend's face. Gray whiskers covered the thinning lines. "Amos?" he called softly.

Amos slowly opened his eyes and blinked. "Myles," he said in a hoarse voice. "You're here. I was just thinking about you."

"You were?" Tears burned his eyelids. He wasn't ready to say goodbye to someone else he cared about.

"Lots to tell you." Amos lifted a trembling hand and pointed at the table behind Myles.

He turned to see the supper tray there. "Are you hungry?"

Amos gave a slight shake of his head. "No, the letter."

An envelope sat near the tray. Myles picked it up and handed it to Amos.

"No," Amos rasped out. "Look who it's from and where."

Myles glanced at the name and address and felt his heart stop for a brief moment. The letter was from Delsie, which wasn't surprising. He'd known she and Amos were corresponding. But the address penned beneath her name wasn't from Pennsylvania. It was from California.

A scraping noise came from Amos. It took Myles a second to realize it was a laugh. "She and her father moved…to California."

"When?"

"End of last month."

Questions fired through Myles's mind, too many to burden Amos with. "Whatever for?" he managed to get out.

"Her father opened a bank there. Wanted to be closer to Delsie's sister in Oregon."

Delsie was no longer in Pennsylvania? She was living out West—where Myles had longed to live for months now. Was it possible this renewed his chances to be with her? He mentally shook his head—he was still a lowly Express rider with limited means to provide for a wife.

"Well, good for her." Myles set the letter back on the table. While shocking, the news still didn't change their impossible situation.

Amos studied him, his gaze more alert than Myles had seen it in weeks. "You need to go there, too, and start your ranch." He started to cough, but he shook off Myles's offer of a drink from the cup on the tray. When he'd finished, he continued, "You go find her and marry her. She loves you still, Myles. And I know you love her."

He ran a hand over his jaw. If only things could be that easy. "That's all well and good, Amos, but I don't have the kind of money I need to build a ranch right now." Boarding Moses at the livery stable all summer and into autumn had eaten into his savings.

"There's something else." Amos coughed again, his face contorting with the pain. Myles looked away. He hated the feeling of helplessness stirring within him. "I know I'm not your pa." The words brought Myles's head back around and renewed the watering in his eyes. "But you, and Delsie, have been the closest thing to a family for me."

Myles reached out and clasped Amos's pale hand. "You've been like a father to me." It was the first time he'd admitted out loud how much Amos's friendship had meant in his life. Myles was better because of knowing this honest, hardworking man of faith for the past seven years.

Amos's mouth curved up into a slight smile. "That's good. 'Cause I got something to give you."

"What is it?" Probably his gun. The older man had already given Delsie his prized pocket watch.

"It's under the floorboards, beneath the bed."

Myles bent and peered under the bed. The space looked rather small. "All right." Lowering himself onto his stomach, he felt around until his fingers touched a hole in the wood. Myles pulled up on the board and it lifted.

"Inside is a knapsack," Amos said.

Moving more by feel than sight, Myles managed to wrestle the sack from the space beneath the floor. He crawled back out from under the bed, brushing dust from his hair and shirt.

Amos caught his eye and nodded. "Open it."

He sat back down and lifted the flap of the sack. Bundles of cash filled the entire satchel. He released a startled laugh. "You rob a bank or something, Amos?"

Another raspy chuckle came from the ailing man. "No. That was earned, from honest work, over the last twenty-something years."

"I don't understand." Myles had assumed Amos was paid as much as the rest of the Pony Express workers, but there had to be at least five or six hundred dollars sitting inside this bag.

"Me and the missus lived simply and we saved."

Amos gestured to the bag. "I want you to have it, Myles. All one thousand and ten dollars of it."

Myles gaped at the money, hardly daring to believe. "But…"

Amos shook his head. "It's for your ranch. Yours and Delsie's."

The words sunk deep into Myles's heart, setting hope to burn anew inside him. "Is this what you meant back in that burned-down cabin in the desert? About the Lord working in mysterious ways?"

Some of the old spark returned to Amos's gaunt countenance. "Maybe it was. Can't think of much more mysterious ways than the Lord blessing you through the riches from one old station worker."

The tears were getting harder and harder to resist. "I can't thank you enough, Amos. But why now?"

"It's time," Amos murmured, his look full of double meaning.

Myles set down the bag and reached for his friend's hand again. "What do you mean, old man? You're tough and stubborn. You'll weather this."

"Not this time." Amos patted Myles's hand in a gesture to comfort him. "You are a credit to your father, Myles. And I'm proud to call you my friend."

Amos's words sounded similar to the ones Delsie had told him four months earlier. Did she really still love him? Could he win her hand once he had his horse ranch running? Everything about his future was changing— again—and it both thrilled and terrified him.

"If you hurry back to Saint Joe," Amos continued

in a voice growing weaker by the minute, "you can get Moses and head West in time to avoid most of the snow."

"I will, but not tonight." He wouldn't leave Amos yet.

Amos closed his eyes. "You don't have to stay."

Myles squeezed the man's hand once, then released it. "Yes, I do."

He let Amos sleep, his mind awhirl with plans and thoughts for how quickly he could find land and horses and start building stables, corrals and a house. When Amos woke again, he asked for a little water, but nothing more, insisting Myles eat the food. Myles obliged, though he couldn't stomach much. What he didn't eat, he shared with Elijah.

Sometime later, he jerked away, aware of the sudden silence and cold. He jumped up and stoked the fire, then moved back to his chair. "Amos?" he said, leaning forward.

The older man's rattling breaths had ceased. His chest no longer rose and fell, and his face appeared relaxed as if in peaceful slumber.

"Amos." Myles's voice broke as the tears he'd held back so long broke free of his restraint. "Goodbye, old man." He gripped Amos's lined hand one last time. "You will be missed."

He knew he ought to go tell Mrs. Guittard the news and see what needed to be done to bury Amos properly. But instead of moving he simply sat, staring at the wall for some time, remembering. Memories of Charles, Amos and Delsie filled his thoughts. He'd had to say goodbye to the three people he cared for most in the world. But one of them might still be waiting for him.

Fresh energy coursed through Myles. He shouldered the sack of money Amos had gifted him and climbed to his feet. "Come on, Elijah. We've got things to take care of." The bird flew to his shoulder as he stepped out of the cabin.

The darkness outside had begun to recede, which meant morning was fast approaching. His future, one made possible by God and the generosity of Hank Amos, awaited him. And with a great amount of work, and even greater faith, perhaps a beautiful dark-haired woman waited for him, too.

California, June 1861

"Morning, Miss Radford." The general-store owner, a Mr. Jasper, smiled at Delsie from behind the long counter. "Here for your weekly letter?"

Delsie nodded. "I have one to post to Lillie, as well."

True to their word, she and Lillie had faithfully written each other, almost every week, since last year. Delsie expected the news any day now that she was an aunt. Had Lillie given birth to her and Clay's first child this week?

She paid to mail her letter and accepted the one Mr. Jasper handed her in return. Before she could tear it open, though, the man spoke again. "That hat you ordered last month came in today." He lifted a hatbox onto the counter and opened the lid.

Peeking inside, Delsie smiled. Her father had insisted she order a new hat from back East for her birthday the month before. Twenty years old now. She could hardly believe it still. While she might have felt ancient at such an age, and unmarried, back in the parlors of Pennsylvania, out West she felt as young as ever. With her whole life ahead of her.

She was content and happy with her life here in California, save for one thing. Her smile faltered a little at the thought. There had been something—or rather someone—she'd really wanted to see for her birthday, silly as it was.

Delsie closed her mind to the foolish hope of once more seeing a certain dark-eyed, dark-haired horseman. Instead she focused her attention on the blue hat before her.

Lifting the creation out of the box, she admired the stacked folds of velvet and the gorgeous white feathers. It was the loveliest creation she'd seen in ages. Although she'd heard from her father, one of the town's most successful bankers, they were to get a milliner here soon, so perhaps fashionable hats would be much easier to come by in the future.

"It's beautiful," she said with sincerity.

Mr. Jasper beamed as if he himself had fashioned the hat. The idea of the white-haired man with spectacles constructing a delicate lady's hat made Delsie choke back a laugh.

"Thank you, Mr. Jasper. I'll see you next week." Looping the string of the hatbox around her wrist, she let herself out the door. She paused on the wooden walkaway outside to tear open her letter from Lillie. Her eyes quickly took in the first few lines until she found what she'd been hoping to read for days.

"I'm an aunt," she whispered to herself, "to a healthy baby boy."

Her earlier bright smile returned to her face. She would hurry to the bank to tell her father that he had a grandson. Delsie kept reading as she walked down the sidewalk, completely absorbed in Lillie's words.

So intent was her gaze and concentration on the paper in her hand that she didn't see the person in front of her until she bumped into a solid shoulder. "I'm so sorry," she murmured, without lifting her eyes. "Please excuse me." She moved a step or two past the stranger.

"I'm guessing that fancy getup you're wearing means you can read," a deep voice intoned.

Delsie froze, her chin snapping up in surprise. That voice; those words. She lowered the letter to her side and pivoted slowly. Her pulse pounded rapidly even before she caught sight of the man's bearded face beneath the shadow of his hat.

"Myles?" The name sounded more like a breathless squeak than anything else.

He removed his hat and smiled at her. That slow, full smile that had the power to weaken her legs beneath her, even after all this time. "Hello, Delsie."

"Wh-what are you doing here?" She glanced around at the other people, who were filing past them as though this were any ordinary day. But it wasn't. The man she'd loved and missed for nearly a year now stood close enough that she could smell soap and sun and leather on him.

"That's a rather long story. But if you'd care to take a buggy ride with me, I'd be more than happy to tell it."

He pointed with his hat to where a shiny black rig and a horse—*could that be Moses?*—stood waiting half a block down the street.

Delsie stared at him in silence, her mind trying to keep up with the reality that Myles was here, asking to take her on a buggy ride.

"If you'd rather not…" He threw her a concerned look and put his hat back on.

"No, no." She shook herself from her stunned stupor. "I would love to, very much. Although, I need to ask my father first. If it's all right…to go."

Myles smiled again, this time in obvious relief. "Fine by me."

"He owns one of the banks. It's not far from here."

"Lead the way."

Delsie began walking, but she kept shooting glances at Myles every few steps. He was really here—alive, well and still incredibly handsome.

Myles laughed. "You're looking at me like you did when I told you I didn't have any sidesaddles for your Express horse."

"Am I?" A blush warmed her cheeks, but she laughed at the memory. Had it really been an entire year since their journey West together? Back in Myles's presence again, the time had shrunk to almost nothing. "I heard about Amos. Mrs. Guittard was kind enough to write and tell me."

"I was with him, at the end," Myles said quietly. "He was the best of men."

"There are still days I think of writing him, only to remember he's no longer with us."

"I've done the same." He placed his hand on her elbow to steer her around a group of women talking in the center of the sidewalk. The touch sent immediate warmth cascading from Delsie's arm to her toes. Oh, how she'd missed him.

When they reached the bank, Myles held the door open for her. Delsie thanked him and slipped inside. What would her father say about Myles? Would he approve of him? Seeing him again had only confirmed the feelings she'd tucked away, but she wasn't sure if Owen Radford would still harbor objections of having an Express rider as a potential son-in-law. Her heart renewed its pounding.

"I'm here to see my father," she told the clerk, then she knocked lightly on the door of his personal office.

"Come in," Mr. Radford called from inside.

Delsie smiled over her shoulder at Myles, with more reassurance than she felt, and entered. "Morning, Papa."

"Done at the general store already?" He stood and came around his desk. "I see the new hat you ordered came in."

"Yes. Thank you." She'd forgotten all about the hatbox. She set it on one of the chairs drawn up to the desk. "I have something to ask and someone to—"

Mr. Radford approached Myles and held out his hand. "Mr. Patton, a pleasure to see you again."

Delsie's mouth fell open as she watched the two men shake hands and exchange pleasantries. "But...how do you...?" She glanced from one man to the other, completely baffled. "Myles is the Express rider, Papa, who helped me..."

"Ah. I suspected as much." A spark of amusement lit his green eyes. "Mr. Patton is also the owner of The B and P Ranch, located about an hour north of here. I've been helping him with his banking needs for a few months now."

"Y-you have your ranch now?" Delsie sank into the empty chair, her mind so full of confusion she could hardly formulate her words. "And my father... You've known him...for...for several months?"

Myles shot her a contrite look. "I promise to explain everything, Delsie. But first..." He turned back to her father. "Do I have your permission, sir, to take your daughter for a buggy ride? I'd like to show her my ranch."

Grinning, Mr. Radford nodded. "Certainly." He bent and kissed Delsie on the cheek. "Have a nice time. I myself have been hoping to see Mr. Patton's spread one of these days."

Woodenly Delsie stood. Her gaze fell to the letter still clutched in her hand. "I almost forgot. You're a grandfather, Papa. Lillie had her baby. A boy."

His grin spread even wider. "Wonderful news. I will write her my congratulations right away." He returned to his desk as Delsie stepped to the door. She looked expectantly at Myles, but he made no move to follow.

"There's something else I'd like to ask your father, before we go. If that's all right?"

She lifted her shoulders in a most unladylike shrug, but she could hardly keep up with all the revelations this morning. Waving absently to her father, she exited the office and shut the door behind her. A nearby chair provided another welcome refuge for her unsteady feet.

How had she not seen Myles around town before now? More important, why had he waited so long before coming to see her? She tamped down her bewilderment, and the accompanying flicker of disappointment, with the reminder that he'd promised to tell her everything. Hopefully, that meant today, during their ride.

At least Papa seems to approve of him, Delsie thought with an astonished laugh. First the news she was an aunt, then seeing Myles again after so long and now learning Owen Radford knew him. It was almost too much to take in.

The door to her father's office opened and Myles walked out. "Ready?"

"Yes. Very much." Delsie rose to her feet. Myles once again took her elbow in hand, re-creating the warm tingly feeling inside her, and gently directed her out of the bank and to his waiting buggy.

"Remember Moses?" he asked as he handed her onto the seat.

Delsie settled onto the pristine leather. "Of course. I thought I recognized him."

Myles gathered the reins and clucked to Moses. Within minutes they were moving down the street, heading for the edge of town. Myles's arm rested firmly against Delsie's, but she made no effort to scoot away. The feeling of comfort and safety she'd so often felt in his presence wrapped itself around her now, and she couldn't bear to shatter it by moving.

"I'm guessing you have a few questions," he said once they'd left the town's buildings behind.

"Just a few," she teased.

He shot her a smile, which resurrected the rapid thrumming of her pulse.

Delsie leaned back against the seat. When was the last time she'd felt this content? Probably not since she'd left Myles, wounded, in the desert. "Why don't you tell me everything that's happened since last summer and I'll throw in the questions as needed?"

"Fair enough." He turned to look at her. "I suppose Amos already told you about my recovering from that arrow and making our way back East?"

Delsie nodded.

Myles faced forward again. "I wasn't sure if I still had a job waiting or not."

"But you did?" She already knew the answer, but she wanted to be sure she hadn't caused him any trouble.

"Yes. That wasn't the only thing waiting for me, though." He cast a sideways glance at her and grinned. "Cynthia came to see me the day I got back to Saint Joe."

The wealthy woman he'd cared about for years? A worm of fear uncurled inside Delsie. "What did she want?"

Myles chuckled. "She actually wanted me back. Told me she was bored with her captain and would use some of her inheritance to help fund my ranch."

The fear grew a little more. "What did you say?"

His eyebrows rose as if he found her question as ludicrous as he did amusing. "I told her no, in the kindest way possible. I knew I didn't care for her in that way and I never would."

Delsie released the breath she'd been holding. Her stomach relaxed, too. "Still, the promise of all that money…"

"Not worth it," Myles said in a firm tone. "After that I continued riding for a few months, until Amos took sick." He licked his lips as if the memory was still a bit raw. Delsie could relate. "It was the night he passed that he gave me something. Something that changed everything for me."

"What?"

Myles shifted the reins to his left hand and reached over to take her hand in his right. The memory of his strong but gentle grip filled her thoughts and her fingers. She hadn't believed she would ever feel his hand in hers again.

"Apparently Amos had saved a considerable amount of money through the years, in addition to the money you gave us." His low voice was tinged with deferential awe. "And since he had no other family, he gave it all… to me." He twisted to face her. "He had over a thousand dollars stuffed inside a knapsack, Delsie."

"A thousand dollars?" She gasped. "Is that what you used for your ranch?"

Nodding, he lifted her hand and kissed her gloved knuckles. "He told me to come West and set up the ranch. Then I was to find you."

Delsie swallowed the lump forming in her throat. Even without her voicing it aloud, Amos had known she hadn't stopped loving Myles. "But how long have you been here? Why you didn't come—" she blushed again "—sooner?"

He rested their joined hands on his knee and gave a self-deprecating laugh. "Believe me, I wanted to. Dozens of times. Especially when I first arrived last October." A reassuring squeeze of her fingers seemed to attest to his sincerity. "But I wanted to have the land and some of the horses purchased and the stables and house begun before I sought you out. I wanted to prove to you that I could get a ranch established."

"I never doubted you, Myles." She placed her other hand on top of his. "So when did you meet my father?" She still couldn't believe he and Myles had not only met one another but seemed to have a good rapport, too.

"I first visited his bank back in February. Though I had to make certain his daughter wasn't in the vicinity beforehand." He threw her a sheepish grin. "I would have waited to meet him until I saw you again, but I figured I could use the financial advice. And I didn't think it would hurt to let him warm up to the idea of me, either."

Delsie laughed. "Yes, that was probably wise. What did he say when you told him you were the Express rider who conveyed me to California?"

"I only told him last week," Myles admitted. "But you know, he didn't seem as surprised as I thought he might after I confessed to knowing you already."

Smiling, Delsie brushed hair from her eyes and studied the scenery around them. She'd come to love this valley surrounded by hills and so different from what she'd known in Pennsylvania, though gorgeous in its own right, too.

So her father had guessed at her feelings for Myles. She'd thought herself clever for keeping them a secret, but he knew her better than she suspected. A sudden thought had her turning to Myles again. "What was it you asked him, before we left? Did it have to do with your ranch?"

"Sort of." His dark eyes reflected hidden amusement. "All in good time, darling."

It was the same endearment he'd called her the last time she'd seen him. Too happy to press him further, at least for the moment, she rested her head on his shoulder.

A few minutes later, he tugged her arm. "There's the ranch, Delsie."

She lifted her head as he drove the buggy between two large corrals, one on either side of the road. A few horses grazed in the left, while a number of foals and their mothers watched them from the one on the right. Straight ahead sat a white two-story house with a wide veranda that ran along the front and sides. Behind it Delsie could just make out a good-sized barn. A carved sign above the porch indicated the property's name in scrolled letters—The B and P Ranch.

"Oh, Myles, it's beautiful," she said as he helped her from the buggy.

He smiled, his expression full of pride. "Finished it last week. We'll start on a bunkhouse soon, though it might be some time before we fill it."

"We?" She followed him toward the house, her hand still tucked inside his, and up the porch steps.

"I hired a young fellow, Joe Cunningham, to help me build the house. He's real good with woodworking and has a knack for horses, too."

Delsie glanced at the two rocking chairs that faced the yard from one side of the veranda. "Did he make those?" She started toward the chairs to examine the handiwork, but Myles gently pulled her toward the front door.

"We'll look at those in a minute. I want to show you the house first."

The inside was sparsely furnished, except for the kitchen and an upstairs bedroom, but Delsie could easily see the potential in each of the rooms. Windows let in plenty of natural light and allowed views of the surrounding valley and hills from nearly every angle.

After the tour, Myles showed her the large barn. There were plenty of stalls to accommodate the many horses.

"I already sold several of the foals to folks in town," he said as they walked back to the front yard.

Delsie took in the beauty once more, shaking her head in wonderment. "It's all so lovely, Myles. You've done a fine job."

He grinned, then tipped his head in the direction of the porch. "I've one last thing for you to see." Still holding her hand, he steered her up the steps again and over to the rocking chairs. "I had Joe carve these. They're identical except for one thing."

Delsie released his hand to run her fingers along

the smooth wooden arms and up the intricately carved spindles at the back. "They're gorgeous."

"Try it out," Myles prompted.

With a laugh, she complied. The seat, though elaborate in decoration, was still comfortable. She leaned her head back and shut her eyes. Rocking the chair with the toe of her boot, she let the gentle morning breeze caress her cheeks as she released a sigh of peace. "I don't think I want to leave."

"I don't want you to, either."

The huskiness of his tone made her open her eyes. He watched her intently, making her heart stutter faster.

"Did you figure out the difference between the two chairs?"

The question took her by surprise. "Oh. Let's see." She studied both rocking chairs, but she couldn't identify any dissimilarities. "I can't see anything."

Myles pointed to the back of the other chair. There in the wood an *M* had been carved, in the same delicate scroll style as the ranch sign.

Delsie twisted to look at the back of the chair she sat in. Instead of an *M*, this chair had a *D* carved into it. One tiny letter, but she knew its significance at once.

Her gaze met Myles's and she did her best to suppress the smile attempting to break through. "I'd say you're rather confident of yourself, aren't you, Myles Patton?"

He knelt in front of her and reclaimed her hand. "I thought I'd take a chance," he murmured. He placed another kiss on her knuckles. "Kind of like you did all those months ago with an ornery Express rider."

"Is that all you remember?" She couldn't contain her

smile any longer. "I remember meeting a good, honest, handsome Express rider. Who—" she waved her free hand "—on occasion might have been…a little grumpy."

Myles laughed, the sound deep and happy and sweeter than anything Delsie could remember hearing in a long time. "All I can say is I'm glad I didn't turn you down that day. And I'm hoping—" he lifted her other hand in his and gently tugged her to her feet "—that you won't turn me down, either. Because I have something to ask you, Miss Delsie Radford."

Delsie's pulse began galloping again. "Yes?"

"With your father's permission and blessing…"

Her eyes widened as she suddenly realized what he'd asked her father earlier. And what his answer had been.

"Will you do me the honor of becoming my wife?" Myles turned her hands over and placed a kiss against each palm of her gloves. "There's no one else in this world I would rather have riding and working and raising a family right alongside me. I love you, Delsie. I think I've loved you since that first time I watched you straddle that horse, with that determined look in those beautiful eyes."

Tears of happiness blurred Myles's rugged face for a moment. These were the words she'd waited more than a year to hear, words she'd long given up hope of ever hearing from this man. "I love you, too."

"So what do you say?" He bent forward, touching his forehead to hers. "Will you marry me?"

There was no hesitation; no need to consider. Delsie

knew exactly what she wanted. "Yes, Myles," she said with a full smile. "A hundred times over, yes."

The grin he offered her, right before tucking her hands around his neck, made her stomach pitch with pleasure. Then his lips met hers in a kiss that filled her head to toe with happiness.

In that moment, Delsie recognized she'd at last reached the end of the trail she'd embarked on a year ago with Myles. Only it wasn't really an ending. This was just the beginning and this time her journey would not be as the Express rider's lady—this time it would be as his wife.

* * * * *

Dear Reader,

It was while driving across Wyoming on a family trip a few years back that Myles and Delsie's story first entered my mind. I could just imagine them racing across the barren landscape, and it wasn't long after that I knew I wanted this story to feature the Pony Express.

Though only in operation a year and a half, the Pony Express has become a legend of the American West. The lone rider on his galloping steed, squaring off against the dangers of man and nature, is an iconic image of the fortitude and lasting impression made by those who came Westward.

All of the Express stations, cities, forts and landmarks named in this story were actual places or sights. The descriptions of Express-related items or information—including the logistics of the Pony Express operation—are also historically accurate. The riders and workers in this story are my own creation with the exception of Mrs. Guittard, who was a real person, though I added my own details to her character for the sake of the story. I'm indebted and grateful to those who compiled detailed accounts and descriptions of the Pony Express and made them available to all. Any errors are mine alone.

While the trouble with the Paiute Indians is also factual—including the burning of stations, the driving off of stock and the killing of Express workers—I took the liberty of setting Myles and Delsie in the middle of this war, when in reality, it occurred several weeks prior to their journey West. The part of the Express line that had closed as a result of these troubles would have been re-opened at the beginning of June. However, I had the line remain closed for the sake of the story and its timeline.

Likewise, for the ease of reading, I've listed the states that made up the Pony Express trail as they are named today. Most of them did not achieve statehood until after 1860, though, and would have been part of various territories at that time.

Folliott Sandford Pierpoint's hymn "For the Beauty of the Earth" was first published in 1864, but its stirring words were too fitting not to reference in this story. Therefore I had Delsie and Amos sing the song during their private worship service, while in reality, it would be another four years before the hymn's publication.

The individuals who worked for the legendary Pony Express were nothing short of courageous, and it's my hope this story will be a tribute to their strength and place in history.

I love hearing from my readers. You can contact me through my website at stacyhenrie.com.

All the best on your own journeys,
Stacy

REQUEST YOUR FREE BOOKS!

2 FREE INSPIRATIONAL NOVELS
PLUS 2 FREE MYSTERY GIFTS

Love Inspired® **HISTORICAL**

YES! Please send me 2 FREE Love Inspired® Historical novels and my 2 FREE mystery gifts (gifts are worth about $10). After receiving them, if I don't wish to receive any more books, I can return the shipping statement marked "cancel." If I don't cancel, I will receive 4 brand-new novels every month and be billed just $4.99 per book in the U.S. or $5.49 per book in Canada. That's a saving of at least 17% off the cover price. It's quite a bargain! Shipping and handling is just 50¢ per book in the U.S. and 75¢ per book in Canada.* I understand that accepting the 2 free books and gifts places me under no obligation to buy anything. I can always return a shipment and cancel at any time. Even if I never buy another book, the two free books and gifts are mine to keep forever.

102/302 IDN GH6Z

Name	(PLEASE PRINT)	

Address		Apt. #

City	State/Prov.	Zip/Postal Code

Signature (if under 18, a parent or guardian must sign)

Mail to the **Reader Service:**
IN U.S.A.: P.O. Box 1867, Buffalo, NY 14240-1867
IN CANADA: P.O. Box 609, Fort Erie, Ontario L2A 5X3

Want to try two free books from another series?
Call 1-800-873-8635 or visit www.ReaderService.com.

* Terms and prices subject to change without notice. Prices do not include applicable taxes. Sales tax applicable in N.Y. Canadian residents will be charged applicable taxes. Offer not valid in Quebec. This offer is limited to one order per household. Not valid for current subscribers to Love Inspired Historical books. All orders subject to credit approval. Credit or debit balances in a customer's account(s) may be offset by any other outstanding balance owed by or to the customer. Please allow 4 to 6 weeks for delivery. Offer available while quantities last.

Your Privacy—The Reader Service is committed to protecting your privacy. Our Privacy Policy is available online at www.ReaderService.com or upon request from the Reader Service.

We make a portion of our mailing list available to reputable third parties that offer products we believe may interest you. If you prefer that we not exchange your name with third parties, or if you wish to clarify or modify your communication preferences, please visit us at www.ReaderService.com/consumerschoice or write to us at Reader Service Preference Service, P.O. Box 9062, Buffalo, NY 14240-9062. Include your complete name and address.

LIH15

*Susanne Collins has her hands full raising her brother's
four orphaned children and running the farm.
When cowboy Tanner Harding offers his help in
exchange for use of her corrals, will he prove to be the
strong, solid man she's been hoping for?*

Read on for a sneak peek of
THE COWBOY'S READY-MADE FAMILY
by **Linda Ford**,
available March 2016 from Love Inspired Historical.

Tanner rode past the farm, then stopped to look again at
the corrals behind him. They were sturdy enough to hold
wild horses…and he desperately needed such a corral.

He shifted his gaze past the corrals to the overgrown
garden and beyond to the field, where a crop had been
harvested last fall and stood waiting to be reseeded. He
thought of the disorderly tack room. His gaze rested on
the idle plow.

This family needed help. He needed corrals. Was it
really that simple?

Only one way to find out. He rode back to the farm and
dismounted to face a startled Miss Susanne. "Ma'am, I
know you don't want to accept help…"

Her lips pursed.

"But you have something I need so maybe we can help
each other."

Her eyes narrowed. She crossed her arms across her chest. "I don't see how."

He half smiled at the challenging tone of her voice. "Let me explain. I have wild horses to train and no place to train them. But you have a set of corrals that are ideal."

"I fail to see how that would help me."

"Let me suggest a deal. If you let me bring my horses here to work with them, in return I will plow your field and plant your crop."

"I have no desire to have a bunch of wild horses here. Someone is likely to get hurt."

"You got another way of getting that crop in?" He gave her a second to contemplate that, then added softly, "How will you feed the livestock and provide for the children if you don't?"

She turned away so he couldn't see her face, but he didn't need to in order to understand that she fought a war between her stubborn pride and her necessity.

Her shoulders sagged and she bowed her head. Slowly she came about to face him. "I agree to your plan." Her eyes flashed a warning. "With a few conditions."